MEET ME AT THE CLOCK

CLOCK

A HOTEL HAMILTON NOVEL

TANYA E WILLIAMS

FIRST EDITION

Cover Photograph by David C Williams

Cover Design by Ana Grigoriu-Voicu

eBook ISBN 978-1-989144-21-3

Paperback ISBN 978-1-989144-22-0

Hardback ISBN 978-1-989144-23-7

Audiobook ISBN 978-1-989144-20-6

For Emily
Thank you for taking an image that existed in my imagination and making it real.

CHAPTER 1

Wednesday, September 14, 1927
Louisa

A crash in the hallway startles me from my daydream. A reverie of my recent role as Cleopatra's servant was occupying my thoughts as I scrubbed my third Hotel Hamilton bathtub of the day. Vivid remembrances of my performances, and the audience's applause, fuel me during mundane days at the hotel.

I smother a groan behind closed lips as I brace waterlogged hands on the now spotless porcelain tub and hoist myself into a standing position. Damp cloth in hand, I lean out the guest room door, swivelling my head toward the sound of plates crashing against one another.

"What on earth?" I dash toward the toppled dining cart. Hazel's backside peeks out from behind the long linen cloth, askew on the trolly after the tumble. Hazel, a fifth-floor maid, is on her hands and knees, surrounded by domed silver lids and the remnants of someone's breakfast.

"Help me, will you?" Hazel's eyes are damp with

desperation. "I can't seem to manoeuvre the carts past these guest room thresholds."

I lift the cart upright, toppling an egg cup and spilling the shell remnants. "I don't think any of us are used to in-room dining yet." I straighten the linen and begin placing crumb-covered white plates in a stack on the top shelf. "I can't understand why anyone would wish to remain in bed for their breakfast, unless they're ill." I give Hazel's shoulder a reassuring squeeze. "No harm done though. We can be thankful they preferred hard-boiled to scrambled."

A man and woman appear from around the corner, walking toward us down the narrow hall. Hazel and I retreat, on cue, pressing our backs into the chair rail and sky-blue walls. I pull the dining cart close as Hazel covertly places a linen cloth over the exposed dishes, hiding the remnants of a half-eaten breakfast.

The guests pass without any indication that they've seen us. I let out the breath I've been holding while Hazel repositions the silver lids atop the plates. Clearing the uneaten morsels out of sight, her voice climbs into a whine. "I don't see why we maids are responsible for returning the dining carts to the kitchen. We are busy enough tending to the rooms."

"As the demands of the guests change, so does our role as hotel maids, I suppose." I offer a noncommittal shrug while pushing the cart back and forth to test out its wheels.

By noon, my tolerant mood has declined. Having spent most of the morning ruminating over Hazel's comment, I am perturbed by the knowledge that the lofty demands of others dictate how I spend my days. I crave the freedom that working in the theatre allows. There, the only thing that matters is the character's plight, and that liberty invigorates me. At least, it did until several months ago.

I release an exasperated sigh as I wander the employee

corridor. The emptiness in the pit of my stomach feels more meaningful than a simple notification of hunger. I meet my sister, Clara, in the lunchroom and force a pleasant demeanour.

"Hazel tipped another cart, I heard," Clara says, lowering her voice.

"Another casualty for the half-eaten eggs of The Hotel Hamilton." My attempt at humour falls flat, but I brush it aside as I bite into my sandwich.

"Hello, ladies." Rebecca Smythe settles into the chair on the other side of Clara, the two of them having developed a friendship in recent months.

"How are things on the eighth floor, Miss Smythe?" I ask between bites. The demands of the hotel guests seem to escalate at higher floors, with the illustrious eighth-floor suites being the very best the hotel has to offer.

"Oh, you know. The usual." Miss Smythe hides a mischievous expression behind a slender hand. "And then some."

Clara giggles as I restrain an eye roll. Lately, what she finds funny, I find disappointing. Even at home, Clara prattles on about the comings and goings of the hotel like a chirpy bird in springtime. Three months into the daily routine of maid life, I find myself wanting more. Much more. We have to blend in with the woodwork of the elite hotel so as not to offend guest sensibilities, and the humdrum existence has me wound tighter than a two-dollar watch.

Clara and Rebecca's conversation filters into the background as my mind wanders, seeking a solution to the question that burns within me. What is there for me to look forward to? What is next?

"Lou?" Clara nudges my shoulder with her free hand. "Louisa, are you listening to me?"

3

"Sorry. What were you saying?"

"Miss Smythe has invited us to tea next week." Clara's delight lights up her face, and I am struck by the realization that a date for tea may very well be the highlight of our week.

"How nice." I rejoin the conversation, though the effort feels akin to pushing one of the behemoth vacuums around all eight floors of the hotel.

On my way out of the lunchroom, Ms. Thompson stops me. "Miss Wilson, I have checked the charts, and it seems you are quite ahead of schedule today. Could I borrow you for a task below stairs?"

"Of course, ma'am." I nod my assent while smothering a weary groan and follow her to the basement.

The cement block basement has captured the chill of autumn, giving off a dank and musty odor that wrinkles my nose.

Ms. Thompson leads me toward the luggage storage room, where several maids are already congregated.

"Thank you for coming, ladies." Ms. Thompson inserts her key into the lock and pushes the door open. "Mr. Olson and I have determined that more storage space is required for our guests' luggage. Few people are traveling light these days, it seems. Their preference is to empty their cases and have their luggage stored during their stay."

Of course that is their preference, I think. The inside of my cheek finds a spot between my teeth to ensure my silence.

"There is a much larger room that will do, down the hall and to the right." Ms. Thompson leans past us as she points a bony finger toward the room beyond our line of sight. "The tasks before you are twofold. First, you will need to document each piece of luggage with its owner's name and room number. We must ensure nothing is misplaced during this transition."

Ms. Thompson meets our eyes in turn, conveying the importance of our first task. "Then we will move the pieces of luggage one by one and arrange them in order of room number. A system has already been established at the new location, so every guest's luggage has a dedicated space, labelled with the room number."

I look past Ms. Thompson, into the room overflowing with hard cases, and cringe. The task before us is sure to be lengthy.

"Now, if you will all come with me, I will show you the new room and explain the shelving system." Ms. Thompson leads the way, and I fall in line with the others. Dressed in matching uniforms, maintaining the same posture and manner, the lot of us have barely a discernible difference. I sigh as we move as one toward the new luggage room.

An hour later, perspiration snakes down the length of my spine. My back is protesting with each movement, given the excessive amount of lifting and finagling required to extract the empty luggage from the small room and haul it through the basement corridors. A whistling tune catches my attention.

George, the affable bellboy with boyish good looks, snaps his head up in surprise as I round the corner toward him. He tips his red-trimmed box hat, placing his free hand near the rim. "Hello, Miss Wilson."

"Hello, George. Haven't I told you a dozen times to call me Louisa?" I lift the corners of my mouth and cock an eyebrow.

"Well, yes, miss. I suppose you have." His cheeks flame with colour.

The red Radio Flyer wagon behind him catches my attention. "What have you got there?"

"Oh, this?" George lifts the square black handle. "Me and the boys use it to move boxes and kitchen supplies and such.

It's a snug fit inside the lift, but it sure beats multiple trips when Chef is hollering something fierce."

A giggle rises as I nod in understanding. His smile widens at our camaraderie, and I can feel him melting into the space where my attention lingers solely on him.

"When Chef's rant transitions from English to French, you know that you best be moving." George chuckles, releasing a nervousness he seems to exude whenever I am near.

I give his forearm a soft pat. "You know, I think perhaps you could be of assistance to me."

"How's that?" A shy nod informs me of his willingness when a ruckus of shuffling and bumping echoes down the hall, turning both of our heads.

I look back to him, then ask sweetly, "George, do you think we could borrow your wagon?"

Four maids appear, struggling with the luggage, exertion painted on their faces.

"Ladies, I've found a solution," I announce.

"I didn't know we were looking for one." Maggie, the gruffest of the group, fires back. Pushing past me, she raises her voice. "Course, if you were helping instead of standing around dallying, we might already be finished."

Perturbed by Maggie's response, I lift the corners of my mouth into a placating smile and raise my voice, directing my words at Maggie's retreating back. "I suppose we could continue on with back-breaking effort, or . . ."

Hazel stops beside me. "Don't worry about her. She's just testy because of the task at hand. What did you have in mind?"

I offer Hazel a sincere smile. "George here happens to have a wagon. I figured we could load up a bunch of suitcases and roll them down the hall." I tap a finger to my lips as I envision the process. "We will need someone to walk beside the wagon to ensure nothing topples, but it's sure to speed things up, while also saving our backs."

"I say it is worth a try." Hazel's words convey a certainty that sets me into motion. "But I suggest someone other than me pull the wagon. You know how clumsy I am when it comes to things on wheels."

"George, may we borrow your wagon?" I ask again, swivelling lightly from side to side, drawing his attention with the sway of my skirt.

He swallows hard. "Certainly, Miss, ah—Louisa. Let me unload this lot first."

I pivot toward the old storage room, calling over my shoulder as I go, "Meet us by the luggage room, and we will set straight to work."

With the help of George's little red wagon, every piece of luggage is securely relocated by the end of the day, garnering a hearty "well done" from Mr. Olson and a "how clever" from Ms. Thompson.

I mention George by name as I explain how we managed the task, not wanting him to think I am unappreciative of the loan and his help.

Despite my aching muscles, my steps are light as Clara and I wander home, the autumn darkness requiring the electric street lamps to turn on earlier each afternoon.

"You seem in better spirits this evening." Clara loops an arm through mine.

"The afternoon was . . . reaffirming."

"Reaffirming? I thought you were in the basement moving suitcases around." Clara's forehead wrinkles.

"Yes, the task was demanding, but I was reminded of how industrious I can be." A trill of laughter bursts from my lips as I recall George and his willingness to be at my service. "I put

7

my charming personality to work, and things fell right into place."

Clara eyes me with a sideways glance. "How so?"

"Well, you see . . ." I tell Clara about George's little red wagon and my idea of how to make the work easier.

"I still don't understand." Clara unlinks her arm from mine and repositions the bag on her opposite shoulder. "How was borrowing George's wagon reaffirming?"

"Honestly, Clara, you've seen me do it a thousand times. You must admit I have a knack for acquiring aid from young men."

"I see. So, using George by way of your female persuasions reaffirms what? That you can manipulate others by winking in their direction?" Clara's flat delivery is accusatory at best.

"No." My nose crinkles in distaste at how the conversation has turned, and I huff. "First of all, there is a difference between charm and female persuasion. George was not manipulated, as you put it. He was merely rewarded with my attention. And I'll have you know that I thanked him profusely and gave him full credit when speaking with Ms. Thompson." I lift my chin in defiance. "By the time we finished the task, he probably thought the whole thing was his idea in the first place."

"Right . . ." Clara drags out the word, questioning my morality with her tone. "Not manipulation, then?"

"Call it what you will. I've learned that life is far easier when others want to assist me." I shrug my shoulders, attempting to appear undeterred by Clara's pointed judgement. "People respond to my joyful personality, and when they do, I show them how valued they are."

"You think it is your personality that garners all that attention?" Clara shakes her head dubiously. "You are a delight. Truly you are. But have you looked in a mirror lately?"

Her words strike at my core, forcing me to hide my instinctual reaction with a scoff. "Don't be absurd." Waiting to cross the street, I turn my attention toward the oncoming traffic, buying myself a moment to recover from the gibe. "Getting what you want in life is all about playing a role. Sure, sometimes that comes at a cost, but the end result is what matters."

"What kind of cost?" Clara isn't finished trying to pin me down.

I sigh impatiently. "I do excel at bringing others into the fold, you know. It's a trait I am proud of. Honestly, Clara, life is a negotiation. I'll admit that every now and then I find myself doing something I am not keen on, but if the final goal is achieved, then I am a willing party to the exchange."

"Give me an example. How much of your soul are you selling on a daily basis, Lou?" Though she doesn't meet my eyes, Clara's words make the hairs on the back of my neck bristle.

"I just gave you one." Exasperation lifts my voice, eliciting a few glances from strangers on the sidewalk. "George and his wagon. I didn't sell my soul, as you put it, by offering George my undivided attention in exchange for his help. Who isn't motivated to assist someone they are fond of? The cost was my time and attention toward him. I don't see how that could be viewed negatively. Besides, he is always happy to help, and I am grateful for it."

"But would you be as inclined to help him should he require assistance? That is what turns a relationship into a friendship instead of a one-sided manipulation tactic."

"I help plenty of people. All the time, I'll have you know." I tug Clara's arm as the traffic clears.

The incredulous look she shoots me lets me know I've annoyed her. Despite our quarrel, pride at my sister's resolve to push back lifts my spirits. Given all that we've been through with Mama's death and Papa's precarious attachment to the drink, I worried she had lost her fire, resigning herself entirely to the role of good daughter and hard-working maid. "We have different approaches to life is all. I am not afraid to be seen and stand up for myself. You, on the other hand, seek to blend in. Heaven forbid you should stick your neck out for something you desire."

Clara's voice squeaks out a tight response. "I don't know how you can say such things when I was the one to seek out a job at the hotel in the first place. Or do you not recall pushing your way into my plans? How quickly we forget."

The Newbury apartment building stands tall on the next corner. I want to remind her that our two salaries are the only reason we continue to have a home, but I bite my tongue. "All I'm saying is that you shouldn't forget to dream beyond your current situation. You could accomplish great things."

Clara's pace quickens and I wonder whether she's called by the warmth of home or the promise of avoiding further discussion on the topic. "Easy for you to say," Clara calls over her shoulder. "You put on another persona like you put on your winter coat."

"Yes." I take two quick steps to reach her, tugging on her arm and meeting her eyes with the truth of my deepest desires. "You know being an actress is all I've ever wanted. Please tell me you wouldn't think to dissuade me of such a dream?"

Clara's eyes flick up toward our apartment building, and I sense unease in her posture. "You know we aren't in a position for you to leave the hotel's employ. Besides, you haven't done much in the way of acting for months. What if you are a maid for the rest of your life, Lou? Would that be so bad?"

"Clara Wilson, how could you say such a thing? Even you, Miss Humdrum must have dreams. I know how you think: I'm fine, everything is fine, I'll just live in my box and never take a chance. How sad would it be if you never dared to hope for a bit of the joy that might be awaiting you." My toe taps hard against the sidewalk despite the ache in my feet. "Dreams don't cost you anything."

Clara pulls on the lobby door of our apartment building. "I am afraid you are wrong, Louisa. There is a cost to everything. Even dreaming."

I shake my head, determined to convince my sister otherwise.

CHAPTER 2

*S*unday, September 18, 1927
Clara

With a sunny Sunday afternoon before us, Louisa and I head out to wander the pathways of Stanley Park. Papa declined to join us. His days working within Vancouver parks have been full and tiring, with the city preparing its green spaces and gardens for the upcoming winter season.

As we stroll along the water's edge, the ocean air breathes new life into me. Though the sound of crashing waves is music to my ears, the towering evergreens located deeper within the park beckon to us. We step onto the beaten trail, its path etched into my mind from frequent visits to the forest. The fresh pine scent grows stronger as we step over roots and wind toward the cluster of trees known as the Seven Sisters.

The drizzle from yesterday has dissipated, leaving Vancouver under the gaze of a brilliant blue sky. The crisp forest air is a welcome change from the warmth of the low-lying sun. Louisa and I grow silent, as is our habit, when we near the site of the cathedral trees. The perfume of the

Douglas fir and western red cedar are a balm to the soul. I can't help but inhale deeply as we stop in front of the grouping of some of the tallest trees the world has ever known.

Time and the city slip away as we become lost in the quiet of this special, majestic place. The towering canopy above us rustles in the wind, sending the best kind of shivers down my spine. I sense the trees possess a wisdom, which settles around us. Despite their looming size, I do not feel small. Instead, their immense presence wraps me in a caring embrace.

In all of Vancouver, this is the place where completeness of self never fails to find me. I exhale the endless pressures, thoughts, and propriety I must live by as a working-class young woman. In this moment, I am simply Clara. I close my eyes, thankful that being myself is enough, if only for a few minutes.

The First Nations legend of the Seven Sisters comes to mind as a tree limb creaks in the distance. As the legend goes, the forest was once haunted by a witchwoman who had been punished and turned into stone. Her power was so strong that her lure continued to confound those who came near the stone, enchanting them to circle round and round indefinitely, unable to find their way out of the forest.

In response to this evil lure, seven of the kindest souls sacrificed themselves by being turned into trees, which were lined up together so all who visited the park could walk safely through the forest. This is what pulls me back time and time again: the feeling of being one. Never more than. Never less than. Their influence could intimidate, but instead the Seven Sisters offer comfort, solace, and a reminder that each of us is worthy of being protected from the evils of the world.

A glance at Louisa tells me she is ready to walk on. I take another deep breath of pine-infused air before following her out of the grove. I glance back over my shoulder once more, with a nod of appreciation and a promise to return.

We move through the park, catching glimpses of filtered sunlight through the treetops. As we step out of the trees' tranquility and into the clearing, the busyness of the park catches me by surprise. Vancouverites of all ages are eager to soak up what remains of the warm-weather season, and Stanley Park is a favourite spot to do so.

The incline up to Prospect Point is flanked by lush flora and fauna but is perspiration inducing nonetheless. The view of the North Shore Mountains from the platform is worth the climb, though, and is the reason we return during each visit.

We are fifty feet from the signal station when a whooshing sound pushes us onto the shoulder of the roadway. A group of riders wearing bicycle club jerseys swarm past us in a rush of air and a whir of colours. At the top of the hill, I tuck fallen strands of hair back into place as Louisa fans her face with both hands.

I smile at my sister's dramatic display of exertion. "Perhaps now would be a good time for a glass of lemonade," I say before reaching into my pocket for the coins I brought along for this very purpose.

"Oh Clara, how clever of you to think ahead. Yes, please, a cold refreshment is just the ticket."

Louisa moves toward the cordoned-off viewpoint as I make my way to the refreshment stand. The line is long, given that most arrived here by the power of their own two feet, with a fortunate few arriving in automobiles. A little brown-haired boy, twitching with boredom, catches my attention. I begin a game of peekaboo with him as we wait our turn. His father offers me a sincere smile of gratitude as we inch closer to the front of the line.

As the boy and his father pay for their order, I take in the beauty surrounding me. The father offers me a final nod before guiding his son away with their drinks.

I raise my hand in a brief wave to the little boy and step under the shade of the temporary awning, ready to place my order. A warm greeting for the vendor lifts the corners of my mouth, before a woman dressed in high-society fashion, without warning, pushes me out of line and takes up a position at the front.

Her expensive silk-chiffon party dress rustles as the woman sways back and forth, her painted nail tapping her pouty red lip as she examines the vendor's offerings on a small sign propped up beside him.

I clear my throat, a meek attempt to make the woman aware of her faux pas. When she doesn't notice me, I remind myself of my station in life and take a small step back, bumping into the man waiting behind me in line.

"Some people," the man behind me grumbles. Though I am unsure whether he is referring to me or the woman who cut the line, I wear the rebuke as my own and shrink even further into my shell.

I am apologizing for my misstep, and my lack of pedigree, when Louisa yanks on my elbow.

"What do you think you are doing?" Her face is pulled into a tight frown.

"I'm not sure what you mean. I'm waiting to purchase our lemonade." I sneak a glance at the woman in front of me, willing her to hurry and make up her mind so I can get our beverages and pull Louisa's discontent away from prying eyes.

"Don't try to deny it, Clara. I saw it all happen with my own two eyes." Louisa inclines her head toward the woman.

"Oh, that." I brush off her comment with a wave of my hand. "Really, it's no bother. It'll only be a minute more."

"You are missing the point. You"—Louisa swings her arm out wide, gesturing to the line of people behind me—"and all of these people have been waiting patiently. She can't simply insert herself and assume everyone will let her."

The hair on the back of my neck rises. I take a quick look at the people waiting behind me and count only five. "I really see no reason to make a fuss. Only a handful of us are waiting, and I don't see anyone else spouting smoke out their ears." My attempt at tempering the tension with a joke does little to convince Louisa.

"If you act less than, you will be treated as less than." Louisa rolls her eyes and lets out an exaggerated huff before turning on her heel and tapping the woman on the shoulder.

I will my body to shrink into the narrow shadow that lies motionless on the ground beside me as the woman twirls with a colourful swish of peach fabric.

"Hello," she says, a sincere greeting enhancing her already lovely features. "Can I help you with something?" Her brows knit, any awareness of her misstep vacant from her expression.

Louisa gestures, an elegant dance-like movement so full of grace that it softens her message. "I'm not sure you are aware, but you seem to have jumped the queue."

"I beg your pardon?" The woman's smile falters a fraction as the vendor garners her attention by raising two bottles of soda pop.

The woman reaches for the bottles as Louisa swivels to face the short line. The heat of embarrassment rises up my collar and licks my face. "All these people were waiting their turn when you hopped, quite gaily, I might add, in your delightful ensemble, to the front of the line."

"Oh my." The woman takes two quick steps away from the vendor, her cheeks growing pink. "I do apologize. It was not my intention." She takes another step, distancing herself from the scene.

I order and pay for our lemonades while keeping one ear trained on the conversation.

"I feel such a fool." The woman takes a step closer to Louisa. "My head is in the clouds today. I didn't even notice anyone else was waiting. You see, we are celebrating Malcolm's birthday," she says, pointing toward a shiny red automobile, with a dashing man leaning against its hood, "and I—oh dear. You must think I am horribly behaved."

"Not at all," Louisa coos, her good nature exerting itself once more. "I merely wanted to make you aware." Placing a hand on the woman's forearm, Louisa continues, "Your dress really is darling. The colour is perfect for your skin tone."

"Oh, thank you. That is sweet of you to say." Her error in judgement quickly forgotten, the woman swishes her skirt. "I admit I am a little in love with it myself. Chris. Chris from Spencer's." The woman's chin drops, waiting for Louisa to recognize the name of the department store owner's son.

"Ah, yes. Chris." Louisa mimics, though I am sure she has never actually met the man.

"Well, he is responsible for spotting the dress and setting it aside for me. He has quite the eye for which items will be fetching on a lady. I truly am fortunate to have him looking out for me when it comes to fashion."

I take our drinks and stand several feet away, not wishing to involve myself in the conversation but wanting to remain close enough to eavesdrop.

Louisa feigns a wide smile. "I imagine you are."

"Yours is quite cute too." The woman volleys her compliment, and I smile at their ping-pong exchange. Two, apparently, can play this game.

"A tad out of date, really," Louisa replies. "But the perfect fabric weight for an afternoon walk."

"Yes, indeed." The woman looks off into the distance

17

before excusing herself. "I best be off before these lose their chill." She leans toward Louisa one final time. "Thank you again for pointing out my error in judgement."

Though her words resonate as sincere, I can't help but wonder if they are laced with a thread of sarcasm.

"Enjoy your afternoon," Louisa calls after her, waiting only a beat before moving toward me.

"New friend?" I can't help but ask, handing Louisa her beverage.

"Very funny." Louisa bumps my shoulder with her own. "I suspect you didn't notice what I gained during my conversation."

"Aside from the confirmation that she is well-to-do and we are not?" I sip my drink, relishing its cool burst against my parched throat.

Louisa inclines her head toward the vendor cart. "Look at the line."

I follow Louisa's gaze but see nothing out of sort. Several people still wait their turn to purchase refreshments. "I don't know what you are referring to."

Louisa's eyes twinkle with mischief. "I kept her talking until all the people who were in line when she jumped to the front had purchased their items and were well on their way."

My puzzlement must be written across my face, as Louisa lets out an impatient whoosh of air. "Don't you see? I made sure her jumping the queue wasn't actually faster. In fact, her butting in cost her an extra few minutes." Louisa hides a giggle behind a flat palm.

"Oh Louisa, you didn't."

"I most certainly did, and you can thank me any time, dear sister. Any time now." Louisa pretends to wait for accolades before bursting into another fit of giggles.

Sipping our drinks, we wander toward the zoo. "Seriously,"

I say, "you really didn't have to worry about me. I was fine to wait in line. I was startled by the intrusion at first, but we got our lemonade in the end."

"What did I tell you before?" Louisa stops abruptly, clutching my arm to gain my attention. "Consider it a lesson in how to get ahead. In life and in line." Louisa grins at her play on words. "All you have to do is be confident in the person you want be recognized as. That'll put you on even footing every time."

"But Louisa, we aren't high-society women with money and power who have a right to demand such things. I wish you'd accept that when you stay in your God-given station in life, there are far less turbulent waters to navigate."

Louisa tilts her head to the side, patting my arm as we stroll forward. "Sweet, sweet Clara. Nobody knows who we are until we show them. That lady back there didn't question whether I was of the same social class as her, because I put on a demeanour she is familiar with in her circle. I am certain it is the reason she apologized so quickly. She didn't want to appear rude to someone she might bump into at a social event."

"I don't think there is anything wrong with who we actually are." I edge the haughty tone from my voice in an effort to keep the peace. "Pretending otherwise isn't for me. My role in society has limitations, I'll admit. But quite frankly, I would rather wait an extra two minutes for lemonade than cause a stir that makes my insides turn to mush." I pick up my pace, determined to leave this conversation behind me. "Besides, I'm sure our outdated walking dresses were a dead giveaway to our lot in life."

"Everyone has something out of fashion in their closet. Some wear them in the garden, and some, as I informed her, wear them for a vigorous walk through the woods." Louisa matches my stride, linking her arm with mine once more. "That reminds me . . ."

I feel a rush of relief at the turn of the conversation.

"Papa told me to make sure you go dress shopping. You can't keep wearing that ratty old thing. We are caught up with the bills for the moment, and according to Papa, he's even managed to squirrel a little extra away for the holidays. You need something respectable to wear, even if your sole destination is the market."

I agree to go shopping but stand my ground on the purchase of only one dress, telling Louisa that we will re-evaluate the financial situation after the holidays.

We move toward the zoo's small animal enclosures, situated in the centre of the park. Approaching the bear enclosure, I can't help but feel sad for the creature in his small, steel-barred pen. My eyes follow his movements back and forth across the width of his prison, and I wonder if he is aware that the same metal bars that afford him a view of the world beyond also restrain him.

As if she is reading my thoughts, Louisa leans over and whispers, "You must know precisely how he feels. Cooped up and watching from the sidelines while the rest of life goes on without him." Louisa shrugs at my sputter of protest, her disappointment in me evident, and wanders toward the park's exit.

CHAPTER 3

$\mathcal{M}$onday, September 19, 1927
Louisa

Monday morning, I leave Clara by the hotel's swinging kitchen door as she checks on the availability of fresh flowers for the hallway tables on the guest floors. The task was handed to her a few short weeks after our employ with The Hamilton began. Though she would argue otherwise, Clara certainly plays the role of eager employee set upon some sort of promotion. She even refused to accompany me to the women's locker room to remove her coat before visiting the kitchen. Forever concerned about others believing she's done a job well, she jumps to extreme worry the moment she's given a directive. If there were an award for following orders, Clara would win it every time.

I make my way down the employee corridor, shaking my head at the contrast between Clara's words and her actions. She steadfastly claims happiness at being just another maid at the hotel while continuing to go above and beyond with every task she completes within its walls.

Hu, a kitchen assistant, walks toward me down the dimly lit hall.

"Good morning, Hu." I offer a broad smile with my greeting, intent to one day convince the man to raise his gaze from the floor and meet my eyes.

We shuffle past one another, Hu nodding a small assent at my presence while once more finding reason to avoid speaking with me. I'll crack his stoic exterior one day, I tell myself, adding a cheerful "Have a great day" as he continues toward the pile of dishes I imagine awaits him in the kitchen.

Laughter filters past the closed locker room door as I press my back against the solid wood and push.

"I mean, she isn't even that pretty, if you ask me." Maggie's husky voice bellows above the chatter. "But that sure doesn't stop her from inserting herself. And to think she assumed we didn't have things handled. The nerve of some people, I tell you."

"You're just sore because you didn't come up with such a clever solution." I recognize Hazel's voice, muffled but distinguishable.

I stop just inside the door, its closing hinges drowned out by the conversation and the commotion of girls readying themselves for the day. Unease pokes at me, and I feel my breakfast sink like a stone in my stomach. I linger out of sight, the overheard words settling uncomfortably under my skin.

"Who are we talking about now?" I hear Jane Morgan pipe in. Her recent promotion to full-time day maid is new enough for me to have forgotten she's now a regular presence in the locker room. I lean forward a smidge to peer around the corner. Jane tilts her body, her face inches from the mirror on the wall, a tube of red lipstick in her hand.

"Why, the oh-so-charming Miss Wilson." Maggie's throaty

laugh echoes off the concrete-block walls and reverberates around the room.

I suck in a sharp breath at Maggie's confirmation. The girl does not like me. My mind spins. I have been nothing but kind and supportive to her, to all the girls. I thought I was making friends.

Jane's lipstick retreats from her lips as she tosses a perturbed look over her shoulder. "Which one? You are aware there are two Miss Wilsons, are you not?"

"Maggie is referring to Louisa." Hazel moves toward Jane, stealing a glance in the mirror as she fixes her maid's cap. "But as I said before, I don't think we should be discussing such things. Especially when Louisa's brilliant idea made a challenging task much easier." Hazel faces Maggie once more, raising her voice for emphasis. "For all of us."

I catch Jane's smirk from my spot in the shadows and draw back in anticipation of her words. Though I have yet to understand why Jane behaves so, her occasional bouts of spitefulness remind me of a cornered cat, its claws out and ready to pounce.

"I don't see the reason for the fuss, Maggie." Jane's voice becomes less audible as she returns her attention to the mirror. "If what Louisa did was helpful, what have you got to complain about?"

I am surprised but buoyed by Jane's sensible remark and lean forward once more, hopeful the conversation will take a turn for the better and my standing within the group will be restored.

"Louisa acts so highfalutin." Maggie places her hands on her hips and attempts to mimic me by batting her eyelashes at Jane's back. "Flirting with the bellboys and winking at the porters." Maggie struts around the locker room with an exaggerated sway of her hips.

23

If her unkind words weren't about me, I might find humour at her antics.

"You know, just the other day, I saw her deep in conversation with Mr. Olson." Maggie pauses for effect, leaning in conspiratorially while waiting for all eyes to fall on her. "The whole thing made me wonder."

"Made you wonder what?" Jane turns her full attention to Maggie, replacing the cap on her lipstick before resting both hands on her hips. Maggie squirms under Jane's direct gaze as Jane repeats her question. "Made you wonder *what*?"

My breath is stuck in my throat, along with my usual self-assured demeanour. My hands grow clammy as I try to recall a conversation with Mr. Olson that might have been interpreted as anything but cordial. I come up empty. I'm torn between my distaste for Maggie's insinuation and my appreciation of Jane's defence of my good name.

"You know." Maggie takes a step back, clearly uncomfortable for having been called out.

"I don't know," Jane retorts with a huff, "which is why I am asking."

"I thought that maybe—" Maggie fidgets with her apron. "Well, I wondered if Louisa might be using her looks to gain an advantage of sorts, you know, in the workplace." Maggie juts out her chin. "Perhaps Miss Wilson is receiving preferential treatment from her overly friendly advances."

"Margaret Adams." Jane steps closer to Maggie and, from my vantage point, appears to be winding up for a battle. "You should be ashamed of yourself. What has Louisa Wilson ever done to deserve such an accusation?" Jane points a finger toward Maggie. "Comments like that can ruin a girl's reputation."

"Oh Jane, don't be so sensitive." Lillian Roberts steps forward, prodding Jane playfully. "I told you there is nothing to worry about. The chatter at The Club went no further than the table we were sitting at."

"This," Jane hisses, her head tipped down in an effort to conceal her words, "isn't about that."

The room falls silent as the air between Jane and Lillian chills. A few moments pass before Jane collects herself, shrugging off the incident by stepping forward and positioning herself directly in front of Maggie. She pumps the neat bun tucked at the base of her neck and says in a softer voice, "If a girl has good looks, I find no fault in her using them to her advantage, especially when the intent is to help others."

Jane turns to tuck her belongings into her locker before facing Maggie again. "Of course, Miss Adams, you may be unaware of what is expected of pretty girls in today's society, given your lack of such appeal, but you may want to think better of looking a gift horse in the mouth."

Jane shoots a dagger-laced look in Lillian's direction before turning on her heel.

I am bolstered by Jane's support of me, though admittedly unnerved by her proclamation that I get ahead by way of my appearance. I'd never do such a thing. Not since that vile director made me question each one of my past successes on the stage. I shake off the memory as my mind races between subdued relief at Jane's impactful words and the worrying comments from Lillian and Maggie. I can't help but wonder if a storm is brewing for Jane and me as I inch back toward the door.

Feeling a small measure of vindication, I stand a little straighter and try to forget my momentary cowardice. I should have immediately stood up for myself. As I have proved to myself time and again, I can continually grease the wheels of compliance when I invoke my charming nature.

My back stiffens as I catch a glimpse of Maggie. I am not

intentionally using my looks to win favours from anyone. Her accusation is distasteful at best, and I can't help but worry that her words may damage my reputation, should she continue to spout such untruths. Any young woman in 1927 Vancouver knows better than to test the ability of gossip to make opportunities vanish. Though I have no desire to be labelled a prude, being branded a tart brings a whole other level of shame to a girl's family. Given my close call with that director, I cringe at the thought.

My elation at receiving Jane's support is short-lived. I see her move in my direction, and panic ripples through me at fear of being caught eavesdropping. I am searching for how to present myself when the door opens, hitting me from behind.

"Oh, sorry Lou." Clara takes a step back through the open door. "I didn't mean—"

"Hush now," I hiss, knowing I will have some explaining to do in the near future. I squeeze Clara's hand in a desperate plea for assistance. "Follow my lead." The words come out in a rush of air.

Clara's puzzled expression pushes me forward, and I pivot, squaring my shoulders while adding a bemused smile to my lips. As Jane rounds the corner, I quip, "In a hurry to get started on the day, are we?"

She shrugs and passes us as we step forward to enter the locker room.

Hazel is the first to speak. "There you two are. I was beginning to wonder if you'd make it in time for roll call." She takes Clara's uniform from her, hanging it over a locker door before untying the apron in what I assume is an effort to lend a hand. "You know how Ms. Thompson can be." Hazel tilts her chin, mimicking the hotel matron's demeanour. "*The early bird gets the worm, ladies.*"

An amused chuckle runs through the group before several

maids filter out of the room, allowing us a tad more space to change and ready ourselves for the day. Maggie is among those vacating, and I breathe a strained sigh of relief at seeing her go, quite certain the words I'd like to fling at her would put me in hot water with Ms. Thompson.

Hazel takes the uniform from my arms in an effort to spur me into action, eyeing the clock on the far wall. "Better hurry, Louisa. Being on the receiving end of Ms. Thompson's frown is no way to start the day."

"No, I don't suppose it is." I feel Hazel's gaze on me and wonder if she has guessed that I overheard the conversation.

Ten minutes later, we are dressed in our matching plain blue dresses, with our hair neatly pinned under the caps I've yet to understand why we wear. Ms. Thompson details our day's duties, assigning guest rooms and passing along any special requests the guests have made in the past twenty-four hours.

Standing in line with the others, my mind wanders back to Maggie's spiteful words, which have left me feeling far more wounded than I care to admit. I had thought Maggie and I were getting on well enough, despite her generally disgruntled nature. I had reasoned that since she worked on the second floor and I on the fifth, we weren't likely to be friends anyway.

Of course, Clara and Miss Smythe, who works on the eighth floor, have become bosom buddies despite a three-floor separation. I think back, searching my mind for a moment where I might have erred in a conversation with Maggie, but nothing that could warrant such unveiled accusations comes to mind.

Ms. Thompson's voice drones on at the opposite end of our straight line. She runs a tight ship here at The Hamilton. We're a crew of sorts, working together, anticipating one another's needs, quickly stepping aside should we encounter a guest en route to or from their room.

I've been fitting in well, dutifully maintaining expectations in my role as maid and colleague. I assumed I was succeeding, always trying to appear willing to toe the line, but Maggie's ridicule cuts deep. My nose tingles as a rim of moisture lines my lower lids. I jut out my chin in defiance and sniff discreetly behind a clenched fist.

Jane, standing three to my left, catches my eye with a sideways glance, her brow creased in question.

I force a smile, not wishing anyone entrance to my private thoughts.

Ms. Thompson is handing out additional tasks, the maids acting like they're dishes of ice cream, thanking her for the opportunity to burden their day with more work than is possible to complete in the allotted hours. I can't help but question the motivation of those standing shoulder to shoulder with me. They truly believe this is the best that life has in store for them.

A pang of guilt seizes my chest. I know I should be grateful. This position has enabled our family to set itself straight. In the beginning, I was keen to work in the hotel, thrilled by the allure of the illustrious new building. I had high hopes of rubbing shoulders with celebrities, musicians, and famous directors. So far, though, I've only brushed up against grime and rumpled bed linens.

A glimpse at Clara fills me with unease. She is bobbing her head in agreement as Ms. Thompson continues with her list. I regret the day I wiggled into what was clearly meant to be Clara's adventure. She is sure to presume I'm being fickle, that I'm unreliable and unable to follow through on my promise of working alongside her. I can hear her rippling disappointment in the corner of my mind.

Shaking off the distasteful melancholy, I bolster my mood with the obvious truth: Maggie must simply be jealous of me. She hasn't been graced with a pleasant demeanour, nor a pretty face. Even her hair frizzes, unwieldy no matter how much effort she puts into securing it in place.

I sniff, angry that I have to bear the fallout of her insecurities and jealousy. My posture stiffens in rebellion of the unpleasant situation before me. I have no desire to work among those who are unable to embrace another's meagre good fortunes and talents. Besides, it isn't as though I had dreams of becoming a maid. The situation presented itself is all. I cringe a little, knowing Clara must see my impulsive leap into the job as exactly that.

I give my head a shake. Girls like Maggie don't matter one bit, I tell myself. She'll probably spend the rest of her life cleaning up after others. I imagine she hasn't even considered an alternative to hotel work.

At least I have my acting. I tilt my chin upward, envisioning the lights, the audience, the applause. I am an actress, and I will prove the naysayers wrong. I must concede that I've never been good at waiting for things to start going my way. Employment at the hotel is merely a distraction keeping me from my true place on the stage. Perhaps it is time for me to take hold of the reins once more.

"Miss Wilson?" Ms. Thompson's voice and a poke in the ribs from the maid beside me pull me from my thoughts. "Miss Wilson, did you hear me?"

"No, ma'am. My apologies, I didn't realize you were speaking to me." Heat races to my cheeks as several heads turn in my direction.

"Very well. I asked that you bring up the large dog bed from the storage room for the guests in room 508. I have no details on the dog's breed, only that he is indeed large."

"Yes, ma'am."

Ms. Thompson flips a page, muttering softly under her breath before addressing the group one last time. "That is all, ladies. If you need me for anything this morning, I will be in my office."

The line breaks apart, and we disperse like schoolchildren at the ringing of an afternoon bell. I watch the other maids scurry, eager to attend to their list of duties.

Wait until they see me on the stage. The thought props up my wounded pride. A spotlight tracking my every move. An audience leaning in for each line I utter. I'll show them all that Louisa Wilson was born to be a star. I am picturing my name in the marquee lights when the disturbing memory of my last audition intrudes on my daydream, causing me to recoil. I let out a weighted sigh and wander toward the linen cupboard to collect my cleaning cart. Even at The Hamilton, it seems, I am judged based on my appearance alone. The question is, what am I going to do about it?

CHAPTER 4

Saturday, September 24, 1927
Clara

The clerk in the dress shop hasn't looked my way since
politely greeting me when I pressed into the cubby of a shop,
the bell jingling. Clutching a plain dress that I am hopeful will
be in fashion for a few years, I check the time on my
wristwatch again.

I've spent the past five minutes glancing about the shop,
my patience wilting as I wait at the counter, ready to pay for
my purchase. Both store clerks are caught in the web of a
woman who seems determined not to decide which dress she
favours most.

An exasperated sigh whispers across my lips as the woman
insists in a high-pitched, grating tone that she "simply can't
decide between the dusty rose or the taupe rose." Both dresses
appear exactly the same to my undiscerning eye. I place my
intended purchase on the counter and rest my elbow, cupping
my chin in my hand. I thrum the fingers of my other hand

against the polished wood counter, hoping to gain the attention of at least one of the clerks. One would have to be blind, or ignorant, not to notice me waiting.

I consider speaking up but recognize my lack of authority. The other shopper—a socialite, I presume, by the way she is carrying on—clearly has sway from the size of her pocketbook. I chide myself for such unflattering thoughts and return to gazing around the shop as I wait.

I check my watch again. The British grocer will be closing within the hour. The grocer is several blocks away from my usual market route, but a telephone call to the shop this morning confirmed the grocer had one box of Atora beef suet remaining. Desperate to get my hands on it so I can make a traditional mince pie, I promised the woman on the phone I would stop in before closing.

This year, the government decided to celebrate Canada's Diamond Jubilee and our annual autumn Thanksgiving on the same July weekend. Louisa and I were both working that weekend, so we agreed as a family to delay our Thanksgiving festivities. With each of us immersed in new employment, postponing our Thanksgiving feast to the traditional time of year seemed sensible. I hadn't considered, though, the difficulty I would have acquiring ingredients, given that the rest of the country celebrated the harvest holiday months earlier.

While the rest of the city buzzed with fanfare over Canada's sixtieth birthday, Louisa and I worked straight through the weekend at a fully booked Hotel Hamilton, barely pausing to glance out the window at the merrymaking below. I wondered if a Thanksgiving turkey or ham still graced every table in Canada on July 3, 1927, or if all our traditions were foregone.

Two more minutes pass without the slightest glance from either clerk. I am considering placing the dress back on the rack and leaving the store altogether when an assured-looking woman leans in beside me, sporting a knowing smile.

"You know, if you act like a wallflower, my dear, people will treat you like one." The woman winks mischievously as her red-painted lips spread into a wide smile.

Without a word from me, she raises a gloved hand in the air, waving it as I imagine a princess might be trained to do. "Yoo-hoo, excuse me. I beg your pardon. I don't mean to interrupt." The woman takes a step in the direction of the undecided shopper and the two imprisoned clerks. Inclining her head toward one of the dresses being scrutinized, she continues, "The dusty rose is the perfect colour for your skin tone, madam. I wouldn't be inclined to let that one slip away."

"Why, thank you." The woman nods to one of the clerks. "I'll take that one." She hesitates a moment before adding, "The other two as well. One can never have too many dresses, I suppose." She hides a sheepish laugh behind one hand.

"Excellent choice. All of them." My newfound champion pivots toward me, amplifying my admiration of her as she gives an exaggerated roll of her eyes in my direction. "Now that you are free, I believe some assistance is needed over here at the counter."

"Yes, ma'am." The younger of the two clerks, pins in hand, stands from her kneeling position on the floor and dashes to the cash register as though she has only this moment realized there are other customers in the shop. Once situated behind the counter, the clerk turns her attention to my rescuer, who has taken up a spot in line behind me.

"This young lady is first." Gesturing to me, I sense her contemplating her next words and am struck by her command

33

of the situation. Without removing her assured smile, she drops her voice an octave, meeting the clerk's eyes. "A friendly reminder, love: this young lady's money is worth just as much as hers." She points a gloved thumb over her shoulder, indicating the society woman with her three dresses. "But if you ask me, it's actually worth more, given how hard she is likely to have worked for it."

My shoulders rise to meet my ears, and I wish I could disappear into the floorboards. I could never be so bold, and yet here I am, under the clerk's scrutiny without having spoken a single word. Embarrassment burns my face. I pay my bill as quickly as I am able before tucking my purchase into my shopping bag. Offering a gracious but quiet thank you to both the clerk and the defender of common courtesy, I slip out the door. As the door closes behind me with the soft tinkle of the bell, her words of advice pursue me like a searchlight seeking a fugitive.

I turn abruptly, in a hurry to extract myself from the scene and to arrive at the British grocer before it closes for the day. In my haste and with my eyes cast downward, I collide with another person on the sidewalk. Words of apology fly from my lips as I lift my gaze to find Cookie standing before me, bundled in a long woollen coat, a parcel tucked under one arm. "Oh, what a surprise." My words race ahead. "Please forgive me, Cookie. I wasn't watching where I was going. You aren't working at the hotel today?"

"Clara, how lovely to see you. They do let me vacate the pastry kitchen every now and again." Cookie winks and motions me out of the way of a passerby. "No harm done and no apology necessary. I imagine it would take more than your little self to bowl me over." Cookie's rosy cheeks glisten in the damp afternoon air. "Now, where is it you are off to in such a hurry?"

I point in the direction of the specialty shop. "The British grocer. They've only one packet of suet left, and I am keen to avoid mixing the stuff from scratch." My nose crinkles in distaste. "After reading Mama's recipe, I must admit I considered tossing the idea of mince pie altogether, but I was desperate to have a practice run before Christmas. Mama always made one for Christmas."

Cookie lets out a hearty laugh. "Can't blame you one bit. Nasty business, that suet-making. A mince pie is sure to brighten your father's face, especially if he is fortunate enough to enjoy two within a few months of each other. There is something satisfying about a savoury pie. Makes my mouth water just thinking about it."

When I told Cookie about our decision to delay our Thanksgiving feast until autumn, she presented me with a recipe the very next day. She guaranteed me a roast chicken made with a recipe from her private collection would soon become a family favourite, with no one missing the traditional turkey or ham.

"Louisa and I both have Sunday off in a couple of weeks, so we are planning to celebrate Thanksgiving then. I know it is a bit excessive having both the roast chicken and the mince pie, but it's been so long since we've had much to celebrate."

"You'll be eating well for days. Mind if I join you at the grocer?" Cookie's delight twinkles in her eyes. "I am always game for a chance to visit the specialty shops."

"I'd be very pleased if you would." Together, Cookie and I stroll toward the British grocer, her lighthearted banter erasing any lingering embarrassment over the events at the dress shop.

The kind lady at the grocer retrieves the package of suet from the backroom as Cookie peruses the rest of the shop. Her eyes are drawn to a shelf of black liquorice candy in tins covered with images of Britain's blue, red, and white flag.

The clerk provides a few instructions on preparing the suet before I pay for it and tuck the brown paper-wrapped box into my shopping bag.

Stepping out the door, Cookie points further down the block with a gloved hand. "Do you fancy a cup of tea?" Her eagerness to continue our visit warms my heart. "The best tea house in all of Vancouver is right around the corner."

"That would be lovely." I incline my head in agreement. "Please, lead the way."

We walk a few blocks, lost in conversation about the comings and goings of the hotel's pastry kitchen. Cookie tells me about a mix-up with the sugar and salt delivery. Her good-natured chuckle puffs little clouds into the chilly air as we stroll.

"This way." Cookie tugs on my coat sleeve, and I realize that we have walked straight into the heart of Japantown.

"Oh, I—ah . . ." My eyes scan my surroundings. Little dark-haired children dash about the street, and old women sweep front stoops with narrow brooms, their day almost at an end, I assume. I sidestep a man pushing a handcart loaded with produce.

"Watch yourself there, Clara." Cookie draws me closer as we navigate the busy street.

"I beg your pardon. I've never . . . well, I suppose the only time I venture to this part of the city is with my father, on the way to a baseball game."

"Ah, your father is a fan of the Asahi?" Cookie weaves her plump frame past a crowded shop entrance, waving a hand in greeting as she passes.

"He is. An avid fan." Two men are seated on a stoop, hunched over a board game in the dwindling daylight.

"Here we are." Cookie pulls on the door, and a light grassy scent washes over me as we enter.

A woman dressed in a dark blue, patterned kimono rushes forward to welcome us. Though her words are foreign to us, her manner indicates familiarity with Cookie. She bows in greeting, a timid but friendly smile upon her face.

Cookie gestures toward me, introducing me as a friend from the hotel. The woman smiles even brighter, adding a quiet "hello."

She shows us to a low table. In place of chairs, four cushions rest on a sand-coloured floor mat. Despite our sitting on the floor, the setting offers a welcome respite from the chill. The woman dashes to the back of the shop before tucking herself out of sight behind a curtain separating the tea room from what I imagine is a storeroom.

"What a lovely treat to have you join me today, Clara. Masao's mother seems delighted to meet you." Cookie removes her wool coat, stuffing her gloves into the pockets before settling herself on the cushion across from me.

"Masao?" My eyebrows lift.

"Yes, Masao. The little Japanese boy who comes to visit the hotel from time to time." Cookie waits a moment for recognition to dawn on me. "The one who enjoys a pastry now and then."

"The little boy? This is his family's tea house?" I can't keep the surprise from my expression. "But I thought he was an orphan and—and that you were being kind to him, since his needs were great."

Cookie's boisterous laugh fills the small tea room. "An orphan? What in the world made you think Masao was an orphan? He has what my granny would have called a hollow leg, I'll grant you, but an orphan he is not."

I glance about the room, ensuring the boy's mother has not reappeared. Despite her Japanese greeting and her shy hello, I can't be sure our conversation in English would not be understood, and I would hate to offend her with my ill-informed notion of her family. "The first time I met him, he was digging through the garbage in the hotel alley, looking for food. He happily retrieved an apple core from the bin. I suppose—well, I may have misunderstood. But why would the boy be digging for sustenance when his mother is clearly more than capable of caring for him?"

"An apple core, did you say?" Cookie smiles. "Clever lad."

Unsure of what she means, I continue, "I even offered him my own apple. To be honest, it took some convincing for him to take it."

Cookie lets loose a guffaw. "Ah, it was the seeds he was after. He is desperate to grow an apple tree as a gift for his grandmother."

"An apple tree?" I realize how wrong my assumptions of the boy were. I glance beyond the moisture gathering on the tea house window. "Wouldn't it take years for an apple tree to produce fruit, especially in Vancouver weather?"

"I imagine it would." Cookie shakes her head, the corner of her mouth quirking upward in amusement. "If anybody can grow a tree in a pot in the middle of Vancouver, I imagine it would be Masao. He is an industrious lad, without a doubt."

Masao's mother returns to our table with a tray of small, dome-shaped cakes I do not recognize, a delicate ornamental teapot, and two small cups stacked one on top of the other.

"*Domo arigato.*" Cookie bows her head in gratitude as the tea is placed between us.

"My pleasure," Masao's mother replies, her voice soft but her English clear. She delivers a gentle bow before leaving us to our tea.

"You speak Japanese?" I ask Cookie as she pours tea into both of our cups.

"A wee bit." A soft shrug conveys her nonchalance. "Masao teaches me a word here and there."

I sip the hot tea, relishing its fresh aroma. "Mmm, you are quite right. This is delicious."

Cookie hands me a treat from the plate. "These are *manjū*, a traditional Japanese treat.

I nibble at the edge of the steamed cake. "So, why is Masao interested in growing an apple tree?"

"Family, I believe. He is a good lad. Curious and adventurous, but his heart is warm and it shines all the way to those dancing eyes of his."

Cookie pauses for a sip of tea. "Masao's grandmother came from the old country a few years after he was born, and the two of them have a barter system of sorts. She teaches him about his heritage, the language, and gardening. In turn, he teaches her English and about life in Canada. Sweetest thing, really. I came to Vancouver on my own, with no one and nothing to my name. I had to learn the hard way how to get by, when to speak. I even learned to tame my Irish brogue so as not to stand out."

"You changed the way you speak? On purpose?" I think back to Mama's English lilt and wonder if she too downplayed her accent to fit in.

Cookie chuckles. "Well, not exactly. I remember the first time I spoke of the rain bucketing down. I thought I was making idle chit-chat about the weather, but the woman at the boarding house didn't have a clue what I was talking about. She looked at me as though I was right barmy."

"I understand." I nod, imagining how Cookie must have felt at being singled out. "Blending in is a simpler way of living." I place my cup on the table. "Louisa thinks otherwise, but I am with you. Rocking the boat just isn't for me."

"Well, I didn't say that, dear." Cookie delivers a playful wink across the table. "I am quite capable of standing up for myself, as I am certain you've witnessed during my squabbles with Chef."

"I see." I take another bite of my cake before sipping more tea. "I must admit, I've always suspected your and Chef's squabbles to be more in jest than anything else."

"Do ya, now? Sometimes you need to make a fuss." Cookie leans in conspiratorially. "Just make sure it's for the right reasons." Her eyes twinkle as she teases me. "Anyway, as I was saying, Masao adores his grandmother and wanted to do something nice for her. He asked me a few months back if I knew how to grow an apple tree, but I'm afraid I haven't the foggiest."

"I can't say I'd be of much help with that either." I lift my teacup, savouring another sip. "Thank you for bringing me here. I am ever so grateful to you for introducing me to this shop, and to Masao's mother. I can rest easy knowing the boy is very well indeed. I would be lying if I said I hadn't worried for him."

"You are a kind soul, Clara. A kind soul." Cookie's expression softens from that of a proud mother hen to something more forlorn. "But life isn't as easy as you may think for those who are Japanese-Canadian. Having a loving family and a roof over your head isn't enough to keep all the city's ills at bay."

I am about to ask what she means when Masao's mother reappears beside our table. "Do you like?" she asks me, inclining her head toward the tea tray.

"Oh, yes. Very much. Thank you." I bow my head, hoping to convey my sincere appreciation of her offering.

Cookie exchanges a few words with her in Japanese before

insisting to pay for our tea, not allowing me the slightest opportunity to argue.

Masao's mother meets my eyes. "You have a good friend in Cookie."

"Yes. I do." I reach across the table and squeeze Cookie's arm.

CHAPTER 5

*M*onday, September 26, 1927
Louisa

Maggie's insinuation that I am a trollop who uses her God-given good looks to elevate her status has pursued me like a bloodhound for an entire week. I've found myself drenched in sweat in the wee hours of the morning, woken from a dastardly nightmare in which both my reputation as an actress and the silky, thin fabric of my nightdress were torn to shreds. In the dream, a mob of angry theatregoers advance toward me, shouting that I am nothing more than a pretty face. In last night's production, the jeering crowd called for evidence of my ability to act at all.

The bad dreams have continued to mock me, their grip tight enough to squeeze the life out of me. Thoughts of the nightmares and the lack of settled sleep have done little for my disposition. A weary body and a sour mood are the least of my troubles though. At The Hamilton, I'm expected to put on a brave face and a cheery smile. Each, unfortunately, is far more than I am currently capable of.

Clara's attempts to cajole me into pleasantness are both heartwarming and infuriating. Sadly, we often lash out at those we love the most. Clara has been on the receiving end of more than one of my prickly responses this week, and even now, when I recognize the need to smooth the turbulence of our conversation, I find myself unleashing a storm of self-pitying anger.

My scornful expression must convey my internal dialogue. Clara, hands on her hips, exclaims with an exasperated tone, "I was only trying to help, Lou."

"Did I ask for help?" My retort is excessive at best, since she only offered to make an egg to go with my breakfast. My appetite has waned as of late, and a slice of toast is all I can stomach. "I am quite capable of knowing what I want to eat, you know."

"I was only suggesting you might feel a bit more energetic if you allowed me to prepare an egg for you." Clara takes her plate and tea to the table, though I feel her eyes on me as I wait for my toast to brown.

I butter my toast and slump into the chair opposite her, my mind ruminating on what I must do, despite my heart's displeasure. I fear I'll lose hold of my theatre dreams—or more pressingly, my position at The Hamilton—due to the frivolous gossip of a bitter girl. I refuse to let Maggie and her fabricated accusations ruin my future endeavours. Even if it means I must tamp down my natural fun-loving disposition in order to blend in.

Last night's dream, a jumbled mess of fears and memories, convinced me that the time has come to take action. I need a plan to ensure my position at the hotel is not in jeopardy. I may not be as happy working as a maid as I'd like, but I can't stomach the thought of losing the position, disappointing my family, and unsettling our newly stable financial situation.

Besides, I have no immediate alternative that will land me on stage, under a spotlight. The last time I sought such an opportunity, it nearly ruined me.

The memory of that cold, damp afternoon in February flickers in the back corner of my mind. The day had started out with great promise, despite having been recently evicted from our cottage on the Murray Estate due to Papa's inability to maintain his job. I was trying to make the best of a bad situation.

I snuck out early in the day, tiptoeing past Clara as she lay deep in sleep. She had been working persistently to turn our less than hospitable apartment into a home. At the bottom of the stairs, I forced my feet into my nicest black pumps, though the day was really too cold for them, and donned my coat before heading out into the brisk city air. My spirits were high as I checked the slip of paper I'd hidden in my pocket, noting the address where the auditions were being held. If we were going to live in the city, I was going to find my way into the limelight.

A sigh sneaks past my lips at the memory of my naive hopefulness, garnering me an imploring look of concern from Clara. I fire an irritated scowl in her direction before returning my attention to the toast and my memories.

Looking back, I realize how unprepared I was for stage life in the heart of the city. I foolishly believed my success in my previous upper-class theatre group to be a sure indicator of future fame and fortune. Despite being the daughter of an estate employee, I was well received in the club after my initial audition. I had, after all, been awarded no less than the top supporting role—and often the lead—in every performance put on by that club, located in the most affluent neighborhood in Vancouver. Little did I know how stark the differences would be.

I arrived home that afternoon, defeated and branded a fool, spending the next several weeks nursing a bruised ego and a broken heart.

Now, all I can wonder is whether my talent for the stage or my good looks secured all those roles. Being beautiful certainly has advantages. More often than not, the benefits outweigh any negatives. Given the situation with Maggie's wagging tongue, though, I am hardly ignorant to the downsides of having a pretty face.

"Are you sure you are feeling well?" Clara's voice pierces my thoughts.

"I am fine," I snap. Regretting my tone, I force a tight smile, aware I am fooling neither of us. "I'll be fine. I believe the downward turn in the weather has me dragging my feet these days."

"If you say so." Clara moves toward our apartment's small kitchen with her dishes, looking as though she wants to say more but deciding better of it as she continues past me.

Clara retreats to the bedroom to finish readying herself for the workday, and I rise from the table, clearing my dishes to the kitchen sink. Taking a final gulp of tea, I resign myself to the situation at hand. The Hotel Hamilton is apparently not the place I am to shine. Instead, I must disappear into the shadows of the rich wood panelling and bide my time until I can sort out my next steps.

Leaving the hotel's employ for the chance at a role in the theatre would be rash and foolhardy, especially since I've been on the outskirts of the scene for months now. I suspect it will take some time to reacquaint and bolster myself. Then I will make an informed decision about where my future truly lies.

In the meantime, I will give Maggie and the others no reason to call me out for even the slightest infraction, real or imagined. I shake my head. Maggie has no authority over me whatsoever, and yet I find myself unable to face her head on. Instead, I am inclined to sidestep her accusations and do my best to avoid the stink they could create.

For years, I've viewed my charisma as an asset. My charming demeanour has gained me plenty of favourable outcomes. Seldom are attitudes toward me anything less than delighted. Yet here I am, shrinking my personality to protect my position at the hotel, all because of another's judgement. I can't control how others perceive my good looks. That thorn is deeply embedded within me, and Maggie's accusations have wiggled into where it rests. I find myself desperate to put things right.

Clara emerges from the bedroom, checking her wristwatch in a not-so-subtle movement meant to hurry me along. I take in her plain features. She tends to dress down, in a manner which appears matronly rather than youthful. Her neat appearance lacks any flair or embellishment.

That's the solution to my problem. All I need to do is behave as Clara does. She would be the last maid in all of Vancouver to be painted as a tart, I am certain.

I hurry toward the bathroom, where I swipe the colour from my lips with a damp cloth. With a heavy hand, I brush through my bouncing curls and tame their natural liveliness. If I wish to go unnoticed, I will need to downplay my looks and conform with the ordinary and the unremarkable.

Clara joins me at the door, wearing a winter jacket in lieu of yesterday's raincoat. The irony of my dilemma is not lost on me as I venture forward. I'm taking cues from my sister, doing the exact opposite of my advice to her. I hold my bottom lip between my teeth and decide not to share this insight. A girl has her limits, after all.

~

By early afternoon, I am exhausted. If I didn't know better, I might assume my tiredness comes from the heavy workload twined with the start of the week. The day has been a trying one—not because the guests are eager to check in and settle themselves for a week of work in the city, but rather because of my new persona. I am intent on steering clear of any action that could elicit an ill mention of me.

The woman with the large dog vacated her guest room on Sunday, but the dog's bedding has yet to be dealt with. I trudge down the stairs toward the laundry, where the oversized bed is waiting for me. I deliver a quick hello to Jing, The Hamilton's impressive laundress, who can remove any stain brought to her. Then I weave toward the back wall of the cavernous room in search of the dog bed.

I am bent at the waist, tugging on a corner of the bed, when a voice startles me.

"Need a hand with that?" George steps forward, the shoulder tassels on his bellboy jacket swaying as he grabs a corner of the bed.

With our joint effort, the large plush pillow slides out, leaving the bed's base hanging precariously off the edge of the shelf. Dust and dog hair circle us, and I wave a hand to disperse the nose-tickling motes.

Although my inclination is to laugh at the humour of our shared experience, I hastily smother the impulse as I remember my decision to remain a meeker version of myself. "Thanks, but I've got it." I drop my end of the pillow to the floor, bracing the stand as I remove it from the shelf.

"I'm here to help." George pauses a moment before adding, with a twinkle in his eye, "Louisa."

I wince at his use of my first name. The name I've been cajoling him to use for months. Here, on my first day of being keenly aware of every word I speak and every action I take,

George finally chooses friendly familiarity over stoic professionalism.

"Thanks, but really, I've got it." I smile, though I know the warm sentiment does not show in my eyes. "I am sure you have better things to do than help me beat a dusty dog bed." Instead of waiting for a reply, I turn my back to him and begin pounding on the overstuffed pillow with both fists. A moment passes before I sense his departure, allowing me to refocus on the task before me.

Dust and dog hair fly through the air as I hammer my fists into the bed, taking out my frustration. I pummel the pillow for what seems like hours, only stopping occasionally to wipe sweat from my brow. I give the pillow a final wipe down with a soft cloth before repositioning it on its stand.

Climbing the stairs, out of breath and coated in grime, my legs are slow and heavy. I peek out the stairwell door, ensuring the hall is empty of guests before dashing to the linen closet. I need a private moment to put myself together for the remaining hour of my shift.

I am pinning my cap into place when Ms. Thompson startles me from behind.

"There you are, Miss Wilson. I was beginning to wonder where you had gotten to."

"I was in the laundry setting the dog's bed straight, as you asked, ma'am." I tuck a loose strand of hair into the back of my hat before meeting her eyes.

"Yes, but I sent Mr. Baker to assist you."

Understanding dawns on me. "I didn't realize you had sent him, ma'am. I suppose—I thought he was merely being kind by offering his help." My cheeks warm with embarrassment over my mistake.

Ms. Thompson's lips pucker in what I assume is displeasure. "I've never known you to be the sort to refuse an offered hand, Miss Wilson." Ms. Thompson looks away, surveying the linen cupboard's shelves as she considers her next words. "Well then, given the state of your appearance, I suppose you should remain here. The others will be bringing in their carts shortly."

I am unsure if I've imagined Ms. Thompson's tsk, but I shrink out of instinct, taking a step back while running both hands down the front of my apron in an attempt to tidy myself. I wonder how I am to be both pleasing to the eye, in the way that is expected of us, while also appearing unremarkable so as to avoid being snared by false accusations.

Ms. Thompson's eyes narrow on me. "No better day than today to ensure the carts get a thorough cleaning. I'll have someone bring your cart."

"Thank you, ma'am." My body folds into an automatic curtsy, the gesture seeming necessary given Ms. Thompson's disappointment.

"As soon as the carts are cleaned, you are free to go for the day." A bustle behind Ms. Thompson grabs our attention.

Clara and the other fifth-floor maids are manoeuvring their carts into the linen closet for cleaning.

Ms. Thompson steps aside, allowing them entrance. She moves toward the doorway but pivots slowly at its threshold, directing one final comment toward me. "Miss Wilson, be sure to vacate the guest floor in the most discreet manner possible."

I nod once before shame at my dishevelled appearance holds my head in place, bowed slightly, looking at the floor. Frustration over my dilemma thrums in my veins. It takes me a moment to regain my composure and address the matron in the expected manner. "Yes, ma'am."

CHAPTER 6

*W*ednesday, September 28, 1927
Clara

Louisa has been moping for days. My first thought was that she should simply get over whatever was eating at her. Heaven knows one can't possibly always get their way in every situation. I am aware that life will present bumps and inconveniences, but sadly, she seems less attuned to this aspect of daily life.

By the time the weekend rolled around, I found myself fed up with her moodiness and lost in unbecoming thoughts about Louisa's expectations of the world. I wondered, since things have always come easily to her, does my sister not understand what the rest of us go through? This unflattering line of thinking came to me as I cleaned our apartment alone, once again, while Louisa slept the afternoon away.

A week has gone by now, and I'd be lying if I said I wasn't the least bit concerned. Our arms are linked, binding us together against the rain and wind as we walk home. Despite our close physical contact, it is hard to dismiss the feeling that we are, in reality, distanced from one another.

A gust of wind snatches my breath. I tug down my toque with my free hand, grateful for both its warmth and its ability to conceal my brow, creased with worry for my sister. The foul weather isn't the only thing discouraging conversation between us, and I wonder for the umpteenth time, what is at the heart of Louisa's unrest?

The small but welcoming lobby of The Newbury is a much-anticipated reprieve from the nastiness of the day. Before climbing the stairs to our third-floor apartment, I remove my jacket and give it a firm shake to release the raindrops that have taken up residence on the garment. My hope is to prevent them from dripping and pooling all the way up the stairs.

Mr. Watkins appears on the landing, ascending from his basement office. "Good afternoon, ladies." He inclines his head toward the darkness beyond the building's front door. "I suppose winter has found us now."

"Hello, Mr. Watkins. Lovely to see you." I offer a sincere smile to the kind man. A few months ago, Mr. Watkins believed in me and gave me the chance to regain my family's good standing with regard to our past due rent. "I suppose you are correct. The winter winds have certainly arrived."

"How are you ladies getting on at the hotel?" Mr. Watkins runs an aged-spotted hand through his greying, rumpled hair.

"Very well, thank you for asking." I believe wholeheartedly in the truth of my answer, but Louisa's almost inaudible grumble makes me think I should not have spoken for her.

I sneak a sideways glance in her direction and decide to hurry us up the stairs, not wishing to dampen Mr. Watkins' day with Louisa's foul mood. "Well, we'd best be off. I think a hot cup of tea is just the ticket this afternoon."

"Enjoy your evening," Mr. Watkins replies as I tuck Louisa's arm within my own and pull her toward the stairs.

We are halfway up the first set of stairs when I turn on the tread and call down to him, "Oh, I almost forgot. I'll be making pie for our Thanksgiving celebration in a week or two. Would you enjoy a piece for yourself?"

"I won't turn down a piece of pie, Miss Wilson. Thank you kindly." The crinkle around Mr. Watkins' eyes arrives before his question does. "But Thanksgiving was this past July, given the Diamond Jubilee. I am sure you were aware of the celebration? There was a parade and such. Sixty years of confederation, the time sure does fly." Mr. Watkins rests a hand on the banister railing and meets my eyes.

"Yes, we both saw snippets of the parade." I glance toward Louisa. "It was from the window of The Hamilton, though, as all staff were required for the weekend of the festivities. Our father was working as well, so we decided to postpone our own celebrations until time allowed."

I take another step down and lean forward with a conspiratorial wink. "If I am being honest, Thanksgiving in July didn't sit quite right with me anyway. I suppose I am a creature of habit."

"Ah, I see. Very clever, Miss Wilson. A Thanksgiving celebration has always seemed fitting at the end of the harvest. I found the sentiment got a bit lost, being mixed in with the Jubilee festivities." Mr. Watkins' face lights up. "I would surely appreciate a piece of your pie, keeping the spirit of the holiday alive and all. Thank you for the offer."

"My pleasure. I will be sure to let you know as soon as I have a slice ready for you." I wave goodbye, and Louisa and I climb the stairs to our apartment.

Closing the door behind me, I reach for Louisa's arm, but she slips past, taking a direct path to our shared bedroom. "I'll put the kettle on for tea," I call out to her as she disappears into the bedroom.

"Tea? Did someone say tea?" Papa appears in the doorway as I hang my drenched coat over the tub, where it will hopefully drip itself dry by morning.

"Papa, you are home early." I kiss his cheek, the warmth of his skin colliding with the cool of my own.

"The weather has us stalled." A nonchalant lift of his shoulders tells me he isn't concerned by the workday being cut short.

"I imagine so." Papa follows me toward the kitchen. "This is the first truly nasty day we've had this year. I don't mind the cold, nor the rain, but put them together with that wind and the day becomes less than pleasant."

Papa chuckles softly as I fill the kettle with water before placing it on the stovetop to boil. I ready the cups, sugar, cream, and tea. Lifting the dish towel off the tray of orange drop cookies, I move three to a small plate.

"I'll get dinner started in a bit." I consider my words carefully. "First, I'd like to coax Louisa out. She's been in a mood for days."

"Ah, so it's not just the storm that has you biting your nails." Papa gives me a knowing glance. "You are not alone. I've made note of her sourness as well. Perhaps between the two of us"—Papa squeezes my upper arm with a comforting hand—"we can encourage her to tell us what the trouble is."

"I think it is definitely worth a try." I place my hand over his, thankful that he has stayed true to his word and left the drinking and the gin joints behind him. I sense that we, Louisa and I, are the fuel that keeps him going these days. Seldom does a day go by when I am not consciously grateful to have him back in the land of the living. The grief over losing Mama five years ago hasn't vanished

53

entirely, but together we share its burden, making it lighter for each of us.

The kettle whistles and I pull it from the burner. Papa takes the cue and calls down the hall to Louisa.

With us seated together at the kitchen table, Louisa blows across the rim of her teacup, steam dancing. Papa clears his throat and begins. "Lou, it seems to me that you are a bit down in the mouth, my love. Is there something we might be able to assist you with?"

"I'm fine, Papa." Louisa's strained smile is a giveaway that she is anything but fine.

I contemplate the situation and decide that with Louisa intent on stoicism, this conversation will surely involve heated words. With an outcome as sure as that, there is no point in wasting time. Therefore, I make a bold decision. With a hint of sarcasm, I say, "Please," drawing out the word. "You've been sulking about for days. You get up, mumble a bit, go to work, walk home—barely uttering two words, I might add—and then disappear into the bedroom until dinner is called."

Louisa's incredulity is written all over her face. "I said I was fine." She spits the words in my direction, and I steady myself against them.

"If you are fine, then why are you so clearly unhappy?" With no reply from Louisa, I continue, "We are doing okay, aren't we? We are covering all of our bills and then some." I reach a hand across the table to Papa and squeeze his forearm. "Papa is keeping his promise, and he is working hard too. I, for one, am very proud of all that our family has accomplished these past four months."

Papa reaches a hand toward Louisa. "What about those theatre classes you were going to resume? You mentioned you were excited to go back to working with the group."

"That is right," I say, agreeing with Papa's line of thought.

"If you could find a class that fits around your work schedule, that would certainly lift your spirits and provide a fresh bit of entertainment."

"Theatre classes have nothing to do with my being entertained, Clara," she snaps. My mouth drops open at her barking reply.

"I did—didn't mean . . ." My words are unexpectedly stuck in my throat, making it all but impossible for me to continue.

"Clara didn't mean to offend you, darlin'," Papa coos in what I suspect is an effort to calm the churning waters of our conversation.

"She doesn't understand. How could she? Clara wouldn't even risk being inadvertently noticed." Louisa pushes her cup of tea away, its contents splashing over the rim and onto the table.

Papa's chin protrudes forward, his fatherly demeanour asserting itself against Louisa's harsh words. "Louisa, no matter how poorly you might be feeling about things, you have no cause to lash out. Consider your words carefully. I suspect you might regret a disagreement with those who are trying to help you."

"I—I thought you enjoyed the theatre," I say. "I was only agreeing that you should find something you enjoy." I dab at the spilled tea with the napkin from my lap. The hair on the back of my neck rises. Louisa is in a fierce mood, and apparently, I am her chosen target.

Crossing her arms over her chest, Louisa slumps further into her chair, no sign of submission evident on the horizon.

Papa and I exchange a look, neither of us knowing the best way to navigate a discussion with Louisa when her knickers are in a knot.

We sit in silence for what feels like an eternity, but when I check my watch, only ten minutes have passed. I drain the last drops from my teacup, gather the empty plate, and stand. "I suppose I will get started on dinner." I step behind Louisa's chair and offer Papa a defeated shrug accompanied by a weary smile.

I barely step out of the way in time as Louisa pushes her chair back. It scrapes the hardwood floor with a squeal. "I assume this inquisition is over, then?" Louisa stands and shoves her hands deep into the pockets of her day dress. Without waiting for a reply, she turns on her heel and retreats to the bedroom, the door closing with a thud.

Without a word, Papa and I begin preparing dinner together. Though it is a welcome treat to have him helping me in the kitchen, my heart is heavy with the reason for his companionship.

"Don't worry yourself too much, Clara girl." Papa slices carrots on the counter behind me, our backs almost touching as we move about the small kitchen. "Your sister is a feisty one. If the past has taught me anything, it is that she spews like a volcano when someone or something has hurt her."

"Do you think I've done something?" My voice cracks with emotion, and my mind races through the past two weeks, worry tightening my chest as I search my memory for anything of significance.

Papa pauses his slicing, turning slightly to look over his shoulder. "If she were truly angry with you, I think we would have heard about it by now. When Louisa blows her top, she does so with gusto."

Scooping his chopped carrots into the bowl beside the cutting board, he continues, "Your mother once said to me, Louisa is like a delicate rose, sturdy in its ability to withstand the wind and the rain and even to resist withering on the sunniest days. But whenever the soil around her roots becomes

56

loose, she finds herself in a state of uncertainty. Without stable earth to ground her, she loses sight of who she is, and all she can do is fight. The empty spaces within the soil at her roots are what threaten her most."

I put aside the onion I have been slicing and turn to face Papa. "I am quite certain I have been on the receiving end of all her thorns this week."

Papa chuckles at my analogy. "I imagine you have." His sigh is weighted with evident concern for us. "Your sister needs to be filled up in order to feel content. I am not suggesting that it is your job to do the filling. I'm merely imparting the wisdom your mother gave me so many years ago. She told me that the feeling of emptiness is Louisa's biggest demon. Her monster in the cupboard, I suppose."

I nod in understanding, though I remain at a loss as to how I might help.

"Something has unsettled her, and until she is willing to share what it is, there is little we can do." Papa eyes me with a wry smile. "Though, I would suggest you stay alert and be ready to duck out of the way at a moment's notice."

We fall into a comfortable silence as we navigate our thoughts, the kitchen, and Mama's chicken casserole recipe.

Louisa emerges when called for dinner and does not add a single word to our evening conversation. I feel my hackles rise when she returns to the bedroom in a huff, without an offer to help with the dishes or anything resembling an apology. A storm is certainly brewing, and I doubt my raincoat will offer much protection.

CHAPTER 7

Thursday, September 29, 1927
Louisa

By the next morning, the storm has blown itself out, leaving the morning air crisp and fresh. I stifle a yawn as Clara and I step onto Georgia Street; a full night's rest should have invigorated me more than it has. The elation at having slept through the night, after more than a week of interrupted slumber, disappeared soon after I woke.

A fog rolled into my brain, engulfing me in weariness as I fumbled my way through my morning routine. Regret over yesterday's harsh words to Clara make me uninclined to speak, unsure of what nastiness might fly from my lips.

Clara, too, is quiet, though I can't blame her for not wanting to talk to me. We walk in silence for several blocks. We are almost in front of The Hamilton when she finally speaks. "I am sorry you are feeling down, Louisa. I don't know what has got you in a jumble, but I am sorry for it all the same."

Stopping mid-stride, I tug on Clara's arm, forcing her to

face me. "I am sorry. There was no reason for me to lash out at you."

Clara smiles, a mixture of relief and love lifting her cheeks.

We pass the hotel's front entrance, saying hello to the doorman as we go. Rounding the building's cornerstone toward the alley and the employees' back entrance, Clara draws me closer, her arm entwined with mine.

"You may not be ready to hear this, but I think Papa is right about you getting back into those theatre classes." Clara stops short of the back entrance. "There must be an evening class offered. Surely, they have something for those who work during the day. I mean, it isn't as though you are making a career out of acting, just a little class for you to enjoy. Don't you think adding something fun to your week would enliven your day-to-day?"

Clara's words punch me in the stomach, rearing me backward. I drop my arm from hers and step away. Anger bubbles within me. "Why do you assume I won't have a career as an actress? You know that being an actress is all I've ever wanted. All I've dreamed about. I have told you countless times about my desire to be on the stage."

"I—I didn't mean to upset you," Clara stutters in a hushed tone as several maids scurry past us, entering the hotel through the back door. "I only thought that, well, one would require more of a leg up than our lot in life provides to be taken seriously as an aspiring actress. I don't suspect our meagre, though happy, upbringing is typical for an actress." Clara takes a deep breath before glancing over her shoulder at the vacant alley. "Besides, you seem to be quite good at the dreaming part, but I haven't seen you actually seek out a role, or even a local theatre group. I figured you weren't really interested in putting in the effort."

"You don't know anything about the theatre, Clara, and

apparently, you don't know anything about me either." I end the conversation with an abruptness that is sure to wound my sister. Her inability to see past society's imposed limits boggles my mind. Hasn't she witnessed me competently skirting such ridiculous rules? After all, they only exist because there are people foolish enough to buy into them. I storm away from her and pull on the heavy door.

The warm air and sweet smell of cinnamon greet me as I enter the hall. A few feet away, Cookie is dancing a jig of sorts near the kitchen entrance, a tea towel swinging overhead as she sings a tune I am unfamiliar with.

The door behind me squeals open before slamming shut with the heft of its weight. I don't have to look to know Clara has come inside.

"Hello, ladies." Cookie whoops as she spins her plump frame in a circle.

Clara steps past me, brushing my shoulder. "What on earth has gotten into you this morning?" Clara beams at Cookie, her delight at seeing her friend in high spirits shoving any upset between us to the back burner.

"Well, I am delighted to announce . . ." Cookie pauses a moment to catch her breath. "Mr. Olson has informed me that I am being promoted." Another squeal of glee erupts from Cookie's shining red face.

"Promoted?" Clara asks, and spite fuels my thoughts. Does Clara think that Cookie, too, is unworthy of improving her station in life due to her social standing? She is, after all, an Irish immigrant woman with no formal training.

I admonish myself for the dejected rumination, pushing aside my disagreement with Clara. I, for one, believe Cookie is capable of anything she sets her mind to. Stepping forward, I stand beside Clara. "Promoted to what?" I ask, my voice lifting to be heard above the din of celebration bouncing around the hall.

Cookie stops her spinning. Using the tea towel, she mops the beads of sweat from her forehead and upper lip. "You are looking at the new head pastry chef, ladies."

"Is Mr. Fournier going somewhere?" Clara reaches for a glass and water jug from a cart beside the kitchen's swinging door. She pours a glass and hands it to Cookie, who tosses the tea towel over one shoulder before accepting the water with both hands.

"He is leaving both The Hamilton and the city. He is moving to Montreal to open a bakery with his brother." Cookie's mouth moves faster than I thought possible, and the words tumble forth with the push of excitement. "I've moved up through the ranks, ladies, and now I'll be calling the shots." Cookie's cheeks blush a deeper shade, and humility creeps into her words. "So to speak."

Chef pokes his tall-hatted head through the doorway. "In the pastry kitchen, that is." His languid French accent draws out his words, though I suspect a hint of joyful teasing is underneath them. "My kitchen remains firmly shut to your ways, madame." Chef's usually stern face softens for a moment, a small smile almost reaching his lips before he adds, "Otherwise, I would also be off to Montreal to escape your madness."

Cookie chuckles good-naturedly, waving him off as he disappears behind the swinging kitchen door.

Clara reaches up and gives Cookie a quick but fierce embrace. "Congratulations. What a fortunate turn of events. You will make an excellent head pastry chef."

I am about to add my own best wishes when I am struck by the notion that Clara appears to have little trouble accepting Cookie's happy news. I wonder if she would be as supportive should my talent for acting also result in success. Though I would like to think otherwise, I doubt that would be the case. I mumble a less than hearty "Congratulations," which seems to fall on deaf ears, given my sister and Cookie do not pause their excited chatter.

"Well now, before you two head off to work . . ." Cookie settles her excitement by running her hands down the front of her apron, regaining her composure with the movement. "I don't want you thinking, 'Ah that Cookie, she is a lucky one.' Though I do always have the luck of the Irish on my side." She lets out a hearty guffaw at her own comment. "I want you to remember this: it takes time to build castles, ladies."

Cookie's words hit me square in the face. I glance at Clara, but she doesn't seem to recognize the importance of Cookie's advice. I, however, do. If I work hard and plan well, success is bound to find me.

"Off you go, then." Cookie shoos us away with a playful swish of her tea towel. "This hotel will certainly not clean itself."

Clara and I hurry down the corridor and then down the stairs to change into our uniforms before roll call. With little time to waste, I help her tie her apron and she mine. We scuttle into position in line just in time to see Ms. Thompson come into view. I breathe a sigh of relief and focus on the blank wall across from me.

The morning tasks go as usual. I am well into reassembling the second of the five guest rooms assigned to me when I finally allow myself to consider Cookie's words of wisdom. "It takes time to build castles." I should have allowed myself more time to find my footing in becoming meek Louisa the Maid, the version of myself that will stop any wagging tongues. If I am to succeed at fitting in at the hotel, I must rein in my vivacious nature and stick to the script.

"That's it." I say the words out loud, I the sole audience member in this guest room. "The role of well-mannered, ordinary maid is just that: a role to play."

Well aware that I am more than capable of portraying unfamiliar characters, I consider my next course of action. This is a task I've accomplished many times over, and quite successfully, I might add. I had no experience or knowledge of Ancient Rome before portraying Cleopatra's most valued servant. Nor did I understand Dorothy's plight upon beginning *Wizard of Oz* as a study course in theatre group. But each time, I explored the intricacies of my character's motivation until I embodied her truest self.

I fluff the pillows, wrapped in fresh linens, before relocating my cleaning cart to the hall and closing the guest room door behind me. I stand behind the cart, ready to push it toward the next room on my list, when a dashing young man saunters toward me, hat in hand. He appears not to have a care in the world.

My heart flips in my chest at the sight of him, all confident and oozing charm. I smother a wide smile as I take on my newly borrowed persona. Dropping my chin, I lower my gaze and tuck myself into the smallest space possible behind my cart, pressing my back against the wall in a demur stance as he passes.

Stealing a brief glance upward, I catch a quick nod and a wink in my direction. This is going to be harder than I realize, I think as the man lets himself into a guest room four doors down from where I stand.

After the lunch break, Ms. Thompson calls Hazel, Clara, and myself into the corridor. "Ladies, I would like you to polish the decorative brass panels and trim around the lift's exterior this afternoon. This task appears to have been neglected in recent weeks." Ms. Thompson's displeasure over the state of the lift's sheen does not go unnoticed. "All eight guest floors will need a good shining. Don't worry yourself with the other floors, I will have someone from the downstairs staff address the lobby and lower levels."

"Yes, ma'am," we say in unison.

"You'll find the polish and rags in the storage room across from my office." Ms. Thompson sends us on our way. "I'll check on your progress in due time. Please begin on the first floor of guest rooms and make your way up."

"Yes, ma'am," we say again before moving toward the stairs that will take us to the basement storage room.

Cleaning the panels of the first lift exterior goes as well as expected, all three of us employing a significant amount of elbow grease to encourage the polish to do its job.

Hazel kneels below me, my tall frame relegating me, by default, to the highest sections. "This is by far my least favourite task." Hazel's complaint comes out as a whine. "And we've got seven more floors to go."

"Hush now," Clara, working opposite me at mid-height, replies cheerily. "We don't want to be overheard complaining. It's part of the job. Well, today's job, anyway."

I compel a lighthearted tone to enter my voice, determined to remain in character. "Working together will lighten the work." My whispered words come off rather stiff, and I catch Clara eyeing me with puzzled bemusement.

Though our polishing rags move furiously up and down the brass panels, they don't reach the narrow grooves where the molded metal creates long thin lines of detail.

"Besides, the lesson will stick with us, no doubt," I add in a low voice, testing the waters with another one of my assumed character's insights.

"What lesson is that?" Hazel cranes her neck to peer up at me.

"I am quite sure I will be inclined to polish the fifth-floor lift exterior every time I spot even the tiniest smudge. In fact, I may tuck a tin of polish and a rag into my cart so I have it at the ready." Enthused by the ease with which I am sliding into the role of well-behaved, hard-working maid, I move my rag-wielding hand faster over the brass.

Twisting my cloth to create a pointed end, I press the polish-soaked tip into a crevice and move the cloth in small circular motions. "Hmm," I murmur as I pull the cloth back to check my progress. "Perhaps, we should . . ." Remembering my intention to maintain a mouselike presence, I stop myself mid-sentence. If I can't hold my tongue and blend in amidst those who know me well, I won't stand a chance at doing so in more uncertain situations.

Ding. "First floor," the lift operator bellows before pulling open the folding grate with a squeal of metal on metal.

The three of us scurry to the side of the lift, pressing our backs to the wall in an effort to remain out of the path of the hotel guests exiting the lift. The lift closes and resumes operation, and we return to our polishing.

"What were you saying?" Hazel stretches her back before crouching low to polish the base of the lift's exterior.

"Oh, nothing." I return my attention to the deep crevice created by the molded brass, sticking to my role like sap to a tree. I mentally will Hazel or Clara to realize that a much smaller tool will be required for the hard-to-reach sections if we are to finish in the allotted time.

Thirty minutes later, we are gathering our polishing supplies and climbing the back-of-house stairs to the second floor of guest rooms. We ensure the hall is free of guests before stepping onto the plush carpet. I have yet to understand the ridiculous idea that a maid is to remain invisible while accomplishing the many tasks required of her.

Working on the second-floor lift exterior, we fall into a productive silence. Hazel, resigned to the task, scrubs furiously, her progress in the small spaces limited by the cloth's thick fibres.

Movement from the hall catches my attention. "You know, there is an easier way to do that," Maggie's voice, husky and low, calls out to us as she pushes her cart into an alcove a few feet from the lift.

"An easier way to do what?" Clara asks.

"Those detailed grooves are all but impossible to reach with a cloth." Maggie reaches into her cart, pulling out a toothbrush. "Here." She prods Hazel aside and demonstrates how the small bristles reach the tight spaces between the brass.

"How clever." Hazel, pleased by the discovery, takes the toothbrush from Maggie's hand. "This will speed up the task."

"Hang on." Maggie retreats down the hall. "I'll get you a new one."

"A new one?" Clara's eyebrows converge.

Maggie returns with a clean toothbrush. "I keep one on hand for all sorts of hard-to-reach places. You can have this one." Clearly pleased with herself, Maggie grins, something I am not certain I have seen before now.

Clara takes the offered toothbrush. "Where are you getting toothbrushes?" Her question is politely delivered, though clearly rooted in her unease at using a pilfered toothbrush.

"The eighth-floor linen cupboard has a stockpile of them." Maggie's smile widens.

"But—but those are for the guests." Clara's concern is evident in the crease above her brow.

Maggie's cheer falters, her expression turning sour, and that is when I see the truth. Maggie isn't set on being nasty, to me or to anyone else. She is simply in need of a little kindness. Friendship even. I stifle a chuckle at the realization. I thought I was the only one adopting an altered persona to fit in, but Maggie has been doing the same thing all along. Sadly, her approach has resulted in fewer friendships given her inherent need to avoid being hurt by lashing out with a sharp-tongue and a nasty disposition. I push an elated appearance into my features. "How thoughtful of you. Thank you, Miss Adams, for saving us a significant amount of time and effort. This"—I take the toothbrush from Clara's hand—"will certainly come in handy."

Maggie's eyes dance in response. "Just be sure to keep the brass polish brush separate, or you'll find yourself scrubbing polish from porcelain."

"We will keep that in mind," I gush, relieved at having figured out Maggie's intentions. "Thank you again."

As the day ends, we have managed to polish and shine the lift's accent panels on all eight guest floors. I've promised Clara I will speak with Ms. Thompson about the possibility of obtaining toothbrushes for cleaning so as not to take those intended for eighth-floor guests. This seems to appease my sister, and Clara remains jubilant from a hard day's work having been completed.

I, on the other hand, am comforted by the positive step I've taken with regard to Maggie. She isn't likely to remain a threat to me now that I know what she is really seeking. Silly me, I should have seen it from the beginning. All Maggie wants is to be included, and I certainly know how to charm the girl into the fold.

CHAPTER 8

Thursday, September 29, 1927
Clara

Instead of changing out of her uniform immediately after our shift ended, Louisa sought out Ms. Thompson to ask about acquiring toothbrushes for the purpose of cleaning.

"She said she would have a toothbrush for every maid by next week, with an extra supply to remain with the brass polish." Louisa pulls on her apron tie, tugging it free from its tight bow. Our conversation is private, given our tardy departure from the locker room. "I was sure to credit Maggie for the idea of the toothbrushes. She will be ever so pleased to be recognized in front of the others tomorrow at roll call."

I am cautiously optimistic that Louisa's foul mood has shifted, unsure of why or how. Louisa is removing the cap pinned to her head as she prattles on about the events of the day.

"I'll be in the kitchen when you are ready," I call over my shoulder as I pull on the door. "I want to check in with Cookie before we head home."

MEET ME AT THE CLOCK

Louisa sends me off with an unconcerned wave of her hand as she hangs her head upside down to give her scalp a good finger brush.

My inclination to leave the locker room with haste is twofold. I do wish to check in with Cookie, feeling as though I perhaps didn't provide enough accolades for her promotion. She has been such a dear friend to me. I wouldn't want her thinking I was in any way unhappy for her. My excitement over the situation should match hers, at the very least, and I intend to ensure she knows that it does.

The other reason I want to leave, though, is for a break from being in Louisa's presence. My sister's flip-flopping moods have made me dizzy. This morning's heated arguments, which I have yet to unravel, have turned into an afternoon of gaiety so sweet I worry I might end the day with a toothache. My head is swimming with questions.

I find Cookie in the pastry kitchen, humming a tune as she ices dainty delicacies. I watch from the open door, amazed by her keen attention to detail. I would expect hands that create such masterpieces to be far more fine-boned and delicate than hers.

Sensing a presence behind her, Cookie lifts her hands from the task and straightens her back, turning to greet me. "Ah, Clara. I thought someone was there. Is it that time already? Are you off for the day?"

"Just about." I step into the small but tidy kitchen. "I wanted to tell you how pleased I am for you. About your promotion. Really, I am." My eyes drop to my clasped hands. "I didn't want you to think I wasn't happy for you or that I wasn't proud of you."

"Why in the world would I think you weren't?" Cookie places the piping bag on the counter and wipes her hands with the corner of her apron.

69

"I was surprised, I suppose. I hadn't known you were interested in a promotion, and well, I guess I hadn't thought that rising through the ranks, as you put it, was even a possibility for the likes of us." My sheepishness holds my words hostage, and I pry them away one by one.

"Ah, I see. Did you know The Hamilton is innovative in more ways than its amenities for guests? Mr. Hamilton, Mr. Olson, and especially Ms. Thompson have their eyes lifted toward the future, you see. They are intent to do their bit when it comes to providing opportunities for their staff to better themselves and their lot in life."

Cookie steps toward the open doorway, inviting me closer with a wave of her arm. "You see Hu over there, washing dishes?"

I meet Cookie in the hall and peek through the round window of the swinging door, into the main kitchen. The view beyond is blurred but visible through the thick glass. "Yes. I see him."

"We don't live in a world where opportunities exist for every individual, and I surely don't believe in stepping on another's back to reach a higher shelf. But I do believe a strong work ethic and an open mind will benefit those who want to succeed."

I search Cookie's face for understanding. "I'm not sure I believe there is anything beyond the limits of my social standing. My father is a labourer, an educated man in his field, yes, but a labourer all the same. To be honest, my ambitions have never included becoming head of anything." I inhale sharply, fear twisting my insides at the thought of being a person of influence or authority. "Not like you've accomplished with becoming head pastry chef."

Cookie inclines her head toward Hu. "Even Hu hasn't let himself be restricted by the societal rules that many folks can't make heads nor tails of. Did you know he and his wife own a small family restaurant?"

"I didn't know that." I clasp my hands over my abdomen in an attempt to still the unease within. I didn't even know the man's name a short minute ago, but I decide not to expose yet another layer of my lack of awareness. "He has never spoken to me, so I suppose I don't really know anything about him or his family."

"Every day after washing dishes and scrubbing counters here, he rushes home to work until closing, cooking meals for his customers. Mr. Hamilton and the rest of the hotel's upper management support Hu's efforts and his desire to make an honest living." Cookie guides me back toward the meagre privacy of the pastry kitchen's alcove. "He is an excellent cook too. Some of the best dim sum in all of Chinatown."

"He is a hard worker, then," I offer, hoping the words are viewed as a compliment, rather than indicating my lack of understanding as to what Cookie is getting at.

"That he is. His dim sum is being considered as a possible menu item for the New Year's Eve reception Mr. Olson is organizing." Cookie's eyebrows lift toward her hairline in emphasis. "All I am saying, Clara, is don't go fencing yourself in by a limited self-view. You may not see it now, but someday, you may find yourself in a position to reach the top shelf." Cookie's face softens.

"You make it sound so easy." I swallow hard to push down rising panic, while coercing a pleasant expression into formation.

"There's nothing to it, dear. If you are willing to put in the effort, there is nothing more to it than that." Cookie grabs my hands in hers, squeezing what I hope is her unbridled confidence into my being.

Louisa appears at the doorway. "Ready to go?"

I look past Cookie and nod. "I am." I give Cookie a quick hug. "Congratulations again. I truly am happy for you."

"I know you are, love. Just remember, remaining stagnant will never move you forward." Cookie ushers us down the hall and to the back door. "Off you go now. Have yourselves a lovely evening."

As the heavy back door closes with a thud behind us, I consider Cookie's words and wonder if being stagnant is as terrible as Cookie deems it to be. Before this afternoon, I hadn't thought my situation to be fixed, but what is wrong with being comfortable with what one has and how one lives? There is safety in knowing where you stand and what is expected of you. I imagine it is far easier to live within those bounds than to accept the uncertainty beyond them.

We round the cornerstone of the hotel and walk toward Georgia Street. The shimmering lights of The Hotel Vancouver to our right and The Hotel Georgia across the street mock me with their display of a life far more fanciful than my own. I can't help but wonder, what if I took a chance? What if I did as Louisa keeps berating me to do and reached for something more?

"How pretty." Louisa hums beside me, her attention drawn through an expansive stone-framed window to the interior of The Hotel Vancouver's lobby, aglow in the light of an overhead chandelier. The darkening sky only adds to the contrast between the lobby and our current location in the chill of the late afternoon. "Makes you want to step inside, doesn't it?"

A knee-jerk response flies from my lips. "In case you've forgotten, we just left a hotel. Why in the world would you want to go into another one?"

Louisa rolls her eyes. "Not as a maid, silly. As a guest." Her voice softens into a wisp, and the sentiment hangs in the air.

I pause near the window and try to view the scene from Louisa's perspective. I cannot deny the allure of the splendour inside, and I consider what it might be like to feel at home in such gatherings of high society. Would life really be that different with money, power, and influence? I watch Louisa's reflection in the glass and know for certain that she thinks it would. My knees wobble at the thought of needing to take charge in order to acquire such a life.

I tear my eyes away from the glimmering view before I can fall prey to its draw. I strong-arm my thoughts and my sister toward the corner, where we wait for the crossing guard to signal us to walk.

Louisa's eyes remain glued to the front entrance of The Hotel Georgia as we cross the street and approach the stately hotel. Having grown familiar with our regular movements past the hotel, the doorman—dressed in a long dark coat, gloves, and a hat—nods to us from behind his stand.

There is movement beyond the door, and he is quick to reach for the handle.

Opening it wide, he greets a well-dressed man and his companion. The couple steps onto the sidewalk in front of us. The woman's short, beaded dress sparkles for a scant moment in the light of the overhead lamps before she wraps herself in a knee-length coat trimmed with fur. My eyes follow her movements as she strides ahead of us with an air of confidence.

Louisa elbows me, her face lighting up at the sight of the pair. Though the city is ripe with nightlife, we seldom find ourselves attending the theatre, opera, or dinner clubs. Our young age and full work schedule rarely allow us to mingle with those living the flapper lifestyle in Vancouver.

Louisa quickens her pace in an effort to keep up with the fast-stepping couple, their dancing feet already primed and ready. I stifle a giggle and feel myself being tugged into Louisa's excitement.

I see now why Louisa is so easily swept up in the thrill of the commotion. The lights, the music, the fashion—they converge into a roar of gaiety and easy spending. The thought of buoyant, untroubled days and nights warms me. A truly bubbling life it might be.

My conversation with Cookie surfaces in my mind as we keep pace with the couple, who remain two short steps ahead of us. Pursuing a glimpse of the high life, I can't help but wonder if I've misjudged my situation after all.

I truly am grateful for my position at the hotel. Until the day I arrived at The Hamilton, I hadn't strived for anything except good grades in school and a helpful disposition. I still prize my role as a prestigious Hamilton maid, but Louisa, and even Cookie, have no trouble with wanting more from life. Whether it be a promotion or a new dress, who am I to judge another's desires? One question presses in on me: what if I, too, want more?

Louisa hooks an arm through mine, a week's worth of moodiness and ill temper washing away with this lighthearted moment. I am looking at Louisa, a wide grin upon my face, when she comes to a sudden standstill, pulling away from me abruptly.

My head spins forward to find the fashionable couple directly before me, and I barely avoid a collision. I am trying to make sense of the unexpected halt in motion when the woman turns in my direction, a look of concern straining her red-painted lips. My forehead crinkles as I lean to the side, peering around her to see what the trouble might be.

There, in the middle of the sidewalk, an ox of a man looms over a crouching, dark-haired fellow frantically gathering groceries scattered on the pavement.

"I told you to be off," the ox bellows, bending at the waist to deliver his command closer to the other man's ear.

A breath catches in my throat as the dark-haired man raises his head, his Asian features and skin tone apparent in the glow of the streetlamp. "I—I am sorry. I am going."

I feel Louisa's arm tense. The couple in front of us exchange a brief look before turning on their heels. They step around us and walk in the direction they came from, apparently preferring to locate another route to their intended destination.

They brush past us on Louisa's side, and I assume she is attempting to move out of the couple's way by stepping forward. I realize my mistake when she bends to help the Asian man with his spilled groceries.

I try to call her name, to warn her not to intervene, but my body betrays me. My lips form words but summon no sound.

"Let me help you with that." Louisa's voice is gentle. Though her eyes never leave the Asian man's face, I sense she is aware of the ox's every move.

"What do you think you are doing?" the ox, who had been pacing a two-step distance, growls at Louisa. His breath bathes everyone near in the scent of intoxication.

Louisa hands a tumbled orange to the Asian man. He nods his thanks and places it into the brown paper bag.

"I asked, what do you think you are doing?" the ox repeats louder, his growl drawing a bigger crowd to the commotion.

Louisa rubs her gloved hands together to free sidewalk debris from the fibres. She stands tall. At her full height, she barely reaches the man's chest, and yet she remains undeterred. "You, sir, are drunk. I am going to give you the benefit of the doubt and assume your poor behaviour is due entirely to your intoxication."

The ox leans closer, laughing in Louisa's face. Though she

doesn't waver in the slightest, I step back out of instinct. "Now listen here, girly, you've got no business butting in."

Fear for my sister's well-being climbs into my throat. I take a step forward, pause, and retreat. The argument inside my head shouts louder than the man's ranting, and that is how I know I have little choice but to quell my fear and ignore the voice that reminds me of my place. I square my shoulders in pretend assuredness and step forward to stand beside Louisa, dragging my timid resolve with me. "Please, sir." The ox's dilated eyes shift from Louisa to me. "My sister meant no harm."

"Then she shouldn't be sticking her nose in something that doesn't concern her." His bellow is sure to be heard all the way to the ocean's edge, and I feel myself cower as his message washes over me.

"If you'll just let us *all* pass"—I glance at the man still crouching on the sidewalk—"we'll be out of your hair in no time at all."

Out of the corner of my eye, I catch Louisa's small hand movement as she gestures for the Asian man to leave. He cautiously begins to stand, but I feel a shift in the night air and realize it is far too late. The situation unfolds quickly. Without warning, the ox winds up and kicks the bag of groceries out of his hands. The groceries scatter once again, raining down on the gathered crowd as they watch in disbelief.

I recoil in horror. What have I done? The Asian man looks over his shoulder at me and then flees the scene. I can't help but assume he blames me for escalating the situation and costing him his groceries. Louisa and the ox stand toe to toe, her eyebrow raised in accusation and his fists balling tighter as each second ticks by. I shouldn't have intervened. I've done no good here.

"Pardon me, coming through." A gruff voice pierces the

tense deadlock. "Out of my way, mate." The voice makes its way through the crowd. A friendly-faced police officer steps out of the crowd. "What seems to be the trouble, miss?" He eyes the ox warily while directing his question to Louisa.

Louisa's posture softens, transforming into that of a polite lady of society in the blink of an eye. She casts a final angry glare at the ox before meeting the officer's eyes. Her hands rise and fall like ocean waves as she animatedly explains the situation to the officer while I stand off to the side, cloaked in shame.

I close my eyes and affirm in my fear-stricken heart that I should not step foot outside of comfortable situations. Staying within my station is a far safer path. Doing otherwise only leads to poor decisions and puts others at risk of getting hurt. A tear rolls down my cheek, and I bite my lower lip to stop its tremble. I shake my head in disagreement at the realization, but know, that which the heart bears witness to, the mind cannot unsee.

CHAPTER 9

Thursday, September 29, 1927
Louisa

I thank the officer for his assistance before looping my arm through Clara's stiff one. We walk toward home, Clara stealing nervous glances over her shoulder with every second step.

"Relax, will you?" I squeeze her arm within mine. "There is nothing to worry about."

"Nothing to worry about? Louisa, you put yourself in harm's way." Clara stops abruptly, forcing me to a halt with her. "That man."

"Which man?" I pull on Clara's arm, coaxing her back into motion.

"The mean one." Her tone is flat, and I sneak a sideways glance in her direction, assessing her as we move toward home.

"What about him?" I look both ways and step into the street. Distracted, Clara falls a half pace behind me.

"He could have hurt you. He was certainly angry enough."

Clara shakes her head. "If that policeman hadn't appeared . . ."

"Do you really think an entire street full of decent people would have allowed anything to happen to two working-class young women?" I roll my eyes at her, purposely skirting the mention of our pale skin tone. I quicken my pace, the evening chill seeping through my wool coat. "Don't be silly. He was a brute, yes, but I wasn't in any real danger." I brush away Clara's concern with a wave of my hand.

As we step onto the curb on the opposite side of the street, a piercing wind barrels toward us, buffeting my face and forcing me to clench my collar with my free hand. A street lamp to our left buzzes and then goes out, plunging the sidewalk into shadowy darkness and sending a shiver up my spine.

My assuredness wavers then dips, but I push forward. I am determined to show my sister that my decision to act was valiant, despite the unfortunate event with the groceries. I take one step and then another.

Jutting my chin, I do my best to conceal the wave of uncertainty that crawls up the back of my neck, undermining the confidence in my stride. I try to convince myself that the burnt-out lamp and the biting wind are playing games with my mind.

I tug Clara's arm with a firm pull and focus on getting us home. Though I try to refuse it entrance, the unsettling reality of what could have been prods me. If I were to give it much thought, I might well agree with Clara's fears. That drunken ox was a beast of a man, no doubt.

I know, however, that his state of inebriation bothers me less than the unspoken truth that neither he nor the police officer addressed: the venom in the ox's words and actions came from disdain for the color of the other man's skin. That thought chills me to the bone.

"What do you think it was about? Their disagreement?" The quiver in Clara's voice tells me she has yet to recover from the incident, her state likely worsened by the darkening sky and blustery wind.

I inhale a lungful of crisp air, unable to voice the ugliness of the drunken man's intentions. Clara, perhaps not comprehending the situation completely, looks like a lamb who has lost her flock.

"You shouldn't have stepped in," Clara asserts, though I suspect the strength in her words rides on the coattails of fear.

"Of course I should have." Pulling her to a quieter side of the sidewalk, I tuck my chin, straining to meet her eyes in the shadows. "Tell me, how would it have been anything but the right thing to do? Every person should feel free to move about the city they call home. The man with the groceries had every right to walk down the street just as we do. I can't imagine him to have done anything to cause such a reaction. What if you were in trouble and nobody stepped in to help you?"

"Why didn't anyone else come forward, then?" Clara turns my relatable example into a much more difficult question to answer.

"I don't know." The words come out as a whisper. "Perhaps because they were afraid." Another response rises into my thoughts, allowing me to regain my footing. "Or perhaps I didn't give them the opportunity to do so, being so quick-witted and all."

"I was afraid. You weren't?" Clara exhales the question.

"I was for a second." I blink slowly, tempering my emotions. "Then, I saw the situation for what it was and knew I could help. So I did."

Clara looks up the street, in the direction of home, her

shoulders sinking under the weight of her thoughts. "I am not sure if that is brave or downright foolish." Her eyes flit upward briefly.

I place my hands on Clara's shoulders, feeling the need to anchor her to me in some way. "Home?"

Clara nods in earnest. "Yes, home."

Ten minutes later, we arrive at the front door of our apartment building, which never looked quite so inviting as it does today.

Clara doesn't even bother removing her jacket before slumping onto the sofa, her bag dropped beside her feet. A sliver of guilt nestles under my skin as I watch Clara slouched in exhaustion, or perhaps something else.

I busy myself with putting away my things and considering the best way to help this evening. Cooking is rarely a task I own, but given my sister's current state, I decide to do what I can. Remembering last night's chicken stew, I open the refrigerator door and retrieve the half-full stockpot.

"Surely, I can heat stew," I mutter to myself as the apartment door opens and Papa steps inside.

"Well, this is a sight," he teases me as I tie an apron over my day dress. "I wasn't aware you knew we had a kitchen."

I roll my eyes, and he plants a kiss on my forehead. "I thought I'd help out." My tone is lighter than my thoughts as I consider the reality. I won't be able to hide Clara's distress from Papa.

"Where's your sister?" Papa places his lunch box on the counter and peers around the wall separating the kitchen from the dining and living rooms.

"She's not feeling quite herself at the moment." I choose my words carefully so as not to panic him.

"Is she sick?" Papa steps past me, toward the dining table.

"Not exactly." My response stops him in his tracks, and he

turns back to me with a question hanging in his raised eyebrows.

"Louisa," Papa says from the doorway, "what happened?"

A weighted sigh leaves my lips, a beat ahead of the slew of whispered words detailing the afternoon's events. To his credit, Papa nods and listens, offering only occasional grunts as I recount the incident. His eyes travel between Clara and myself as he considers the situation.

"I can understand why she might be unsettled. I don't imagine she's ever witnessed prejudice quite like that." Papa's concern for Clara is written all over his face. "You've told me everything?"

"After the police officer dispersed the crowd and sent the man on his way, there really wasn't anything more to do. I'll admit things got a little heated, especially when the groceries went flying, but in the end, nobody was harmed."

"Can you manage heating the stew?"

"I think so."

"Then we will eat as soon as it is warm." Papa steps softly toward Clara, then perches on the edge of the sofa. "Hey there." He cradles Clara as she folds herself into his embrace. "Oh honey, it's okay. Everything is going to be fine."

Clara's sobs hit me like pelting rain as I stir the chicken stew. I was certain I was doing the right thing, taking the prudent course of action to ensure no harm came to the man with the groceries. I hadn't considered my stepping in would bring harm to someone I love.

The stew bubbles as I place spoons at each place setting. I fill three glasses with water from the tap and ladle steaming stew into bowls before signalling to Papa that dinner is ready.

At the table, Papa squeezes Clara's hand. "Eat, darlin'. A full tummy will help you feel better, I promise."

Clara obediently sips a spoonful of stew, her eyes fixed on the bowl.

I blow the steam from my spoon and wait, listening to the quiet slurps of stew. Truthfully, I crave Papa's reassurance too, but I am not currently his primary concern.

Placing his spoon in the empty dish, Papa moves his bowl to the side and folds his hands on the table. "Clara?" Papa waits for Clara to raise her head. "Louisa told me what you encountered on your way home."

Clara's blank expression has me biting my lower lip, uncertain of what to expect from this conversation.

"Clara, girl," Papa coos as he leans toward her, one hand reaching for both of hers. "Tell me, what is troubling you most?"

Clara's gaze meets mine before dropping once more. We sit in silence, Papa allowing Clara the time and space to gather her nerve and her thoughts. He never wavers. Holding her hands, he offers all of his attention and strength.

I am in awe of his gentle nature. Never demanding. Seldom quick to anger. I am certain his words will carry weight. They will help Clara rise up and understand that what I did today was necessary and helpful. Papa will make her see that we should stand up for others. Yes, I think as I sit a little straighter in my chair, I can feel the vindication of my actions, and this awareness settles me so.

Tears brim in Clara's eyes, and my heart instinctively lurches. Papa gives her an encouraging squeeze of his hand. "Go on. You are safe. Nobody can hurt you here, Clara."

Clara steals a look in my direction, and for a split second, I wonder if she fears me. But I quickly dismiss the surely absurd notion.

"I made a mistake. I am so sorry, Papa." Clara's words are choked with emotion.

"Why do you think you made a mistake?" Papa shifts a fraction closer, giving her hand another reassuring squeeze.

"I shouldn't have stepped in. I thought I was being helpful, but the man lost his food because of me. What if that one bag of groceries was all he could afford for an entire week?" Like a boulder pushed from the top of a hill, Clara is unable to stop herself. Her previously unspoken questions tumble forward, one after the other. "Why did Louisa have to be the one to help? Why couldn't the man with the groceries help himself? Why was that man so cruel? Why did all those people crowd around and do nothing when he was yelling at Louisa?" Clara's voice dwindles with the last push of air from her lungs. "I made a mistake. I promise not to step out of line again."

"Do you think this was your fault?" Papa scoots his chair closer to Clara, wrapping her in a tight embrace. "None of this is your doing. I wish I could give you a reason for why things like this happen, but I've yet to make much sense of it myself."

Several minutes pass. Clara dries her eyes with her napkin and picks up her spoon. Each of us is lost in our own thoughts, and only the occasional scrape of a spoon against a bowl breaks our silence.

Just when I think it is appropriate for me to speak, Clara stiffens in her chair. "You're right, Papa. If Louisa hadn't confronted the man, none of this would have happened." Clara's words arrive with a punch.

"What? How can you say that?" Heat snakes up the back of my neck. "I was only doing what was right."

"Well, it's true. If you hadn't decided to intervene, we wouldn't have been caught up in a situation that was none of our business."

"Now, girls." Papa raises both hands in an effort to

maintain the peace. "Let's not start lashing out at one another."

The skeptical look on Clara's face is enough to encourage Papa to continue. "Louisa"—Papa gestures toward me—"is an adventurous spirit. Wouldn't you agree?"

Clara nods.

"What makes you uncomfortable may be different from what makes Louisa uncomfortable. This does not diminish your courage or your goodness as a human being. No two people are exactly the same." Papa straightens his posture. "As your mama used to say, that is the beauty in all of it. Diversity is the purpose and the loveliness of this world."

"So, I am right to do what makes me comfortable, then?" Clara frustrates me with her inability to see reason.

"That is a question only you can answer." Papa's smile is sincere.

"Good. I am glad we have that settled." Clara meets my eyes with a determined look before wrapping her arms around Papa in a fierce hug.

I find myself wanting to say otherwise. Wanting to tell her that you should, without question, feel comfortable standing up to ugliness. You should be aware of what is happening around you. Frustration builds at my sister's aversion to step beyond her carefully crafted box of propriety.

Though this afternoon's events might have seemed rash or irresponsible when viewed through Clara's eyes, I was quite aware of my intentions through it all. Even without the benefit of hindsight, I recognized my actions as deliberate and sensible. I suck my bottom lip between my teeth, knowing that saying as much now will only unsettle our family once more. My doubt remains though. Someone must stand up for what's right. How can Clara not see the most obvious question of all: if not us, then who?

CHAPTER 10

Friday, September 30, 1927
Clara

By the following morning, Louisa's disgruntled mood has returned. Her gloom hangs over our breakfast table, mirroring the low-lying storm clouds beyond the window. I stifle a yawn before taking a sip of tea.

Yesterday's commotion on the sidewalk and our subsequent family discussion are surely at the root of our subdued morning. Louisa's curls are a mess of beautiful tangles as she nibbles at the toast I set before her. Even a night spent tossing and turning hasn't diminished her good looks, despite successfully souring her disposition. I assume the lack of a good night's rest is the reason for her quiet this morning. Given my own drowsy state, I enjoy the silence, finding no need to interrupt it with invented cheeriness.

If Papa were here, I would make more of an effort, I reason with myself. But given that he was awake and readying himself for the day before dawn broke, I have little inclination to coax enthusiasm for the morning from either Louisa or myself.

I brush the crumbs from the table and onto my plate and then move to the kitchen to pack our lunches for the day. Having enjoyed the two previous Saturdays and Sundays off from The Hamilton, this week and next are sure to be long ones. The cool autumn weather brought sniffles and coughs for a few of the hotel's maids, and tomorrow will be Louisa's and my only day off.

Counting myself fortunate to have avoided sickness, I muster the desire necessary to do as Mama would instruct, if she were here, and simply *get on with it*. Serrated knife in hand, I slice four pieces of bread. I open my mouth to ask Louisa if she would prefer chicken salad or peanut butter, but as I turn my head to speak, I catch the swish of her dressing gown as she leaves the table, not bothering to clear any of her dishes. "A foul mood indeed," I murmur under my breath as I retrieve the peanut butter from the cupboard and spread a healthy portion onto her sandwich.

The walk to work has us ducking our hooded heads against the wind, a persistent presence the past few days that has made using umbrellas or carrying on conversations impossible. The gusts sweeping up the streets from the waterfront push us off course. In an effort to steer us straight, I tug Louisa close, linking her arm within mine. The look she shoots me makes me think twice about my intended consideration.

As we round the corner of The Hamilton, the tall building blocks the wind. Louisa unlinks her arm from mine and slides off her hood. "Blasted wind." Her words, laced with annoyance, are presumably directed at the weather, but I can't help feeling their sting—as though I alone am responsible for the nastiness of the day.

I let out a slow breath, deciding it is in my best interest to bolster Louisa's mood. A more favourable disposition from her is likely to make both of our days easier. "Winter is right around the corner, it seems." I remove my own hood, hoping to find common ground between us. "I suspect we should be grateful the snow has yet to fall."

Louisa's scoff indicates another misstep on my part. I search my brain for an appropriate response, but my attention is drawn by movement further down the alley.

"Miss Clara. Miss Louisa," Masao calls with an excited wave of his arm.

"Aren't you supposed to be in school, young man?" Louisa teases the boy as he hurries his steps to reach us.

"No school today." Masao grins, clearly pleased with his announcement.

"Why is that?" I ask, trying to assess whether we are being fed a tall tale.

"My mother needs help in the tea shop today." Masao shrugs in apparent nonchalance, but his delight remains evident in the mischievous grin fixed upon his face. "So, no school for Masao today."

"Well, aren't you the lucky one." Louisa ruffles his dark hair before turning toward the back door of the hotel. "Would love to stay and chat, but we really should head in before roll call."

I pause a moment, allowing Louisa to go ahead of me. "Cookie tells me you are growing an apple tree."

Masao nods enthusiastically at the mention of his project.

Louisa huffs indignantly before leaving us in the alley. I release a strained whoosh of air and try to ignore my sister's hostility. "How is it going? The tree, I mean."

"Not so well, Miss Clara." Masao kicks a stone with the toe of his shoe. "I have tried many seeds for months now, but not one has come up through the dirt. I don't know what I am doing wrong."

"Maybe there is a trick to it," I say, tapping a gloved finger to my lips, "you know, like a secret way that only apple trees grow."

Masao's face drops into a frown.

My brow knits as I consider a way to help the boy. "Have you tried looking for a book at the library?"

Masao slaps his forehead with the palm of his hand. "Thank you, Miss Clara. That is an excellent idea. I will go to the library and look for a book."

The back door creaks open, and Cookie's flushed face pokes out. "Ah, there you are. I've been waiting on you, Masao. Your mother is in a hurry to have you back at the shop today. I've got what she needs inside."

"Thank you, Miss Cookie." Masao offers a slight bow from his waist and follows her inside.

Cookie inclines her head in my direction. "Shouldn't you be well on your way, Clara? Fridays are always busy, with everyone coming and going for the weekend. We don't want Ms. Thompson to be put out of sorts, thinking another of her maids has fallen off the roster with illness."

"No, I suppose we do not." I squeeze past my friend, patting her arm as I move beyond the open door.

I head toward the locker room as Cookie puts an arm around Masao's shoulder, guiding him toward her pastry kitchen.

Louisa is alone, pinning her cap in place and grumbling at her reflection in the mirror, when I step into the locker room.

She doesn't say a word, but I feel her watching me as I shrug off my coat and change into my uniform.

I am tying my apron at my back, trying to piece together

how I've blundered, when the tornado that is Louisa descends upon me.

"Do you even realize how hypocritical you are being?"

My head snaps up, sending my cap askew. "What are you talking about? I am not being hypocritical about anything."

"Really?" Louisa turns away from the mirror and slams her locker door shut. "You play nice with Masao but couldn't be bothered to help another who's just like him." Louisa's toe taps out an angry rhythm. "In the street last night." Her cheeks flush with anger. "I don't know what you'd call it, but to me, that is a fine example of hypocrisy."

"Masao is just a boy." I am stunned by Louisa's fury, and I fumble with my cap while trying to pin it in place.

"A Japanese boy," Louisa fires back at me.

I check my watch. "We will have to talk about this later. We are going to be late for roll call."

Louisa pushes past me, huffing as she moves through the door and up the stairs. I catch up with her on the landing, my short legs pumping to keep up with her long strides. When she reaches for the door handle, I place my hand on top of hers to gain her full attention. "Masao is a Japanese-Canadian boy." I say the words with conviction. "He was born here."

Louisa cheeks puff out in exasperation. "Oh, I see. So you plan to interrogate every person in the city who's of Asian descent to determine their place of birth before you offer to help them?"

Pinching my hand in the process, Louisa swings the door wide open and steps into formation as Ms. Thompson eyes us from the opposite end of the hall.

I follow suit, standing at the end of the line, frustration with my sister building within my chest. I stare straight ahead, intent on ignoring Louisa and her condemnation.

"Glad you could join us, both of you." Ms. Thompson

steps our way. "If we weren't so short-staffed, I'd take a moment to remind you that being tardy seldom begins the day right." She waves her free hand in the air, dismissing our lateness, while the other holds onto her trusty clipboard. "Consider yourselves fortunate that we do not have the time to tend to such matters this morning, as we are three maids down for the fifth floor alone."

Ms. Thompson steps in front of me, meeting my gaze with a question lingering behind her eyes. "We all need to pitch in with the extra duties today." Checking her clipboard, she continues. "I've decided we should work as a team for the quickest results. I'll have you pair up. We will start with the rooms that have already been vacated this morning but will be the first to have new guests this afternoon. Then we'll move on to rooms whose guests are staying through the weekend."

Ms. Thompson rattles off the list of top-priority guest rooms before dispersing us with instructions to find a partner and get straight to work. "Ladies, one more thing. We must have all the rooms with expected guests completed before we break for lunch today."

Murmurs of discontent rumble through the group.

"I know. I am sorry, but we have no other option but to ready the rooms before the check-in hour." Ms. Thompson unbuttons the cuff of her sleeve and begins rolling it up. "You won't be alone in this. I will be joining in and working with you, side by side, until the rooms are complete."

I nod with an appreciative smile. I admire Ms. Thompson's work ethic and her dedication to remaining fair to the girls under her charge. She is one to go down with the ship, and for that I am grateful.

Maids bustle about the hall, pairing up and grabbing carts. I turn toward Louisa. Despite our disagreement, I have no doubt she will prefer to work with me, given how efficiently we work as a team.

I cannot hide my disappointment as Louisa turns her back to me, striding directly to Jane Morgan's side. The two exchange a few words, and then Jane smiles at Louisa. They retrieve a cleaning cart, Jane laughing at something Louisa has said. My heart sinks and moisture sprouts in my eyes.

"Well, it looks like it will be you and me, Miss Wilson." Ms. Thompson follows my gaze down the hall, toward Louisa's retreating back. She places a warm hand on my elbow, guiding me toward the last remaining cart. "Sometimes, I find putting all my attention on a task to be a good way to puzzle out a problem. What do you say? Shall we give it a try?"

I dab discreetly at my eyes, doing my best to regain my composure in front of Ms. Thompson. "Yes. Thank you, ma'am." I follow the matron to the first room on our list. As she unlocks the door to the recently vacated guest room, the question that has been circling me presses forward, landing with a thud in my heart. How did I become the villain in Louisa's story?

CHAPTER 11

Friday, September 30, 1927
Louisa

I hide my annoyance at Clara's daft view of inequality behind the friendliest banter I can muster as Jane and I tackle the first guest room on our list.

"Let's start with the bed." I place the fresh linens on the bench seat positioned against the footboard. Then I motion to Jane to help me move the low-backed settee a few feet away from the bed frame.

Together, we strip the bed, tossing the rumpled sheets into a tidy pile near the door.

"You know," Jane begins, her eyes flitting up to mine as the bedsheet billows in the air above our outstretched arms, "I am glad you sought me out as your partner today."

"Of course." The sheet settles delicately over the mattress, and we each begin tucking and folding our corners with the efficiency we have come to take for granted after months of daily practice. "Why wouldn't I choose you as a partner?"

We move to the settee and manhandle fresh pillowcases

onto the four pillows that will line the bed's intricately carved headboard. "Well, Clara is your usual choice." Jane places a newly encased pillow back on the bench while she moves on to the next one. "Don't get me wrong, I would choose to work with someone as capable and familiar as well, if given the chance."

"Do you have a sister, Jane?"

We each take two corners of the duvet, spreading it wide between us as we walk it toward the waiting mattress. "I do. I have two in fact."

I nestle the bottom edge of the duvet into the space between the footboard and the mattress. "Lucky you." The words slip out with more sarcasm than I intend. "I mean, how fortunate to have two sisters. Double the dresses to choose from, I imagine."

Jane catches my eye with a questioning glance.

With the duvet smoothed, we place the pillows gently, careful not to muss the aesthetic of the fully made bed.

"Anyway." I wave a hand dismissively. "Is there a particular reason you are pleased to be working together today?" We return the settee to its spot at the end of the bed, and I move toward the cleaning cart.

"Well yes, actually. I was hoping to ask your opinion on something."

I cover my surprise by unlatching the vacuum from the cart and heaving it onto the floor. "My opinion?" I hand Jane the feather duster and incline my head toward the bedside tables.

Jane begins with the lamp atop the night table, dusting the shade and then the body. "Don't be so surprised. We are more alike than anyone else might imagine, and you know it."

I concede this point with a nod of my head. "I suppose there are similarities in how we view our place in the world."

"Well, anyway, I seem to have found myself in a bit of a pickle." Jane avoids my eyes by focusing on lifting the lamp to dust beneath it.

"What kind of a pickle?" I bend at the waist, unwrapping the long, thick cord from the back of the vacuum before walking its plug end to the electrical socket.

Jane moves around the bed to dust the second table. "Well, it seems I came across as overly friendly to a certain gentleman at The Club a couple of weeks ago. You know the place?"

I nod. Though I've never been there, I am aware of its location and its reputation as an anything-goes nightclub for the young and wealthy.

"I mean, I didn't intend to give him the wrong impression." Jane's bottom lip begins to tremble. "I didn't intend to give him any impression at all, really. I had seen him around my social circle on several occasions, and I was merely hoping for a bottle of champagne for the table. He seemed quite keen to go along with it. We were just having a bit of fun."

Not wishing to drown out Jane with the loud vacuum, I wipe down every inch of the wardrobe with slow, methodical movements. "He must think otherwise." I swivel my head in Jane's direction, my eyebrow lifted. "Hence the pickle?"

"I've been told the man wishes to court me." Jane sighs, her shoulders slumping. "His intention is to have a whirlwind courtship before seeking permission from my parents to marry."

"Has he said as much? Is this not what you want?" I stand and face her. "In all honesty, Jane, I thought you were looking for a suitable husband."

"Well, I am intent to marry, but . . ." Jane fidgets with the duster's wooden handle. "Oh, I don't know. Perhaps I am being silly."

95

I stuff the cleaning rag into my apron pocket and step toward her. "There is something you aren't saying. Is this man not the desirable sort?"

Jane releases a forced laugh. "Well, he is well to do and certainly travels in similar circles. My parents would love him."

"But you don't?" I cock my head to the right, encouraging her to continue.

Jane shakes her head no. "I could never love a man who claims me as his in public while quietly threatening to ruin me if I don't take him up on the offer."

"Jane." I draw out her name, uncertainty wrapping around my words. "How could he ruin you?"

"Don't look at me like that, Louisa. I've seen him at The Club a few times is all. We've shared a few laughs, but I swear, it has always been in the company of others." Jane brushes past me, returning the feather duster to the cleaning cart before grabbing the handle of the vacuum with more force than necessary. "I haven't done anything so unbecoming as to be labelled a trollop." Jane's hand drops from the vacuum as she covers her face. "Only, that is exactly what is happening."

"What is happening? How has he threatened you?"

Jane's bottom lip quivers. "He knows."

"Knows what?" The hairs on the back of my neck stand to attention.

"He knows that I refused to marry that old codger my parents set their sights on. He knows that my situation within my family is precarious at best. He knows that I am in no position to go against him. He has probably even met my father in business settings." Jane releases a weighted sigh. "He knows he has control over the situation and I do not."

The warmth seems to leak from the room as the reality of Jane's problem settles over me. "What does he want?"

Jane's shoulders shake as she attempts to fend off a

downward spiral in decorum. "He has decided that I should be his wife. Apparently, he is in need of a boost to his status, and the Morgan name would do just that. If I do not concede, he will represent me as a woman with loose morals to my friends and family. It wouldn't take long for such a rumour to ripple through my social circle and destroy any chance I have of marrying well in the future."

"Can he do that? I mean, surely not everyone would believe his lies."

"He already has."

"What do you mean? What has he done?"

"There is a whisper going around my group of friends. I could tell the moment I returned to the table that night." Jane wipes a tear from her cheek. "The avoiding eyes. The immediate shift in conversation when I approached my seat. You know that feeling when you realize people are talking about you?"

I nod in understanding, my back tensing as Jane's story unfolds.

"That sort of thing is hard to ignore." Jane glances around the room before meeting my eyes again. "Lillian, I mean Miss Roberts, tried to assure me that the chatter never left the round table at The Club—but a murmur, especially a scandalous one, can quickly become a landslide."

"So, this man has said that if you marry him, all this nonsense will go away and he will somehow save your reputation?"

Jane wrings her hands, her worry over the situation creasing her forehead. "Pretty much, yes."

I cannot smother my opinion of the man. "What a swine." Before the words have even left my lips, I know I will do whatever I can to help set things right for Jane. This is what Clara does not understand. Our responsibility as human beings is to help those in need, regardless of their class, race, or gender.

"Knock, knock." As though summoned by my fiery thoughts of her, Clara stands in the guest room doorway, holding a stack of fresh towels.

"Yes?" My irritation with my sister has yet to subside, and my arching eyebrow makes sure she knows.

"Ms. Thompson asked me to bring these to you." Clara takes a tentative step forward, offering me the towels. "Something about a delay with the laundry."

Apparently, I pause a moment longer than is polite, as Jane moves past me to accept the towels from Clara. "Thank you," Jane says. "We are just about to start on the washroom."

Jane looks from Clara to me before adding, "Please, thank Ms. Thompson for the consideration. You've saved us a trip to the basement, that is for certain."

Clara glances once more in my direction and then offers Jane a tight smile. "Okay then, I will see you later."

When Clara has left, Jane turns to me. "What was that about?"

"Just a difference of opinion between sisters." I may disagree with Clara's ways, but I have no intention of sullying her name in front of Jane, at least if I can help it.

Jane shakes her head. "Remind me not to get on your bad side." She adjusts her grip on the vacuum. "You have a look that could slice a person in two."

My smile emerges, tugging an idea along with it. "Jane, I think I know how to help you."

"You do?"

"Were you planning to go to The Club tonight?" My mind spins as a plan begins to form.

Jane pushes the vacuum to the far corner of the room, following our training. We always start at the furthest location from the door. "No. I figured he wouldn't have much recourse if I didn't show up. Though, I suppose he could just arrive at my door." A panicked expression strikes her face. "You don't think he would come to my house, do you?"

"Probably not so soon into this charade of his, but I do have an idea that might put this all to rest in no time."

"What?" Jane leaves the vacuum and stands before me, her hands reaching for mine. "Please, Louisa, tell me your plan."

"Just be dressed and ready. Meet me at the clock at seven, and I'll fill you in on our way to The Club."

"Oh Louisa, you are a lifesaver." Jane squeezes my hands as she gushes.

"But first, we have four more rooms to clean before we can break for lunch. What do you say?" I grab the washroom cleaning supplies and raise them in the air.

"I say, you tend to the washroom and I'll finish the vacuuming." Jane's relieved smile bolsters my enthusiasm. I am doing the right thing by helping her, a concept Clara wouldn't understand.

Five hours later, as the rest of the fifth-floor maids gather in the lunchroom, gobbling their sandwiches, I take a moment to borrow the phone in Mr. Olson's office.

"Hello Miss James, this is Louisa Wilson." I pause while the theatre club's kind receptionist responds. "I know, it's been ages." I nod as she inquires as to why she hasn't seen me recently. "Yes, we moved into the city a while back, so unfortunately, it became impossible for me to partake in the theatre's productions." I laugh lightly at her compliment. "Thank you, that is very kind of you to say. Yes, I do miss it terribly."

I wait for Miss James to stop talking so I can ask my question. "I was wondering if you could get a message to Thomas Cromwell? Yes, that is right. Do you know if he will be at the theatre this afternoon? The message is somewhat time sensitive. He will? Fantastic! Thank you. The message should read, Thomas, meet me at The Club at seven fifteen this evening. I require your assistance in setting someone straight. If you are up for an impromptu performance, please bring your Jimmy character with you. I'll be waiting inside. Hope to see you tonight. Louisa Wilson." I listen as she reads the message back to me. "Yes, that is it. Thank you, Miss James. Goodbye." I hang up the phone, pleased to have set the wheels in motion.

CHAPTER 12

Friday, September 30, 1927
Clara

I return to the fifth floor and meet Ms. Thompson in the linen closet. I wait patiently as she scans the papers on her clipboard.

"Ah, Miss Wilson, there you are."

"Yes, ma'am."

"I have to say, the fifth-floor maids are top-notch. Give them a challenge, and they know no other way but to rise to the top." Ms. Thompson beams a rare full smile, her eyes dancing with delight. "We have made excellent headway, so this afternoon should go quite well."

"Yes, ma'am."

"Is everything all right with you, Miss Wilson? You seem a little down in the mouth today." Ms. Thompson lowers her clipboard, taking a step closer. "I noticed a bit of tension between you and your sister earlier."

"I am sure everything will be just fine, ma'am." I force a

smile and try to shrug off thoughts of Louisa's harsh words. "You know how it sometimes goes with sisters?"

"Yes, I certainly do. I am fortunate to have both a brother and a sister." Ms. Thompson leans in conspiratorially. "My sister and I were absolutely inseparable growing up, until we— well, I suppose until we grew up into two separate individuals."

Ms. Thompson's words catch me off guard. I hadn't considered there might come a time when my relationship with Louisa might change irrevocably.

"I didn't mean to alarm you, Miss Wilson." Worry knits her eyebrows together. "It is only natural to have your own thoughts and feelings about life as you age, and they may differ from those of a sibling." Ms. Thompson places a gentle hand on my forearm. "But your childhood memories will always bind you together, dear."

"Yes." I hide my concern over this new realization behind a tight smile. "Thank heavens for that."

"A word of advice, Miss Wilson." She glances over her shoulder to ensure our conversation is private. "Change is the only true constant in our lives. Nothing remains the same forever. Try not to be afraid of it. I promise you, the wider you open your arms to change, the easier your life will be."

"Thank you, ma'am." The words are surely an unsuitable response, but they are all I can manage at the moment.

"Well then, shall we continue on?" Ms. Thompson examines her clipboard once more. "We have rooms 510 and 512 to tend to before the check-in hour is upon us."

I direct the cleaning cart toward the door and follow Ms. Thompson down the hall. My mind spins like the cart's wheels as I ruminate on Ms. Thompson's insights.

By the end of the workday, I have thought long and hard about the disagreement between Louisa and myself. Though

Ms. Thompson's words ring true, I am determined to ensure that Louisa's and my relationship will be the exception to the rule. Though I suspect that I, as I always have, will be the one who needs to adjust. To make that dream a reality, I will have to meet Louisa where she stands. Her soapbox seems always to be a tad taller than my own.

Walking home, I make an effort to draw Louisa into conversation. Convincing myself that our disagreement has been caused by missing facts, I edge around the topic. "I spoke with Ms. Thompson today about our next Sunday off."

"Mm-hmm." Louisa remains a hard nut to crack.

"She said we could both have October ninth off so we can celebrate Thanksgiving as a family."

"Fine." Louisa slows to a stop at the corner of Georgia and Howe, barely glancing at The Hotel Vancouver to our right.

"I thought you'd be excited. You know, to plan our Thanksgiving." I nudge Louisa's arm with my elbow, attempting to be playful. The notion falls flat as she steps off the sidewalk to cross the street.

"Do whatever you want, Clara." Louisa's miffed-sounding voice sails over her shoulder as I play catch-up with her long strides.

We pass The Hotel Georgia in silence, both of us acknowledging the doorman with a discreet wave.

I gather my courage over the next two blocks and then test the waters again. "You know, I'd like to talk about this morning." I steal a sideways glance in an attempt to gauge her reaction. "I think we may have gotten off on the wrong foot."

Louisa pulls up her jacket collar while letting out a long, slow breath.

"I was thinking that, well, maybe we've simply misunderstood one another is all."

"You've thought about this all day and that is what you

came up with?" Louisa spits out a strangled laugh. "And here everyone assumes you are the smart one."

Louisa's words sting, causing me to stop walking. "I never said you weren't smart. I—I think you are very smart."

An exasperated sigh billows from Louisa's mouth in a visible cloud, but no words follow.

Flattery is certainly not going to win her over this time. I try complete, unfiltered honesty instead. Balling my fists at my sides, I force the words out. "I am not as brave as you."

"This has nothing to do with bravery." Louisa's hardened features soften a little.

"You may think that I didn't feel heartbroken for the man with the groceries." This catches Louisa's attention. "The truth is that I felt horrible for him. My insides sank as low as they could sink, and then they sank some more." A tear prickles at the edge of my eye, and I blink to release it down my cheek. "I am not a monster, Lou. I don't wish for bad things to happen to anybody, regardless of who they are."

Louisa's thumb brushes away my tears. "I didn't say you were a monster."

"You sure are treating me like one."

Louisa sighs again, but this time she inclines her head in agreement. "I suppose you are right about that. I never meant to make you feel that way, Clara. It's just, well, I want the world to be something other than what it is."

Louisa gestures to a bench tucked under a tree half a block from our usual route home. We sit on the bench, our knees almost touching as we angle our bodies to face one another.

"I see injustice all around me in this city," she says, "and I can't help but wish that every man, woman, and child had the same opportunities and fair treatment."

"I wish I never had to see it." My words are demure, and though they are truthful, I recognize the cowardice in them.

"That is the point." Louisa's gloved hands ball into fists on her lap. "Turning a blind eye doesn't make things better. To me, it seems to indicate acceptance."

I consider her words, wondering how to walk that line between doing what is right and doing what is prudent.

"I realize that I may be asking the impossible." Louisa's face twists with frustration. "I became angry with you because I couldn't understand how someone who I know has such a kind and loving heart would choose to look the other way."

Tears trickle down my cheeks as my sister's honesty cuts through to my core.

Louisa's shoulders fall under the weight of our conversation. "I suppose there has been injustice ever since the world began. If there is one thing history has taught us, it is that humankind tends not to be very kind at all."

We sit in silence for a moment, our breath creating clouds as it mixes with the cooling air. "But how do we, as working-class girls, have any impact on things I can't even comprehend?" My voice wavers, already knowing the answer will not be an easy one.

"I don't know, Clara. All I can do is take on one circumstance at a time. I just pray that somewhere down the line, the pebble of kindness I toss into the water of humanity will ripple out and touch more hearts than I ever could on my own."

My head bobs slowly. The autumn chill, along with the remnants of our conversation, settles uneasily under my warm winter coat. My questions remain unanswered, and the one thing I feel with certainty is that I am not brave enough for this.

Louisa breaks the silence. "We should get home."

"I suppose so." I stand and tighten the jacket belt at my waist. "I was thinking chicken pot pie for dinner. Might take me a bit to roll out the crust, but it should be a cozy meal for a chilly evening. Then maybe we can play a round of gin rummy or pull out one of Mama's old puzzles."

"Oh, I meant to tell you." Louisa is already a step ahead of me, leaving me hurrying to keep up with her once again. "I won't be home for dinner."

"You won't? Where are you going?"

"I'm helping out a friend."

"Does Papa know?" We cross the street, and I see the brick face of The Newbury a block ahead of us.

"He will as soon as I tell him."

"Do you think he will have any objection? I mean, it isn't as though evening outings have been a usual occurrence."

Louisa pivots to face me as we reach the corner. "Need I remind you I am only a couple years shy of being able to vote? Most girls my age are marrying and having children. I don't think I am being presumptuous when I make plans with a friend on a Friday evening."

I've been put in my place, once again. "So, you don't want anything to eat? Maybe just a nibble?"

Louisa places a hand on my shoulder. "If you would like to make me a cup of tea and a biscuit while I change, that would be most appreciated."

I can tell she is placating me with her request, so I bite my bottom lip and refrain from pressing further. The last thing I want to do is upset the apple cart we have only recently re-established.

"Now all I have to decide is what to wear." Louisa's pace picks up as we near home. "I had thought to wear my latest winter dress, but it is two seasons past its prime."

I tug open the front door to the apartment building and Louisa strides through, her focus shifted to rifling through her closet in her mind's eye. "I suppose I could wear the short-sleeved dress. That is the most fashionable one that I own."

"Will that be warm enough?" We trudge up the stairs, unbuttoning jackets as we climb.

"Probably not." Louisa slides an arm out of her coat sleeve, warmed by the building's heating system and our efforts on the stairs. "But I think it's worth the sacrifice." Louisa slides the jacket off her shoulder to carry it as we reach the third floor.

I insert the key into the lock, more than a little curious of why there need be a sacrifice at all. Instead, I remind myself of my desire to maintain a relationship with my sister—on her terms, of course. I dismiss the edge the sentiment brings to my thoughts and decide to keep my lips sealed.

CHAPTER 13

Friday, September 30, 1927
Louisa

Dressed and powdered, I step from The Newbury, the wind snatching my breath. Wrapping my winter coat tight around me, I double knot the tie at my waist. Though I don't look toward our apartment window, I feel Clara's eyes on me as I skip across the road to catch the streetcar.

Ticket in hand, I board the trolley and move closer to the rear exit doors, eager to disembark and set things in motion. The streetcar stops a half block away from the clock, so I grip my collar with one hand and duck my head against the wind.

I arrive first, glancing at the clock's large, round face, its hands indicating I am a few minutes ahead of schedule. I pace with small steps, trying to keep the brisk evening air from chilling me to the bone.

Jane's sleek, chauffeured car pulls up and parks in front of the clock. The uniformed driver hops out and moves quickly around the front bumper to open the door for Jane, offering her a tip of his cap and an extended hand. Jane's black evening shoe touches down on the sidewalk, its beads catching the light of the streetlamp as she stands.

"Thank you." Jane inclines her head toward her driver before hastening toward me. "I'm so nervous I could burst."

"You've nothing to be nervous about." I squeeze her hand, which is wrapped in an elbow-length fashion statement. My own gloves are woollen and meant only to block the night's chill. "We will have you sorted out in no time at all."

I explain my plan as we walk toward The Club. "When Jimmy arrives, you act like he is the love of your life. Leave the rest to me."

"What if he doesn't show?" Jane's nerves are bubbling to the surface when I spot the neon sign illuminating the entrance to The Club.

"Don't worry. I won't let that man bully you into a dinner date, let alone a marriage." My attempt to lighten her mood goes unnoticed, so I stop to gain her full attention. "Jane. You can trust me."

"Why are you doing this for me?" Jane's eyes rim with moisture. "I mean, I am grateful, truly. It's just—it isn't as though we are close friends. Our history is quite the opposite, really."

"You've got too many friends, is that it?" I tease, looping my arm with hers and tugging her closer. "If I don't try to help you, who will? Shouldn't we always try to help when we are able?"

"I suppose. I guess I've never really been the helping kind." Jane's eyes examine the sidewalk as we stroll. "I wasn't raised to look out for others, only for myself and the interests of my family."

"Perhaps now you will begin to see places where you can offer assistance."

Jane nods thoughtfully, and I feel as though one of my pebbles might have just created a ripple, right before my eyes.

Mere steps away from The Club's entrance, I toss her a mischievous smile. "If it makes you feel better, I am hoping to get something out of this arrangement too."

Jane's head snaps up, a question lining her porcelain complexion. "Do tell."

"I'm looking for more excitement in my life, and this"—I splay my free hand to indicate the nightclub—"could very well be the place to start."

Jane cocks her head to one side. "I knew Louisa Wilson was in there somewhere. This may sound crazy, but I actually feel reassured knowing that the quick-witted, bold, unstoppable Louisa I've come to know has got my back." Jane glances at the wide wooden door of The Club. "Shall we?"

We check our coats, slipping our ticket stubs into Jane's slim clutch purse and step down a few stairs into the darkened lounge. A five-piece band on an elevated stage plays a jazz beat with a life of its own. I place a hand over my stomach to steady myself, the unfamiliar tune pulsating through my body.

My eyes roam the expansive room. Men and women are nestled into booths lined with dark, plush fabric, sitting closer than is socially permissible in public. Cocktails and champagne flutes are scattered atop nearly every table in the joint. The dance floor is alive with moving feet and swinging hips that make beaded flapper dresses come to life.

I scan the crowd and spot Thomas resting on a stool near the back of the club. I excuse myself to the ladies' room, intent to fill him in on tonight's plan.

A few minutes later, I return to find Jane a few feet away from where I left her, waiting nervously for me. "We're over here," she says and leads me to a round table near the dance floor.

Several well-dressed young women with red-painted lips eye me warily as Jane introduces me to each one in turn. I take note of a Sarah, who is perfectly dazzling in a silver, beaded dress I saw in the Spencer's department store window last week. The pricey dress was on display for less than twenty-four hours before the mannequin was disrobed of the latest in flapper fashion. I suppose I now know who did the snagging.

Even the few men in the group are dressed in formal fashion, with vests, jackets, and hats. As Jane introduces me, each of them leans forward in turn to kiss my bare hand. A Paul, dressed in black tie, catches my eye with a wink direct enough to bring colour to my already rouged cheeks.

A familiar face pulls my attention: Miss Lillian Roberts, whose daddy used his connections to get her a job at The Hamilton. Miss Roberts eyes me but addresses Jane. "What is she doing here?"

Jane steps forward and lowers her voice, hurriedly explaining my presence.

Miss Roberts twists her lips in what I assume is contemplation. "Fine," she hisses at Jane as she steps forward, extending her hand for me to shake. "Nice to see you again, Louisa."

"You as well, Lillian." I press my luck by addressing her by her first name.

Jane returns to my side, inviting me to sit. I am pulling my chair closer to the table when I hear Jane suck in a sharp breath. "That's him." She ducks her head behind a raised hand.

I pretend to cast my eyes about the room, bobbing my head to the music. When my eyes lock on him, I can't help but smile. The man would be difficult to miss, even if Jane hadn't given me a detailed description. He's tall and dashing, with slicked-back dark hair and a brilliant smile that I'm quite certain has broken a heart or two.

Despite Jane's attempt to remain undiscovered, the man scopes her out like an animal in his crosshairs.

"I see him," I whisper behind a well-placed palm. "He is coming this way."

"What do we do?" Panic rises in Jane's voice. "What do we do, Louisa?"

Thomas, or rather Jimmy, for tonight's theatrical purposes, steps confidently into the lounge. Though I suspect he has not set foot in the establishment prior to this evening, he seems perfectly at ease. He catches my eye just as Jane's dashing but conniving suitor approaches our table. I signal with a barely noticeable wave of my hand, which he acknowledges with a slight nod.

"The cavalry is here." I dip my chin and whisper in Jane's ear. "Just act natural. Remember, he is the love of your life."

"I was hoping we'd bump into one another this evening." Jane's bully of a man reaches us first, craftily covering his domineering side with a suave demeanour. "Care to dance? I believe we have some important things to discuss."

Before Jane can utter a word, Thomas is at her side, wrapping her in a tight embrace that lifts her to her feet. "Darling, I've missed you." Pulling back, he meets her eyes and tilts her chin up with a gentle finger. "Please say you'll forgive me. Father wouldn't let me escape last weekend." Thomas rolls his eyes with an exaggeration that almost sends me into a fit of giggles. "Buried. Simply buried under a mound of paper."

Jane lets out a nervous laugh.

"I told him yesterday that there was absolutely nothing he could say that would keep me another week from my girl."

Thomas wraps his arm around Jane's shoulders, giving her an extra squeeze for emphasis.

As if suddenly realizing there are other people in the room, Thomas offers his free hand to the other man. "How rude of me. Jimmy. Jimmy Fuller. Nice to meet you."

The man, looking slightly stunned, returns Thomas' handshake. "Robert Murphy."

"So, how do you all know each other?" Thomas raises the uncomfortable question before signalling to a passing waitress. "Miss, could we get a bottle of champagne for the table?"

"Yes, sir. Whose account should I charge it to?" The waitress glances between the two men.

"You can charge it to mine." Thomas' smile broadens, and I know he is up to something. "The account is under James Fuller the Third."

Thomas looks back at Jane, squeezing her into him. Jane, gaining her footing in the charade, places a hand on Thomas' chest while gazing into his eyes adoringly.

I decide it is time to play my part. "Mr. Murphy?" I keep my voice demure and bat my eyes. The man remains confounded, staring with an open-mouthed expression at Jane and Thomas. "Excuse me, Mr. Murphy." I place a hand on his forearm. "This might be a tad forward of me, but I've never been to a club this nice, and I'll just be kicking myself in the morning if I don't get out on that dance floor."

Mr. Murphy recovers himself, sending me a debonair smile that doesn't quite reach his eyes, ensuring its only effect is to make me wonder what he is playing at. He offers his hand and I take it. "Of course, Miss . . . ?"

"Wilson. Louisa Wilson."

With his hand on my back, he guides me onto the floor. A slow, soulful song has us swaying together, close enough to feel one another's breath. "So, Jane tells me you've expressed an interest in marrying her."

Mr. Murphy pulls back sharply. "She told you that?"

"Relax, Robert." I wave my hand as though none of it matters, ensuring I gain the upper hand in our conversation. "May I call you Robert?"

He nods his assent, though I suspect he would rather I didn't.

"Listen, here is the thing. She isn't in love with you." I peek at the table where Thomas and Jane remain in character as love birds.

"But I can make her love me. If she would give me a chance." Robert's words come out less confident than I am certain he would prefer.

"No, you really can't. Even if Jimmy weren't in the picture, you're barking up the wrong tree." I raise a single eyebrow, challenging him. "You wouldn't be happy in the end. Trust me on this. Wouldn't you rather find someone who adores you, instead of someone who fears what you might do?"

"She told you about that?" Robert's shoulders hunch. "Most certainly not my best moment, I'll admit."

"See." I tilt his chin up with my index finger. "I knew there was a decent guy in there somewhere."

Robert's smile is shy. "My father has been pressuring me to marry well and fast." His voice deepens, mimicking his father. "Choose a bride, Robert, who will lift the Murphy name high for all of Vancouver to know."

"I see. I understand how hard it must be, living up to the expectations of one's family. So, is it likely that Jane was mistaken about your intent to coerce her into marriage?"

"No, she wasn't mistaken." Robert's eyes drop from mine. "I was desperate, and my father . . . I'm sure he means well, but he didn't seem concerned that I marry for love. I figured the whole situation was a losing one."

"You might just deserve more than that." I offer him a sympathetic smile. As the song shifts to an upbeat tempo, we move apart and fall into step with the other dancers on the floor.

As we dance, I notice a few of the girls at Jane's table following Robert's every move. When they catch me watching, they shrink back, pretending to be in conversation with one another.

The music slows again, and I let Robert pull me toward him. "Can I tell you something?" I whisper close to his ear. He nods. "I think you've been focused on the wrong girl."

He pulls back to look at me. "What do you mean?"

I shrug my shoulder discreetly toward his admirers. "You've got more of a following than you may be aware of."

Robert's cheeks flush with colour, endearing him to me even more.

"I'll make you a deal. You agree to keep the threats and marriage talk away from Jane, and I'll help you become even more irresistible to those ladies over there."

"How exactly do you plan to do that?"

"Oh Robert, you have a lot to learn about women." I laugh. "Deal?"

"Deal, Louisa. I may call you Louisa, I presume." Robert's eyes twinkle as a true smile lifts his cheeks, lighting his handsome face.

Robert and I finish a run of songs, laughing and carrying on as though we are old friends. By the time the band pauses for a break, I am glistening with sweat, and Robert's tie is loose around his neck.

I slip into a chair beside Jane and shoot her a confident

wink. She relaxes visibly, releasing her hand from Thomas' to squeeze mine in thanks.

Thomas leans in. "Looks like you've worked your magic, Lou."

I follow his gaze to Robert, who is pouring champagne into Sarah's glass.

"I couldn't have done it without you." I quench my dry throat with a large gulp of water.

We allow enough time for Robert to head out onto the dance floor with Sarah. The girl is beaming at her good fortune. Robert has finally noticed her.

"You know," Jane says as she watches the couple, "they are perfect for one another."

"He's really not a bad guy." I bump Jane's shoulder with my own. "Misguided by duty to his father, perhaps, but not a bad guy at all. He won't be threatening you anymore, or marrying you, for that matter."

"Thank you, Louisa. I don't know how you did it, but thank you." Jane stands, pulling me up with her and wrapping me in a tight embrace. I am once again reminded that people are just people. We all falter from time to time, but we all have the same opportunity to recover ourselves too. Sometimes, all we need is a little encouragement to find our way.

"Come, let me give you both a ride home." Jane tugs on Thomas' sleeve. "It's the least I can do."

"I won't decline a ride in this weather." Thomas leaves with our coat-check tickets and waits patiently at the door as Jane says farewell to her friends.

Thomas slips Jane's coat over her shoulders before turning to help me shrug into mine. His fingers graze the back of my neck as he adjusts my collar, sending a shiver the length of my spine.

We reach for the door at the same time, and I find myself

catching my breath when his warm hand brushes mine. I cover the emotion with a nervous laugh.

The three of us pile into Jane's chauffeured automobile. The driver looks at us through the rear-view mirror. "Where to, miss?"

"Oh yes, where is home?" Jane looks at me and then Thomas expectantly.

"I'm at The Newbury. The corner of Thurlow and Robson." I do my best not to be embarrassed by our home's address.

Thomas clears his throat. "Really?"

I nod, wondering if I have given away more than I should about our family's financial situation.

"I'm in Washington Court." He smiles and says to the driver, "Thurlow and Nelson, please."

"Excellent," Jane says to her chauffeur. "First to Louisa's and then to—" She stops. "I'm sorry, I don't actually know your real name. I assume it isn't Jimmy."

We all burst into laughter, gaining us an amused expression from the driver.

We are still giggling as we pull up to my apartment building. "Listen, Louisa." Thomas puts a hand on my sleeve. "I was hoping we could get together tomorrow. There is something I've been wanting to talk to you about. Until you left that message, I didn't know how to locate you."

"I have the day off tomorrow." The cool air rushes into the back seat as Jane's chauffeur opens the door and waits patiently while I dawdle.

"Great. How about ten o'clock? The diner just up from the library?"

"Sure. The least I can do is buy you a cup of coffee." I can't stop myself from smiling. "Thank you again for playing Jimmy tonight."

"Please, it was my pleasure. Have a good night." Thomas' smile makes my heart skip a beat.

I wave goodbye to both of them and walk toward my building.

The driver's mouth quirks up on one side as he opens the building's front door for me. "You should know, miss, I haven't seen Miss Morgan this happy in quite some time. I am glad to see her laugh again."

"I am very pleased to hear that."

The driver waves me inside. "Good evening, miss."

"Thank you," I reply as the door closes behind me.

CHAPTER 14

Saturday, October 1, 1927
Clara

Louisa arrived home later than I expected last night, but then again, I suppose I had no idea what to expect. She hadn't told me where she was going, what she was doing, or whom she was meeting. I toss the thick blanket off my legs and slide my feet to the cool wood floor.

Her light snores indicate a truly restful state. Watching my sister sleep softens my view of her, and I resolve to coax out the details of her evening while we tend to the day's household chores. I tiptoe from the bedroom and silently close the door behind me.

It's too early to start making a ruckus, so I settle in with a cup of tea and reread Aunt Vivian's most recent letter. Given the ocean that separates us from Mama's sister and our cousin, Josephine, letters have become a lifeline between our two worlds.

. . .

Thursday, August 18, 1927

    Dearest Clara,

    I was so delighted to receive your previous letter. It sounds as though things are going quite well for you and Louisa at the hotel. I am pleased to know that my and Josephine's little gift and words of insight helped set you on your way to becoming maids. I pray the opportunity is precisely what you were seeking.

    Summer is nearing its last hurrah here in London. The days are hot and sticky and quite often unbearable. The nights, however, have begun to cool, hinting at the autumn weather to come. The hotel is far quieter this time of year, as those who can afford to travel are heading out of the city to cottages by the sea.

    The furthest we have ventured this summer was to Kew Gardens. Josephine and I packed ourselves a picnic lunch and spent the day roaming the beautiful grounds. I don't know if your father mentioned it, but The Gardens are where he and your mother met. If I remember correctly, he was visiting the area for a summer-long botany program. Your mother once said she found his interest in flowers charming.

    Once acquainted, they spent every spare moment in each other's company. In hindsight, I knew she had one foot out of England the moment I learned she was being courted by a foreigner. Here I go, sure to find myself in trouble with your father for telling tales. All that is truly important is how dearly she loved him, and I am quite certain you are already aware of that fact.

    Josephine had some questions about your upcoming Thanksgiving. We do not have such a celebration here in the UK, but your mother mentioned it in her letters. Her description of the dinner menu made my mouth water from across the pond. Your mother was a fine cook, and just her written words were enough to make one's stomach rumble. I wish you all a lovely celebration. May you find peace, love, and thanks in spending the day in one another's company.

    On that note, I do hope you will indulge Josephine and myself with a detailed writing of your festive dinner. I am a glutton for punishment, it seems, as I know I will be hungrier than ever after reading news of your Thanksgiving meal. If you would be so generous to include a recipe or two, that truly would be appreciated. The other day, Josephine and I were talking about Christmas and discussing what a wonderful addition one of your mother's dishes would be to our holiday table.

Well, it seems the hour I set aside to compose this letter has come to a close. I had best ready myself for the day ahead. I am genuinely grateful for correspondence from you. I have missed hearing news since your mother's passing, and it warms my heart to know that you are picking up where she left off. Please know she would be so very proud of you, Clara.

With love and hugs,
Aunt Vivian and Cousin Josephine

I FOLD THE LETTER AND TUCK IT INTO ITS ENVELOPE, MAKING A mental note to send a few of Mama's favourite recipes after our Thanksgiving dinner.

The sun is beginning to rise in the morning sky, a welcome respite from the rain and wind that have been assaulting us in recent days. I step toward the window and draw back the curtain. A gull floats on the breeze, his wings adjusting with a dancer's ease as he navigates the current.

"Looks like a beautiful day." Papa emerges from his bedroom, appearing well rested and with a grin upon his face.

"Nice to see the sun, isn't it? Perhaps it won't be too long of a winter after all." I lift the teacup in my hand. "Can I make you a cup of tea? Maybe some toast or eggs?"

"Thanks, but I am heading over to the Murrays' for an early meeting. I wouldn't want to spoil my appetite, as Mr. Murray has promised me some of Tildy's famous biscuits and gravy in exchange for guidance on an English-inspired garden he is hoping to add."

"Well, look at you. Breakfast and garden planning. I can't

imagine a more perfect morning for you to enjoy." I return my cup to the kitchen as Papa grabs his coat and shoes. "Please give my best to the family and all. Let them know how much we've missed them since our move into the city."

"I will be sure to do that." Papa reaches for the door. "I expect I'll be home by mid-afternoon at the latest." He pauses a moment. "And Clara, be sure to get outside and enjoy the sunshine. It would be a shame to miss out on the gift of a beautiful Saturday."

"As soon as the chores are handled, I'll see if I can convince Louisa to join me on a walk along the water."

Papa tilts his head in question.

"I promise, I will." I laugh and press a kiss to his cheek. "Now off you go, or you're sure to miss that breakfast."

Two hours later, I've kneaded a loaf of bread and covered it with a towel to rise on the counter. While I wait for the bread, I mix the dough for a batch of scones, which will serve as quick breakfasts as Louisa and I head back to work for another seven days straight.

Though these long workweeks are not ideal, our willingness to help when Ms. Thompson needs us has ensured our ability to host our family Thanksgiving next Sunday. Last week, I spent my evenings going through Mama's cookbook again before finalizing the menu. Although I am eager for the celebration, I am a little apprehensive about the cooking. I elected to add a few special dishes to the mix, and the preparation is sure to take a full day.

As I shape the scones, I remind myself that Louisa will be here for moral support, if not actual assistance in the kitchen. I contemplate making the mince pie in advance. Though I know I'll be tired from the long workweek, I can't see any other way of having enough time with the oven.

I am sliding the scones in to bake when Louisa finally

appears from the bedroom. "Hey there, sleepyhead. I thought you might stay in bed all day."

She offers me a weak smile with a roll of her eyes.

"Scones are in the oven. Should be ready in twenty minutes or so." I wipe my hands with a tea towel before checking the progress of the rising bread.

"Oh, I can't stay."

I turn to face my sister, noticing that she is wearing one of her best day dresses, and carrying a matching handbag to boot. "What do you mean?" My arm swings wide, gesturing around the apartment. "We have chores to do. With the long week ahead, I assumed you understood that today is the only time we can tackle the cleaning."

"I didn't get the chance to tell you. You were asleep when I arrived home," she says, like it is my fault for not being awake. Classic Louisa—she can turn any situation on its head so she comes out shining.

"Maybe that is because you arrived home after waking hours." My hands go to my hips as I feel the tide turning within me. "Is that lipstick?" I step forward. "Where exactly are you going?"

"It's just a little gloss." Louisa pushes past me to the coat rack. "If you must know, I am meeting a friend for breakfast."

"Is this the same friend you were out with last night? Is there something you are not telling me, Louisa? Do you know when you will be back?" The questions roll off my tongue in rapid succession.

Louisa raises her eyebrow. "Which one of those would you like me to answer?"

My gaze falls to the floor, disappointed and annoyed that I am being left to take care of our home by myself. "When will you be back?"

"I don't know." Louisa stops my next words with a raised

palm. "But I will be back as soon as I can, and then I will help you with the chores."

"But—"

"But nothing, Clara. This is the best I can offer you." Louisa folds her arms across her chest and taps her toe, a sure sign that she's done discussing the point and is simply waiting for me to agree.

"Fine." The word flies out of my mouth. "I am not doing your laundry. So if you wish to have clean clothes, you'll have to sort that out yourself."

"I think I can manage that." Louisa shakes her head at what she has apparently deemed childish behaviour. "I'll see you later."

The apartment door closes with a soft thud. My enthusiasm for the day plummets. Dejected, I slump onto the sofa and manage a convincing imitation of a pouting three-year-old.

An hour ticks by as I wait for the bread to finish baking. Seeing how everyone in my family has abandoned me for better options, I let the time pass, unmotivated to do the tasks that make their lives easy.

I glance at my wristwatch, letting out a long, slow sigh as I lift myself from the sofa to check on the bread. As I'm pulling the loaf from the oven, my wrist grazes the hot oven door, causing me to jerk my arm away. The movement is too abrupt, and the bread pan slides from my towel-wrapped hands and skids across the kitchen floor.

I let out a frustrated holler that can certainly be heard by all of our third-floor neighbours. I reposition the towel and rescue the bread to the cooling rack. I am running my wrist under cold water when the phone startles me.

Though the phone was installed over a month ago, it seldom rings. And when it does ring, it is never for me. Papa decided to install a phone in the apartment so we could contact him if we found ourselves working late at the hotel. Truth be told, I suspect he was keen to provide us with the convenience our neighbours have been making use of for some time.

I wrap a cool cloth around my wrist and lift the receiver from its slot on the dining room wall. "Wilson residence."

"Clara? It's Rebecca. Did I catch you at a bad time?"

"No, sorry." I pull the cloth from my wrist to peek at the red slash of skin. "I just burned myself on the oven, so I was a little preoccupied." I toss the cloth back into the kitchen and position myself in front of the phone's mouthpiece. "Wait. Did you get a phone?"

Rebecca giggles over the line. "We did, and I wanted you to be the first person I called."

"Well, I am honoured." I can't help but smile at Rebecca's joy and her warm thoughts of me.

"I was actually wondering if you wanted to join me for a walk? With it being such a beautiful day, I figured a walk would do us both good. Of course, only if you are up to it. How badly did you burn yourself?"

"I'm quite certain I will survive, though it may leave a mark." I feel my mood lifting and am once again thankful for the opportunity to work at The Hamilton. The hotel is the reason Rebecca and I met. "A walk sounds absolutely perfect."

"Fantastic news. Do you want to take the streetcar and walk at English Bay?"

"I haven't done that in ages." I consider the time our adventure will take but quickly dismiss the worry. If Louisa can take the day for herself, then so can I. "Yes, that would be wonderful."

Rebecca and I set a time and location to meet. I place the bread upright on the cooling rack and leave the pan in the sink to scrub later. Changing out of my worn dress and into the one I recently purchased at the shop, I pull a Louisa move and add a swipe of gloss to my bottom lip.

I scrawl a brief and less than informative note to Louisa about my whereabouts, wrap my jacket around my shoulders, and head out the door.

CHAPTER 15

*S*aturday, October 1, 1927
    Louisa

Stepping away from The Newbury, I make a concerted effort to tamp down my guilt over leaving Clara to tend the household on her own. She isn't wrong in her assessment of the manner in which the day's events are unfolding, but I remind myself that Clara's view is often unnecessarily narrow. Perhaps I am helping her see that not everything can run according to her plan.

The sun's warmth seeps through my coat as I walk, helping my shoulders relax while easing thoughts of Clara and laundry. Vancouver is most beautiful in the glimmering morning sun, and though the trees have been battered by days of rain and wind, a few tenacious colour-infused leaves sparkle in the glow.

I move quickly through the streets, the scent of fresh bread permeating the air outside of the bakery. The library on the corner of Main and Hastings is one of my favourite buildings in the city. Since Carnegie's fifty-thousand-dollar donation built the city's first library in 1903, it has served as a stunning example of fine architecture.

I peer through the expansive window of the diner and spot Thomas seated at a corner table. At my quick tug on the cafe door, the sound of the jingling bell fills the cozy space. A waitress in a dull grey day dress, mostly covered with a full white apron, greets me with a menu.

"Thank you. I see my friend over there." I point in Thomas' direction and am met with his friendly wave. He stands to invite me to the table, waiting until I've seated myself before sliding back into his own chair.

"I'm glad you could make it." Thomas' wide smile sends a delightful warming sensation through me.

"Coffee?" The waitress appears with a pot at the ready.

"No, thank you." I glance at the menu. "I'll have a cup of tea instead." She refills Thomas' cup and leaves to fetch my tea.

"The pancakes are great here." Thomas directs his chin toward the menu. "If you are hungry."

"That sounds good." I push the menu to the side as the waitress returns with tea and a small pot of hot water.

"What can I get you?" she asks me, with her pencil poised over a pad of paper.

"I'll have the pancakes, please."

"Do you want whipped cream with that?"

My eyes flick up to Thomas, who is watching me with a curious grin. "Yes, please."

The waitress looks expectantly at Thomas.

"I'll have the same."

"Alrighty then. Won't be long." The waitress retreats toward the kitchen, hollering "order" as she nears the pass-through window.

"I assume good pancakes aren't the reason you wanted to meet." I hide my nerves by adding sugar to my tea.

Thomas chuckles. "You will thank me after."

"I should be thanking you now." I blow the steam off the top of my cup. "For last night."

"I was happy to help. Besides, bringing Jimmy to life again was fun." Thomas stirs a spoonful of sugar into his coffee. "Jane explained the reason for the ruse as she drove me home. You are a good friend."

My cheeks warm, and I resist the urge to cover them with my hands, instead hiding behind my cup of tea. "I am not certain Jane and I are what you would call friends, but she was in need of some assistance. Besides, Robert isn't all bad. Misguided, definitely, but not a bad person entirely. Anyway, it all worked out in the end." I take another sip of tea, aware that Thomas' eyes have yet to leave mine. "Oh, that reminds me. The champagne?" I lift an eyebrow in question.

Thomas lets out a low, soft chuckle. "A friend who works at The Club owed me a favour." He lifts his shoulders with an unconcerned air. "He repaid me with a bottle of The Club's finest. I felt it might be necessary to really sell Jimmy's character." Thomas winks mischievously. "I think it worked."

"I agree, it most certainly did. But why do I get the feeling that you made the extra effort for another reason?" I lower my teacup to the table.

"I could never pull one over on you, Lou." Thomas pauses while I fill my cup. "I didn't know how to reach you after you left the theatre group. I tried to track you down, but nobody knew where you'd vanished to."

"I didn't exactly vanish." My lips purse at the sentiment, as though I'd slinked away with my tail between my legs. "We moved is all."

"That's the funniest bit. I could hardly believe it when I

129

realized you'd been living only blocks away from my own apartment. I've spent months looking for you." Thomas shakes his head. "You were right under my nose all this time."

"Why were you looking for me?"

"That's the reason I wanted to meet with you this morning. I am directing a play, and you were the first person I thought of for the role. To be honest, I haven't been able to think of anyone else since."

The waitress arrives with two steaming plates of pancakes covered in whipped cream. "Here you are. Enjoy." She leaves us to dig into the sweet, fluffy stacks.

"What's the role?" I ask, hiding my excitement as I place a napkin in my lap.

Thomas cuts into his stack of pancakes, whipped cream melting onto the edges of the plate. "Harriet Craig."

My hands hover over my pancakes, holding a knife and fork. "As in Harriet Craig from *Craig's Wife*?"

I can see Thomas is as ruffled as a hen with a fox inside its coop, but he hides it well beneath a veneer of suave certainty. "The one and only." He takes a bite of pancake and watches me intently as he chews.

"Oh my." I place my fork and knife on the table. "That is quite the role." A thousand questions dance through my mind.

"Yes, Harriet Craig is an enormous role, but I know you can handle it. I bet you read every review when the play hit the stage a couple years back."

I nod, recalling how fans and critics alike talked of how the play pushed societal boundaries, raising questions of what is appropriate for an upper-class married woman. I was captivated by the character of Mrs. Craig, this force to be reckoned with.

Thomas reaches his hand across the table and touches

mine. "I wouldn't have mentioned it if I didn't think you were perfect for the role."

I am caught between exhilaration and sheer panic. "Who played Harriet Craig on Broadway again?"

"Crystal Herne."

"Oh, I adore her. She is beautiful."

"She is. And so are you." Thomas squeezes my hand.

My guard goes up in an instant. "Is that why you thought of me? Because of my looks?" My voice quavers.

Thomas straightens abruptly. "No. I thought of you because Harriet Craig is a commanding character and you would make her shine, even if all you did was raise that eyebrow of yours."

I nod, more solemn than ecstatic, contemplating his words. "Tell me more about the production. What are you thinking?" Realizing that my question may not have been what Thomas was expecting, I lighten my tone and usher into place a confident smile.

Thomas relaxes and returns to his breakfast, explaining his vision for the play between bites.

"I've filled the role of Mr. Craig with an up-and-comer whose performances, from what I've seen, have been outstanding."

I take a bite of pancake, my stomach turning as the overly sweet concoction hits my tongue. "Anyone I know?"

"I don't think so." Thomas shakes his head. "He's not from around here. Toronto, maybe. Honestly, I can't remember. I was just pleased he agreed to join the production."

I nod and let him continue, politely adding the occasional comment while my mind runs rampant. A starring role in a real theatre production is the opportunity I have been dreaming about. But the memory of my last ill-gotten lead role haunts me like a bad dream.

Thomas cleans his plate with speed. A hum of excitement fuels the rhythm of his words. He has secured most of the cast. The set and even the wardrobe are ready and waiting for rehearsals to begin.

My stomach is in knots. Pushing my plate to the side, I dab the corners of my mouth with my napkin. "And where is all this taking place?"

Thomas' grin widens. "Just up the street. I figured we could stop by so you can see the theatre and read for the part."

"I see. So this wasn't about breakfast, then? Your plan was to bamboozle me into an audition this morning?" I tease him while pushing the plate a little further away, the smell of the sweet pancakes souring my stomach.

"You are perfect for this role, Lou." Thomas stares at the table as he gathers his thoughts. "I have a backup, but I've been holding off on getting the contract to her." He pauses, locking his eyes on mine. "Since the moment I decided to direct this play, I've pictured you as the lead. I am set on you."

Visions of the stage and the lights dance freely in my mind's eye. I can hardly believe this is happening, given that only days ago I made the decision to chase my dream. No more making beds and scrubbing bathtubs. No more wagging tongues or maid's hats. No more Hotel Hamilton.

This is precisely what I want. In fact, it is all I've ever wanted. Yet, as Thomas watches me and waits for me to speak, I can't help but wonder if my acting ability is truly what Thomas is seeking.

He's never given me any reason to doubt his motives. Thomas is a few years my senior, so I crossed his path less frequently than others. But each time we worked together at the theatre group, he was respectful and kind. My mind continues to whir.

Though I've never intended to use my appearance to gain

a role, I haven't met a man yet who wasn't swayed by a toss of my hair or a dazzling smile. How can I be sure I haven't given Thomas the wrong idea? Am I fooling myself? Is Thomas likely to be any different from the last director?

I would be a fool to let this opportunity pass. However, it is the quietest voice in the recesses of my mind that I cannot help but hear. It asks, what if I have no talent at all? What if I have been skating through life with my God-given good looks?

The memory of my last audition sneaks into my periphery. I was elated during the first read-through and then the second. The final callback after lunch had me happy enough to do cartwheels. I still remember the director's parting words to me. *You, Louisa Wilson, will go far.*

By the end of the day, I had secured the lead role. I was told to return the next day to sign the paperwork, with rehearsals to begin the following week. The theatre was nearly empty as I gathered my things and headed for the door. Flushed with excitement, I walked half a block along the theatre's brick facade before stopping to slide my arms into my coat. I was buttoning up, with the playscript tucked between my knees, when I overheard a few of the cast members chatting in the alley, their cigarette smoke drifting through the cold February air.

The man is predicable. Even if Miss Wilson does have talent.

I recognized the voice of the male lead. *Yeah, but it's not her talent he's interested in. His plays always have a pin-up girl as the lead. He prefers trophies to real actresses.* His voice softened. *I feel sorry for the girl, really. She probably doesn't know what she's gotten herself into.*

I shake my head in defiance of the memory. Despite the crushing disappointment I felt that day, I continue to find myself drawn to the spotlight. The first time I stepped onto a stage, I fell head over heels in love. It's thrilling to have permission to be someone else for a while. The feel of the audience's eyes on me and the applause they so graciously offer make me feel whole, complete, worthy.

I feel the warmth rise to my cheeks and know that raw emotion is colouring my face. "Well, I suppose it couldn't hurt to read a few lines."

Thomas slaps a couple of bills on the table. Grabbing my hand, he pulls me out the door, waving a hearty thank you to the waitress as we leave. Off to the theatre we go, with Thomas' beaming face leading the way.

CHAPTER 16

*S*aturday, October 1, 1927
     Clara

I return to the apartment as the clock nears two, refreshed and toting a much better mood. The walk with Rebecca was just what I needed, and though the chores still await me, I am buoyed by my outing. Even the laundry seems less daunting than it did this morning. A little bit of sun goes a long way when the Vancouver weather begins its descent toward winter.

I busy myself with the washing of Papa's and my clothes, staying true to my warning that Louisa will have to wash her own clothes this week. I suspect the task will be accompanied by a copious amount of whining and muttering from my sister. With the clothes positioned on the drying racks, I move back to the kitchen to scrub the bread pan. I have prioritized the list of chores, coming to terms with the fact that not everything will get done. The dusting, for example, is last on the list. I can squeeze it in one evening after dinner next week, if time and energy allow.

I scrub the bathroom, including the tub, before sweeping the entirety of our apartment's floor in preparation for a once-over with the mop. An hour later, a rare thankfulness at the small size of our home washes over me as I dump the contents of the mop bucket into the kitchen sink. I check my watch. Three fifteen. Both Papa and Louisa should have returned home by now.

So much for Louisa's offer of assistance. A frustrated sigh escapes my lips as I plunk myself down at the kitchen table. With a pad of paper and a pencil, I detail my Thanksgiving Day plan of action. Sifting through Mama's recipes, I calculate the timing, listing the dishes in the order I will prepare them.

With the list before me, it's clear that I will be short on time, no matter how early I begin cooking Sunday morning. Turning the paper over, I start again. I'm determined to serve Mama's beef mince pie, for the sake of family tradition. I will have to bake both the mince pie and the apple pie after my Saturday shift at the hotel. My nose wrinkles and my mouth twists, unable to see another way. I will be baking late into the evening, before rising early the next day to continue the dinner preparation. I tap my pencil on the table and decide there is no way around it. I write *Saturday* at the top of the page before listing *mince pie* and *apple pie* underneath. Then I finish the list with Sunday's plan of attack.

"The effort will be worth it," I say out loud. "A real Thanksgiving we can be proud of." A resolute nod of my head affirms my commitment to the celebration. I stand, scooping up the recipes and placing them in the order I have listed. I take a moment to appreciate our family's accomplishment. We have food in our cupboards and a secure roof over our heads. That was not always a guarantee, and I am thankful every day for our family's recovery from the dark period of near penilessness.

136

The apartment door swings open, wrenching my attention away from the kitchen. Louisa steps into the short hallway, barely breaking stride to drop her bag on the floor.

"Clara?" she calls out with breathless excitement, her head swivelling around the living room before finding me straddling the distance between the kitchen and the table. "There you are."

"Here I am." My eyebrows converge, crinkling my forehead.

"I got it. Can you believe it?" Louisa is giddy enough to take flight.

"Got what?" I bite my bottom lip, not certain where this announcement is going.

"I auditioned for a play today and I got the role." Louisa squeezes me into an embrace, exuberance spilling out of her.

My arms are trapped by my side, imprisoned by Louisa's hug. I force the words out with a shallow breath. "You didn't mention you'd be auditioning for a play."

"I didn't know." Louisa pulls back, though her hands still grip my shoulders. "Isn't it crazy? I went out to meet Thomas and . . ." Louisa's thoughts seem to lack direction. "Did you know he's been looking for me all this time?"

"Louisa." I raise my voice to gain her attention. "Slow down. I have no idea what you are talking about."

"Let's sit down and I will tell you all about it." Louisa pulls me toward the sofa and settles herself as much as her excitement will allow.

I wait expectantly, well aware that the day is growing short and the list of chores is far from complete.

"Thomas." Louisa dips her chin, her eyes imploring me to remember the connection. "From the theatre club."

I nod and push myself back into the corner of the sofa.

"Apparently, shortly after I left the club, he decided to put his time and money into directing and producing a play. As soon as he settled on *Craig's Wife* as the play, he knew I would make the perfect Mrs. Craig. I was his first choice for the female lead. He told me so this morning. Thomas has been looking for me ever since." Louisa takes a deep breath before launching in again. "I am amazed. I can hardly believe what good fortune it was that I called the theatre and left a message for him about Friday night."

"Friday night?" I ask, realizing that today's news is somehow tied to Louisa's mysterious Friday evening excursion.

With a wave of her hand, Louisa continues. "That is another story altogether. Anyway, Thomas asked me to meet him this morning, but I had no idea he wanted me to audition."

"That's great." I nudge a little enthusiasm into my words. "I suppose getting back in touch with the theatre was a good suggestion, then."

Louisa sniffs the air sharply, impatient with me for not keeping up. "You don't understand, Clara. Thomas is putting on a real production. He has it all organized. The play will take place at a theatre downtown. The one just up from the library. The costumes have been acquired, along with the lighting, the music, and most of the cast. For goodness' sake, there will be a paying audience and an opening night. I will be earning my first wage as a professional on the stage." Louisa lets out a squeal of delight. "This is exactly what I was looking for. Something to take my career to a new level." Her expression falters, the elated smile vanishing like the sun behind a storm cloud, before reappearing with her next words. "Of course, I didn't agree to the lead role, but who knows where I will go from here."

"I am happy for you, Lou." Even as I say it, I recognize the lack of truth in my statement.

"But . . . ?" Louisa draws out the word, her delighted demeanour shifting behind a guarded gaze with a slow, deliberate blink of her eyes.

"But what?" I try to hide my concern, but I know it is on full display.

"You have something else to say." Louisa's eyes narrow a fraction. "I can read it all over your face."

"I guess I am wondering how you will fit such a production into your work schedule." My hands clasp and release repeatedly in my lap. "You do plan to continue working at The Hamilton, don't you?"

"For now." Louisa smooths her dress over her lap with both hands, shooting me a knowing look. "I knew you'd be worried about that. Even though I've just told you I'll be paid as an actress." Leaning forward, she takes my hand, softening her tone. "You don't have to worry, Clara. I have already sorted it out with Ms. Thompson. That is the reason I am so much later arriving home than I anticipated. As I already told you, I didn't accept the part of Mrs. Craig, as Thomas was hoping I would."

Louisa waves off her comments with a flutter of her hand, leaving me no room to question why she turned down the lead for a smaller role. "After I accepted the part, I went straight to the hotel and found Ms. Thompson. I have arranged to have my schedule altered to accommodate the rehearsal and performance calendar."

"That is very responsible of you." I weigh my words carefully, sensing I am still missing details of this arrangement.

"The thing is"—Louisa's eyes roam the room, avoiding my face—"I have to work Sunday."

Before I can even register the information, Louisa plows ahead, apparently trying to smother my objections. "I promise

I will come straight home from the hotel and help with dinner. I promise I will."

My face slackens, inviting my mouth to hang open unceremoniously. I couldn't hide my disappointment even if I were inclined to try. "You mean to say that you won't be here to help with the Thanksgiving dinner we've been planning for weeks?" Heat rises to my cheeks, warming my entire body in a sickly, feverish way. "Louisa, how could you? This dinner is important to our family. We haven't had a celebration like this since—" My words are hindered by the emotions spilling out of me.

"Since Mama died," Louisa finishes.

We sit in silence for several minutes. I wrestle with my whirling disappointment, while Louisa assumes a demure expression to pacify my anger. It doesn't work.

Our silence is interrupted by the opening and closing of the apartment door. Both our heads swivel to acknowledge Papa's return. He strides into the living room, a brown paper bag in his arms and a wide smile lighting his features. "Hello, girls."

I push myself up from the sofa. Avoiding eye contact with Louisa, I plant a kiss on his cool cheek. "Welcome home." I move toward the kitchen. "Looks as though you had a good day."

Papa's smile wavers as his gaze shifts between Louisa and me. "Hang on a minute, Clara. What's gotten you two looking so glum?"

I call over my shoulder as I step past the dining table, "Louisa can fill you in. I've got dinner to make and a list of tasks longer than my arm." I shoot Louisa a pointed glare. "Apparently, it's getting longer by the minute."

"Don't be so dramatic, Clara." Louisa's voice hitches up a

notch, her impatience with me evident as she stands, both fists clenched.

"Yeah, I'm the dramatic one." I shake my head in disbelief. "You've no idea, Lou. No idea what goes into keeping this home running." I pivot to face her straight on, my hand gripping the back of a dining chair. "There is an order and a method to staying on top of the chores. Bread doesn't simply appear, you know. Though I suppose it does for you." My scoff tastes bitter, even to me.

"Order," Louisa almost shouts. "That is all you know. Certainly, it wouldn't hurt you to step beyond your little box. I swear it's getting smaller every day."

A bubble of anger rises within me. "I am not in a box." The words are eager to spew, but I control them as best as I can, not wanting Louisa to see that she's gotten the better of me. "One of us has to be mindful of the things that need doing."

"Girls." Papa steps between us. "I've no idea what's gotten you so upset, but surely we can sit down and have a level-headed chat about it."

Words fly from my lips before I can stop them. "What's the point?" My shoulders lift and fall in defeat. "Louisa's made up her mind, and as usual, she's only considered herself." I fix a steely glare on my sister. "Dreams, as I've said before, are foolish endeavours. Louisa is going to follow her whims, whatever they may be, while the rest of us adjust and pick up the pieces."

Louisa cocks her head, a fire burning behind her glare.

My words are laced with ice. "Of course, I suppose it won't be much of an adjustment, after all, given that she's never contributed to the running of our home."

Papa is about to interject, but Louisa beats him to the punch. "How dare you say I don't contribute. How dare you."

Louisa mimics my crossed arms, her toe tapping the floor. "I consider the needs of this family every single day. I even went as far as arranging things with Ms. Thompson so that I could continue to bring in a steady wage—in addition to what I will be earning from the play, I'll have you know." Louisa's chin tilts up, her defiance leading the charge. "I may not be as inclined as you to cook and clean and shop, but you can't say I don't contribute. You know very well that I do what I can."

A strangled laugh escapes me. "So, you expect me to take care of everything at home while maintaining the exact same job as you do at the hotel? How is that even remotely equal? When did housework become my sole responsibility?"

Louisa's anger dissipates, and I know her next words are going to sting. "The house became your responsibility, Clara, when you decided you needed to control it. I thought you would have learned that by now."

Papa places the brown paper bag on the floor as though about to say something. However, Louisa isn't finished speaking her mind. "You view yourself as the sensible one, Clara," she says, her tone calmer and more soothing. "You alone chose that road. You may not be comfortable with the idea of reaching for something beyond your station, but you could at least pretend to be happy for someone else."

"What is that supposed to mean?" My anger is slow to submit.

Louisa steps past Papa and squeezes my upper arm. "I know the news that I'm moving on to explore my dreams makes you quiver inside." Louisa lowers her chin to meet my eyes. "You could strive for more too, if you wanted to."

I whisper my next words, for fear of hearing them spoken out loud. "I don't think so, Lou. One of us needs to remain steady. Mama told me to take care of the family. I am only doing what she asked. This is what others need from me."

My bottom lip trembles under the threat of tears. "Even you."

"You said it yourself. Adjustments need to be made." Louisa squeezes my arm a little tighter. "How do you know how things might change unless you try? If you ask me, it sounds like you've been telling yourself stories about a future that hasn't happened yet. Sometimes you need to get out of your own way to imagine different opportunities."

My only response is a shrug. All I want is to be angry with my sister, to punish her for taking a risk while leaving me behind. But I can't deny the halo of truth around her words. Maybe I am letting fear get in my way.

"Lord knows I can't force you to do anything." Louisa's laughter fills the apartment before her tone turns serious again. "But I do hope you consider what I've said."

Papa wraps an arm around each of us. "This reminds me of what your mama used to say when I was all caught up in a problem: The future is yet to happen. Why do you assume you know the outcome?"

I nod in understanding, feeling defeated by the logic but propelled by the whirring of my mind. My thoughts spin with the tasks ahead of me. Although this conversation has taken a turn, the reality is that Louisa will not be present to help with Thanksgiving nor with the everyday chores. My life is unlikely to change anytime soon, and that burden remains heavy.

I retreat to the kitchen, partly out of duty and partly out of a desire to be left alone. I prepare dinner while Louisa and Papa settle themselves on the sofa, where she tells him about her new opportunity. Excitement oozes from Louisa's every pore, her voice climbing in volume as she talks.

What if Louisa is right? What if I am meant for greater things too? I travel down that line of thought as I chop carrots into small rounds.

I am yanked from my ruminations when I nick my thumb with the knife. I press a dish towel to the cut, stemming the trickle of blood. Running my hand beneath cool water from the tap, I force myself to come to my senses.

Stop it, Clara, I tell myself. Stop it right now. You should be grateful for all that you have. You are a maid in a fine hotel. Your family is safe and well nourished. Nothing good comes of stepping beyond your station.

CHAPTER 17

Thursday, October 6, 1927
Louisa

Several days have passed since my announcement and subsequent disagreement with Clara. Though we are polite to each other as we move about our small apartment, there remains an underlying tension. This unwelcome shift strains our relationship, despite my many attempts to smooth the disagreement.

I thought my prudent decision to square away my work schedule would be far more appreciated. After all, I took steps to ensure we would maintain our financial stability while I venture back into theatre life. It seems, though, that I have underestimated the importance Clara has placed on our Thanksgiving celebration. Even so, she doesn't need me to get dinner to the table. We are both aware how she delights in planning and cooking, so I'm not sure why my presence will be missed before the actual feast.

Even within the walls of the hotel, Clara remains moody and indifferent toward me, sulking like a child over melted ice cream. Her avoidance of me has become the status quo these past few days, a situation that has caused more than one raised eyebrow among our gaggle of fifth-floor maids. Yesterday, Jane pulled me aside to inquire if all was well in the Wilson home. I can't help but think that if Jane noticed, being famously unaware of others, then everyone must have.

I gather another bundle of soiled linens from outside a half-closed guest room door and add them to the laundry cart. Collecting the fifth-floor laundry this morning is the perfect task to accompany my contemplative mind. The discontentment between Clara and me runs through my thoughts on repeat, gaining no resolution and weighing me down. Normally, I would be less bothered by Clara's coolness, but I can't shake the notion that my sister, of all people, should be happy for me.

Pushing the laundry cart toward the service lift, I let out a defeated sigh. Thinking over the past few weeks, I continue to be pulled back to the situation on the sidewalk. I've asked myself a dozen times if Clara's recent unsteadiness is about my new opportunity in the theatre or about what transpired that day. Perhaps seeing the way that drunk man treated the Asian man with the groceries struck a nerve in Clara. If I know anything, it is that once you've seen injustice up close, you simply can't unsee it. Everywhere I look around this city, I become more aware of the pecking order, and I can't help but wonder how it all came to be.

The lift arrives, and I squeeze myself and the cart inside. I press the button for the basement and feel the rush of cool air brush my skin, eliciting goosebumps up my arm. The laundry room is located at the far end of the dank basement, warmed by the heat of the oversized drying racks.

I say a friendly hello to those hard at work and position my cart in the long line to wait my turn to deposit the dirty laundry. Being a maid has many drawbacks, but each trip to the bowels of the building reminds me that things could be worse. I could have been relegated to laundry detail. Before the thought is fully formed, my awareness of those working within the room shifts into focus.

Not a single Caucasian face exists among them. They're all female. Their ethnicities vary, but they all have warm skin tones that no Canadian winter could erase. Accents and languages I cannot decipher flutter above the din of constantly moving contraptions that take up most of the room's footprint. I watch for a moment and notice that every woman has her eyes locked on the machine before her. A safeguard, I suppose, to avoid injury.

With vivid imagery of disfigurement slinking into my imagination, I turn abruptly and leave. Away from the machinery, the cool basement air slaps me in the face, along with the realization that my situation could most certainly be worse—and much more dangerous.

I take the back-of-house stairs to the fifth floor. The rule is to take the lift when transporting something larger than oneself. Otherwise, stick to the stairwell for efficiency's sake. I arrive on the fifth floor slightly out of breath but ready for the next task, eager to hurry along the day's work so I can move on to the main event.

I push all disappointing thoughts of Clara from my mind and focus on this evening's rehearsal. I can barely contain my enthusiasm. The day of our first rehearsal has finally arrived. Thomas is gathering all supporting cast members in hopes of getting a jump on the smaller roles before focusing on the main characters. I've spent the week memorizing my lines to portray Mrs. Craig's niece, Ethel. Though I have only a handful of lines, I am determined to deliver each with gusto.

As I pass by room 508, Jane pokes her head out the door.

"Psst, Louisa." She motions me back with a wave of her hand. "You help me with this one and I'll help you with yours?" Her smile lingers, a sure sign that Jane would like a little company to help ease the day's duties.

My left eyebrow lifts in a teasing challenge. "I've got a double next on my list. Are you sure you want to share the load?"

Jane giggles, her softer side much easier for me to coax out now that we've shared time and purpose together. "Only for you." Jane widens her eyes in mock exasperation. "But don't tell the others. I'd hate for it to get out that I enjoy working alongside someone."

I follow Jane into the room. "Yes, that would be a real disgrace, wouldn't it? Jane Morgan, a suitable working companion." I can barely keep the smile from my words, and I stifle a giggle as I poke lighthearted fun at her. "Or perhaps Jane Morgan, the best partner a maid could have."

Jane hides a laugh behind a raised palm before handing me the duster from her cart. "I haven't had a chance to dust anything yet. If you can start on that, I'll tackle the bedding."

"Yes, ma'am. Louisa Wilson at your service." I salute Jane by putting the feather duster to my brow, resulting in a series of sneezes that momentarily incapacitate me.

We putter around the room, returning items to their proper place. "Are you excited about tonight?" Jane asks, remembering a conversation we had earlier in the week about my new adventure.

"I am." I reposition the lamp on the bedside table and give the tabletop a final swipe with the duster. "I can hardly believe my future begins tonight."

"You know, I would have thought you'd have gotten the role of Mrs. Craig. I bet you'd make a good one." Jane plumps a freshly cased pillow into place. "Did I ever tell you I saw the original on Broadway?"

I stop moving and meet her eyes. "Really?" I resist the urge to sit down on the freshly made bed and immerse myself in the coming story.

"A couple of years back, when it was all the rage." Jane waves it off, as though traveling to New York is an everyday affair. "My father had business in the city and took me along to visit with his great aunt in Manhattan." Jane plops another pillow onto the bed. "You know, come to think of it, I am pretty sure he brought me so he didn't have to visit with her himself. She is, how shall I say . . . a vibrant woman, who resembles a thunderstorm rolling across a prairie." Jane pauses for dramatic effect, and I wonder if she has ever considered a role in the theatre. "And that is when she is getting her way. I can only imagine how things might escalate should someone decide to tell her no."

"What was it like?" I move to the other side of the bed and distractedly dust the second lamp and table.

"New York or the play?" Jane pulls the bench seat away from the bed frame and eyes the bedding from the floor.

"The play. New York. Both, I want to hear it all." I dust the dresser, the frame of the mirror, and even the baseboards as I listen to Jane talk about her trip to a city I've only dreamed of visiting.

Another hour passes as we work in tandem, chatting all the while. With a final glance about the room, we declare the guest room well-appointed and push her cart into the hall, tucking it into an alcove before proceeding to the next room on my list. The double-bedded room is not the usual set-up for The Hamilton, but a few such rooms have arisen from guest requests, given the hotel's limited number of rollaway cots. Parents, it seems, are toting their children with them as they travel to Vancouver, the summer being our busiest season for families.

Our conversation covering all things New York comes to an end as I manoeuvre my cart over the plush grey-blue carpet. Jane offers to tackle both beds while I deep clean the washroom.

I am lost in fanciful thoughts of the big city as I scrub and scour a particularly nasty case of tub ring. I tilt back on my heels as I consider Jane's initial comment about the play. She thought I'd make a good Mrs. Craig.

My worry and regret are instant companions in the small, half-cleaned washroom. What if I made the wrong choice? What if this was my big chance and I blew it by opting for the safer, smaller role? My intention was to choose a place on stage where I won't be singled out for my looks.

I'll admit, my refusal of the lead felt akin to pulling a coat of armour over my heart. Could I have taken Thomas at his word? He said that he chose me because of my talent. Perhaps I didn't give him the opportunity to demonstrate his integrity on the matter. If I'm being honest with myself, when it comes to Thomas' heart-stopping attention, my view is clouded at best.

Doubt over my decision to shrink from the limelight has plagued me since the day I made it. I reason that I would be better off earning a career through hard work and talent instead of having it handed to me for my looks. Now, I can't help but wonder if that is even possible. If I had trusted Thomas, would my appearance truly not have been a factor? A sigh slips through my lips, the weariness of repeated thoughts taking their toll.

Truth be told, I am happy with my pleasant appearance. I fear life would be far less kind if I were a homely girl. But surely, a career built on talent, perhaps with the benefit of good looks, must be long and healthy.

I stand and stretch my back before eyeing the tub from several angles to ensure all signs of soap scum have been removed. I catch my appearance in the mirror and tuck a few rogue hairs back beneath my cap. Then I set to polishing the faucets.

The afternoon's tasks are suitable company for the butterflies gathering in my stomach. Mama was right, a busy hand does indeed quiet a busy mind. I arranged to work through lunch, opting to leave the hotel a half hour earlier than usual to arrive on time for the first rehearsal. The decision, it seems, was a good one. Given my nervous state, I would likely be unable to eat a bite.

As four thirty nears, I tuck my cleaning cart into its spot in the linen cupboard and head toward the lobby to confirm my early dismissal with Ms. Thompson. I hug the dark wood panelling near the registration desk, trying to become invisible to mingling guests. Ms. Thompson is speaking with a petite, middle-aged woman in a striking ensemble that looks as though it was ripped right from this month's fashion magazine.

I catch Ms. Thompson's eye and she gestures for me to wait a moment. Ms. Thompson hands a room key to the man behind the desk before shaking the woman's gloved hand.

As the woman walks toward the front door, Ms. Thompson strides over to me, her posture conveying her command over this hotel. "Thank you for waiting, Miss Wilson. I realize you are in a hurry this afternoon."

"Yes, ma'am. Thank you for allowing me to leave early for the day."

"All your rooms have been situated?" Ms. Thompson asks. "Nothing has been left unattended?"

"No, ma'am. Everything is in order."

"Very well." She offers a quick nod. "Good luck, Miss Wilson. I'm sure——"

"Sorry to interrupt." The woman with a fashion sense I can't help but admire closes the gap between us. "I did have one more question."

Ms. Thompson turns to the woman, her lips stretched into a forced smile. "Yes, how can I assist you, Mrs. Barnes?"

The woman tilts her head back as she looks me up and down. "Well now, you are a knockout, aren't you, dear?"

Ms. Thompson stiffens beside me. "Miss Wilson was just leaving." She smiles at Mrs. Barnes before saying to me, "Off you go now. We wouldn't want you to be late."

My cheeks flame, and I turn to retreat from the hotel's lobby.

Mrs. Barnes' voice echoes past me as I near the entrance to the back-of-house corridor. "What floor does that one work on?"

I steal a glance over my shoulder and see Mrs. Barnes pointing a finger in my direction.

"Miss Wilson is one of our most accomplished fifth-floor maids." Ms. Thompson's words are polite but terse.

"In that case, my husband will stay on the eighth floor. The suite you showed me will do just fine." Mrs. Barnes continues, "I'll have to keep my eye on that."

I reach the door that leads to the corridor beyond, but I am stalled by a trolly of afternoon tea cakes.

I hear Ms. Thompson's voice, lowered with concern. "Keep an eye on what, Mrs. Barnes?"

Mrs. Barnes dismisses Ms. Thompson's question. "I know we agreed to a regular room, but if you can arrange for an eighth-floor suite, I will ensure the rate is paid prior to my husband's arrival."

I sneak a final glance in their direction before sliding

through the door. Ms. Thompson's expression appears unsettled, but without knowing who this Mrs. Barnes is, I can't understand exactly why.

Before I can dash to the locker room to change out of my uniform, Cookie stops me with a crushing embrace.

"Are you off, Lou?" Cookie releases me just as fiercely. "We are so proud of you." She beams, her cheeks glistening with beads of perspiration.

"Thank you." I squeeze Cookie's hands, overjoyed that someone is glad that I'm moving my life forward, even if my sister isn't. My disappointed thoughts vanish when I spot the clock on the wall. "Oh my, I best be off or I'll be late for sure."

"Off you go, then." Cookie hollers after me, "Opening night will be here before you know it. I can't wait to see you up on that stage."

Cookie's words trail after me as I dash down the hall toward the locker room, more than ready for my next adventure.

CHAPTER 18

S unday, October 9, 1927
Clara

With my hands coated in flour, I use my arm to sweep the damp hair from my forehead. Fatigue from my pre-dawn start to the day creeps in, reminding me of Mama's warning about burning the candle at both ends.

The poem "First Fig"—a favourite of hers since she read it in Edna St. Vincent Millay's book of poetry, *A Few Figs from Thistles*—would slip from her lips like a song. Mama had a way of making even the most mundane reminders sound beautiful. Her enchanting English accent would accompany the cup of tea she placed before Papa as he prepared for a long day of work during planting season at the Murray Estate.

My candle burns at both ends;
It will not last the night;
But ah, my foes, and oh, my friends—
It gives a lovely light!

. . .

I SMILE AT THE MEMORY, THANKFUL FOR ITS COMPANY THIS morning as I work my way through Mama's recipes in preparation for our Thanksgiving feast. Yesterday, I baked late into the evening after a full day at the hotel. My work yielded a traditional mince pie and the sweet cinnamon-scented delight of a nearly perfect apple pie.

After Louisa informed me I would be cooking the meal without her assistance, Papa did his best to convince me to scale back my plan for Thanksgiving. "A roast chicken," he said, "will be more than enough for our celebration." I dismissed his advice, reasoning that I had already purchased the suet and the other ingredients. I had known from the outset that my vision for Thanksgiving was ambitious. Deep down, I crave the reassurance of seeing how far our family has come. Our Thanksgiving Day feast is a celebration of our accomplishments and a memory I am sure to tuck away for future comfort.

The five years since Mama passed have held no milestones, no celebrations, and very little in the way of traditions. This Thanksgiving is an opportunity for us to reclaim those moments. Though events from here on out will be coloured by Mama's absence, I know in my heart that she would want us to pause and celebrate every one.

As I scan the cluttered counter of our small kitchen, I have to admit that my well-intended enthusiasm might have gotten the better of me. I pour boiling water over tea leaves and let it steep to a dark brown colour, willing the hot beverage to perk me up as I reach for my list.

With the mince pie tucked into the icebox and the apple pie resting on the kitchen table, I check the dinner rolls baking in the oven. For what feels like the twentieth time today, I run

155

my finger down my list of tasks. I take a sip of hot tea and decide the scalloped potatoes will be next.

With no counter space left for peeling and slicing the six potatoes I acquired from the grocer on my way home from the hotel yesterday, I set to cleaning the kitchen and organizing a fresh set of ingredients. Scalloped potatoes are a new dish for me, and though Cookie talked me through the crucial steps, my stomach tightens as I begin work.

Cookie's voice rings in my memory. *Take your time with the potatoes. This is where so many stray. They need to be thin like paper. Use your sharpest knife, and be sure to have a bright kitchen to work in so you can see what you are doing.* Gesturing with her hands, Cookie pretended to slice imaginary potatoes on her pastry kitchen countertop. *Slow and steady, Clara, is all it takes.*

"Slow and steady." I say out loud to myself as I peel the first potato.

An hour later, I have a baking dish layered with gooey goodness and ready for a spell in the oven. Cookie assured me that cooking the potato dish ahead of time and then warming it while the chicken rests would be most efficient.

With thirty minutes to fill while I wait for the potatoes to bake, I gather my recipes and a few sheets of stationary and settle myself at the table. I promised to send Aunt Vivian a few of Mama's favourite recipes, and the prospect of sitting down for a moment is more than a little appealing.

Dear Aunt Vivian and Josephine,

Today is our Wilson Thanksgiving celebration. I felt it was only fitting to include both of you in our festivities, so I am enclosing Mama's recipe for mince pie, as well as her famous apple pie recipe.

One afternoon when I was a young girl, she told me a story as she rolled out the dough and I waited to help her crimp the pastry's edges. At the time, I thought she was teasing me with a funny story, but given your continued interest in the pie recipe, I wonder if she was in fact sharing a secret with me. This memory warms my heart more than I can tell you. I hope you smile just as brightly with the recipe in your own hands.

Josephine, in the event that Aunt Vivian leaves out the details, please let me explain to you what my Mama told me. She said that while growing up, she was the baker in the family. She delighted in the task of making mouth-watering goodness from only a few ingredients. I am sure it will come as no surprise that her apple pie was a family favourite here in Canada too.

The story goes that Aunt Vivian, who was never one to bake, according to Mama, harassed my mother to no end for the apple pie recipe. While she and your father were courting, he would occasionally come to dinner with the family, and he said my Mama's apple pie was his favourite dessert.

Aunt Vivian was so eager to please her beau that she pestered Mama for months about the recipe. I should mention that as my mother told me this story, she had one of the most devilish grins I'd ever seen. In the end, Mama told Aunt Vivian that she wouldn't divulge her apple pie recipe until Aunt Vivian straightened up and agreed to marry the poor boy.

I am not certain of the circumstance that led to her never sending you the recipe, but I can tell you that I will forever treasure Mama's apple pie for so many reasons beyond its deliciousness. You will find the recipe included with this letter. May it warm your heart and your home as it does ours.

In other news, my adventure-seeking sister seems to have found herself a new opportunity to explore. I know I should be polite and simply relay the details of Louisa's new undertaking, but I am still annoyed with her as I write this letter. You see, she fancies herself an actress. I will not deny that she is talented, but she is keen to make a living in the theatre. The theatre, of all things!

She recently arrived home with a role in a real production. I know I should push my worry to the side and let Louisa be Louisa, but I can't *help but be concerned. What if she loses her position at The Hamilton due to scheduling conflicts with her rehearsals and performance dates? What if she does find success and leaves us forever?*

THE PENCIL CLATTERS TO THE TABLE. TEARS SPRING TO MY eyes as the realization dawns on me. I am upset with my sister not because I worry she won't succeed, but because I fear she will. All along, the problem has been me. I don't want her to leave. My head drops into my hands as tears tumble down my cheeks. This is what Louisa meant about me being stuck in a small box, unable to see beyond.

My mind flashes back to the night on the sidewalk with the Asian man and his groceries. She was the brave one. While I made a mess of the whole situation, she risked her own safety for another. All this time I've been viewing Louisa as impulsive and unthinking, but she knows exactly what she is doing. I've never spent much time looking beyond my lot in life, but Louisa has. It is time for me to start trusting my sister as the intelligent woman she is.

I am still sitting at the kitchen table, head in hands, when Papa returns home. I try to wipe my tears, but my red blotchy face is a sure giveaway. He kneels before me in concern.

"Clara, girl, what is the trouble?" His soothing tone is enough to elicit even more tears.

"I've been so wrong." The words give themselves up as reluctantly as a sunny day in February.

"Wrong?" Papa's brows converge. "Wrong about what?"

"About everything. Louisa. This dinner. Even my path in life." My shoulders fall as an exhausted sigh deflates my body.

"Oh, darlin', it can't be as bad as that." Papa reaches into the bag that has dropped from his shoulder. "Look, I went to Stanley Park, special for you." He pulls out a handful of colourful leaves larger than his palm. "I found one of almost every variety in the park." He places them gently onto the table. "Look here, I've got a big-leaf maple, a black cottonwood, a choke cherry, a red alder, and even your favourite, a Pacific dogwood. I thought you'd enjoy something special to decorate the Thanksgiving table with."

I finger the purple and red Pacific dogwood leaf, shimmering with autumn colours.

"I have a few boughs of evergreen too. I thought you might like to arrange them the length of the table and place the leaves among them." Papa extracts a handful of pine, their fragrance filling the air.

"They are beautiful. Thank you." I lunge forward, embracing him in a fierce hug.

My nose catches a whiff of something other than the forest scents, and I pull back from Papa, lifting my wrist to check the time. "The potatoes!" I stand abruptly, almost making him totter. I move with urgency toward the oven and sigh in relief as I remove the baking dish. The steaming scalloped potatoes have not a single singe. "I almost forgot about them. Dinner would have certainly been ruined."

"No darlin', I think you might be missing the importance of Thanksgiving. Dinner is about us and all we have to be thankful for. Now, I am grateful for the food and all your effort. The grumbling of this old stomach of mine confirms that." Papa steps closer, wrapping an arm around my shoulders. "But it isn't everything. We have each other, and that is more important than anything else in this world."

Papa steps back and surveys the kitchen. "Now, what can I help with?"

"Why don't you arrange the table, and I will set to work on the chicken and vegetables." I check my watch again, having already forgotten what time it is. Heeding Papa's words, I am intent to be thankful for our family, even when we disagree. "Louisa should be home in a couple of hours. I think it will be nice to have everything ready when she arrives."

Papa's expression turns serious. A flash of grief darts across his face before he hides it from sight. "Thank you, Clara." He washes a hand over his face, and I know he is feeling the absence of Mama's presence in our world. "Thank you for filling our home just like she would have."

I squeeze his hand in mine, pushing aside my weariness. My life may not be as glamourous as Louisa's, but I have done right by my family.

CHAPTER 19

Wednesday, October 12, 1927
Louisa

With a cold chicken sandwich made from Thanksgiving leftovers tucked into my bag, I stifle a yawn as I pull on the theatre's heavy door. The concrete-coloured sky does little to encourage my early start to the day. With many of the play's cast members working other jobs, Thomas has been forced to be creative with the rehearsal schedule.

Tuesdays and Wednesdays are long days that begin with the rising sun and end only after Thomas is satisfied with the current scene. During the remainder of the week, Thomas shuffles cast members as he pieces together each actor's after-work availability. I am convinced the man is not only a director with a vision for the production, but also a magician.

I shake off the morning chill as my shoes clack rhythmically across the tiled lobby floor. "Good morning, Mr. Johnson." My cheeks lift at his brilliant toothy grin, all the more welcoming for its contrast with his dark skin.

"A good morning it is, Miss Wilson." His broom doesn't stop moving. "You have a blessed day now, you hear?"

"Thank you, kind sir. I will do my best."

Our shared banter is only days old, and yet I can't help but feel a kindred spirit in him. It began last Thursday, as I dashed through the theatre's doors, trying to outrun the rain. The tiled floor, polished to a shine, was like Lost Lagoon frozen in winter. My hurried steps into the lobby sent me slipping and sliding across the tile. Mr. Johnson, anticipating my collision with the floor, grasped me by my arms with two strong hands, steadying me and setting me straight.

I thanked him profusely as he guided me through the lobby, to the plush carpet of the auditorium. On our short walk to the stage steps, I learned he and his family have lived near Park Lane for several years. Mr. Johnson has two boys, aged nine and eleven, and a wife who apparently sings like an angel. I was instantly taken in by his joyful disposition and have since found his presence within the theatre to be welcome and comforting.

I step quickly along the slight downward slope toward the stage. On the opposite side of the stage, Thomas is flipping through his notes. From his ruffled dark locks and his rolled-up sleeves, I can tell he has been here for several hours already. I say a quiet hello to a few cast members lounging in the first few rows and make my way toward Thomas.

Pulling a flask from my shoulder bag, I clear my throat to elicit his attention. "Thought you could use some coffee." I lift the narrow bottle to eye level. "Had it filled at the diner down the way."

"You are a godsend, Lou." Thomas takes the coffee from my hand and doesn't waste a moment. He twists off the cap and pours the strong, dark liquid into the cup's lid before meeting my eyes again. "Thank you."

His eyes scan the room, squinting into the low light as he sips. "We'll get going as soon as Gerald arrives."

I nod but sense there is more that Thomas would like to say. Taking his cue, I pause a moment, allowing him time to say what is on his mind.

Instead, he seems to decide better of it, running a hand through his rumpled hair as his face erupts with a boyish grin. Thomas' smile makes my stomach somersault. I wonder, not for the first time, if he has always had this effect on me or if his new role as director has caught my interest. I feel a blush warm my cheeks. "I'll wait over there with the others."

I wander back to the group but notice the female lead, Sarah, sitting by herself. I approach her with a sincere "Good morning."

"Good morning, Louisa. Have I got that right? It is Louisa, isn't it?" Sarah's round face lights up like a ray of sunshine, and I wonder how this sweet-looking creature will transform into the unflinchingly confident and sometimes cold Mrs. Craig.

"Yes. That is right." I motion to the seat. "May I join you?"

"Of course." Sarah moves her bag to the empty seat on the opposite side. "I didn't mean to come off as unwelcoming. I—I suppose I needed a moment to gather myself."

"Gather yourself?" I settle into the velvet-cushioned seat and angle my body toward her. "That sounds like a bit of a task for this early hour."

Sarah sighs, her eyes roaming the theatre. "I don't want to seem ungrateful. I am thrilled for the opportunity to play such a challenging role. It's just . . ."

I lower my voice to a whisper. "Just what?"

Sarah looks over her shoulder again, toward the

auditorium doors. "I haven't been getting on well with Gerald."

I cock my head, inviting her to continue.

"Not on or off the stage." Sarah fiddles with the strap of her bag.

"I am sorry to hear that."

"I am trying my best to be professional, but the man seems to have a negative comment for my every word." Sarah lets out a long breath. "I know Thomas is counting on me to bring Mrs. Craig to life. That alone is as much of an uphill battle as I've ever encountered in the theatre. Add to that the challenge of a lead actor who enjoys pointing out every possible flaw as I deliver my lines."

"I didn't realize." I place a hand on Sarah's forearm. "Thomas has had the rest of us sequestered as we work on our smaller roles."

"Yes, today will be the first rehearsal for all to see." Moisture gathers in Sarah's eyes. "I imagine that is why I am a little undone at the moment. Today, everyone will see for themselves just how unsuitable I am for the role."

I squeeze Sarah's arm in support. "Don't say that. I know Thomas wouldn't have chosen you if that were the case." I decide it best to omit Thomas' words about seeing me in the role of Mrs. Craig from the get-go. "Surely your other acting successes have led you here. Can you draw on other characters you have portrayed to help you deliver a convincing Mrs. Craig?"

Sarah taps her bottom lip with a pink-painted fingernail. "I did play the Wicked Witch in *The Wizard of Oz* when the original actress came down with a case of the mumps."

"There you go. That is something. I bet you could—" My words are cut off by the slamming of the inner auditorium door, a quite surprising sound, given the door's hushed closing mechanism.

"Apologies for my tardiness, everyone." A man, who I assume is Gerald, saunters toward the stage with a smug expression stretched across his face. "I was accosted by fans outside the theatre." He tosses his jacket onto an empty seat before smoothing his slicked-back hair with both hands.

"Right. Okay then." Thomas drops his stack of papers onto the stage with a thwack, setting the *let's get to work* tone. "We are starting with the scene in the Craigs' living room, so let's have Aunt Ellen and Mr. and Mrs. Craig on the stage first. Mazie and Mrs. Harold, stand by to run through the opening scene."

I sneak a glance at Sarah and can see her polite nature fighting against her disapproval of Gerald. I nudge her arm and mouth the words "You've got this."

I sit with the rest of the cast in the audience as Thomas directs the actors into place. Before Sarah has uttered a single line, Gerald is already criticizing her posture—or her lack of posture, as he sees it. At his loud and accusatory comments, Sarah instantly looks defeated, and I begin to understand her concern. She has been dealing with this behaviour for several days. No wonder the poor girl has lost confidence in herself. As desperate as I am to make a name for myself, even I don't envy her situation.

Thomas steps between the two. With his back to the audience, his words are muffled and inaudible. He moves to the side and calls to begin again. "Take it from the top."

The actress playing Aunt Ellen delivers her line. The second time around, the actors gain momentum, until Gerald's Mr. Craig enters the scene.

"No, no, no," Gerald huffs from the side of the stage.

"Mrs. Craig needs to command the room. She needs to be perfectly prim and—"

"Gerald." Thomas' voice cuts through. "You do remember that I am the director and not you."

A murmur of chuckles emerges from the rest of the cast, seated in the audience. A stern scowl from Gerald turns everyone mute. "Then why the devil haven't you stopped this catastrophe?"

Thomas takes in a lungful of air. "Listen, I know you are used to having input." Gerald opens his mouth to speak, but Thomas' raised palm stops him. "You agreed when you signed on for this role that you would not have creative license over every aspect of the production."

"Yes, but—" Gerald seems to lack even the least bit of restraint. It occurs to me that he is more like Mrs. Craig than the charming character he portrays.

"Let's take it from the top." Thomas runs a hand through his hair before adding, "Let's try to make it to the end of the scene, shall we?"

By the time we break for a very late lunch, tottering on the edge of the dinner hour, the tension in the theatre is as thick as molasses in wintertime. I am torn between wanting to boost Thomas' mood and needing to ensure that Sarah is okay after taking quite the verbal beating from Gerald.

I flash Thomas one of my most reassuring smiles and then follow Sarah up the aisle, toward the theatre lobby. "Hey," I call out to her as she pushes the dark-panelled door open wide. "Are you hungry?"

Sarah is close to tears, and her voice trembles with emotion. "Honestly, I am not sure I can eat."

"Come on, let's get out of here." I turn away from the stage and pull her through the door by the elbow, determined to find a quiet spot where two girls can talk things through.

We find a diner and sit at a table overlooking the street. Since it's between the lunch and dinner rush, the diner is ours alone, save for one man sitting at the counter, digging into a sandwich while reading the newspaper. Despite my rumbling stomach, I order only half a sandwich and a glass of water, knowing Clara's worry over our family's financial status has yet to be alleviated.

Sarah orders a bowl of soup and a cola. "You must think me such a ninny," she says, fiddling with her napkin.

"Nonsense. I don't think anything of the sort. What I do think is that Gerald is doing a fantastic job of playing the louse. Plain and simple. I mean really, he was interrupting your lines when he wasn't even in the scene." My chin tilts up in indignation. "I've never seen such rude behaviour on the stage."

"Thank you." Sarah's cheeks pink with embarrassment.

"Here's what I think you ought to do." I wink conspiratorially. "If you want to put our leading man in his place, that is."

Sarah's ardent nod is enough encouragement to keep me talking.

"Sometimes, you have to play a role in order to coerce a desired outcome. You need to determine what Gerald is after. What is his best-case scenario here? Once you have established that, then you can"—I lower my voice and lean across the table—"give him what he thinks he wants. With any luck, he'll be so enamoured with himself that he'll leave you to do your job on stage."

By the look on Sarah's face, I assume I've been about as clear as mud. I try again. "For example, he may want your adoration of his talents. So, you could put on your best *I adore you* act and see if it sticks. Act like you are in awe of his raw talent." I shrug. "You never know. He might be convinced that he does indeed enjoy your adoration. He is certainly full enough of himself to fall for something as vain and direct as that."

"Do you really think it will work?" Sarah's spirits appear to rise. When her soup is placed in front her, she begins to eat as though she hasn't seen food in several days.

"I think it is worth a try," I say between mouthfuls. "It's hard to know for sure, but I don't think it wise to continue as things are right now. If Gerald is allowed to consume rehearsal time like he did today, there won't be a production at all." I point my sandwich-holding hand in the air. "And I am not about to let that self-absorbed man ruin my opportunity to act in this show."

Sarah giggles at my enthusiasm, then nods in agreement. "No, we certainly cannot let that happen."

We return to the rehearsal more jubilant than we left. I find my seat in the audience as Sarah endeavours to take Gerald on. I watch her bat her eyelashes at him as she asks sweetly if he had an enjoyable lunch break. My lips twist with disappointment when he eyes her with skepticism and removes himself to the opposite side of the stage without a word.

Within ten minutes, Gerald's incessant need to interrupt and criticize has once again derailed the rehearsal. I marvel at the man's ability to consume all the air in the theatre with his drivel and constant complaints. The other actors on stage roll their eyes and release frustrated sighs.

Thomas, a normally patient man, has run his fingers through his hair so many times I worry he'll be balding by nightfall. All I can do is offer him a kind smile from afar as he wrestles with the words needed to direct the cast amidst the lead actor's temper tantrum.

Twenty minutes later, Thomas throws an arm in the air and surrenders. He dismisses the cast in a rush of "We'll pick this up tomorrow" and "Don't worry, it will all come together in the end."

I slide the empty coffee carafe into my bag while wishing Thomas a good evening. Then I head out the door and toward home. As I drag myself up the slight hill to Georgia Street, I can't help but wonder if only Sarah is unable to prod Gerald into a nicer disposition. But then again, Thomas isn't having much luck either, and he is in charge of the play. I shake my head, concern for Thomas creasing my brow. Tickets for opening night have already been printed. If Gerald doesn't fall in line soon, Thomas risks losing his shirt and his reputation.

CHAPTER 20

Friday, October 14, 1927
Clara

By eleven o'clock in the morning, the hotel is buzzing with guests. Those having spent the week in the city for work are clearing out and heading home, while the weekend crowd arrives to enjoy Vancouver. We have little time between guests vacating rooms and new guests wishing to check in, sending every maid, porter, and bellboy running through the back-of-house corridors like stampeding horses.

The mayhem unfolding in the lobby filters up the stairs to the fifth floor. Pausing her flurry of directives, Ms. Thompson pulls me into the linen closet for a private conversation.

"Miss Wilson, I need you to gather and organize the others. We need to prepare the rooms as quickly as possible. The slew of early arrivals are currently taking up the entire lounge area."

I am only capable of uttering, "Ma'am?"

"Have I not made myself clear?" Ms. Thompson's brow furrows, the sight of her displeasure making my palms sweat.

"I—I am not sure I am the one for the job, ma'am. I'm not much good at rallying the troops, so to speak." I glance at my shoes, shame over my inability to take charge coming home to roost. "I would hate to disappoint you, but I fear I am not deserving of such a role. Perhaps, Louisa would be—"

"Miss Wilson, I do not have time for this wishy-washy attitude. I did not ask your sister. I asked you, and I expect my request to be obliged."

"Yes, ma'am." My insides turn to mush with worry over how the other fifth-floor maids will respond to me giving them direction.

Ms. Thompson tilts her head to the side, examining me. She lets out a sigh, and her expression softens a fraction. "All right, Miss Wilson, all you have to do is convince everyone to work together. You won't come across as overbearing or bossy, or whatever you are worried about being cast as. The girls will pull together for you. You can trust me on that."

"Yes, ma'am."

She hands me her clipboard with the fifth-floor roster. "I really must go and tend to the other floors. Spread the word for everyone to meet here, and then set to it." Ms. Thompson turns to leave, pausing in the hallway to offer a final word of encouragement. "I wouldn't have asked you, Miss Wilson, if I didn't think you capable of the task."

I take a few deep breaths and muster my courage. I poke my head into the hallway and tell the first maid I see to gather everyone.

Waiting for their arrival, I take deep breaths and review the tasks at hand. I smile sheepishly as the others trickle in. Gathered together in the linen closet, I explain the situation. Pushing aside my fear of seeming like a bossy goose, my voice wavers at first. "Ms. Thompson has asked me to convey the urgent need for all of us to work together in order to ready the rooms."

I search the faces before me and notice that none of them appear anything but ready for further instruction. My shoulders relax a fraction. "I think we might be most efficient if we each focus on the task at which we are most accomplished. Everyone who excels at vacuuming, please raise your hand." I jot down the names of four maids on the back of Ms. Thompson's roster.

"Who can tackle a washroom from top to bottom with the utmost efficiency?" Five more hands go up, and I add them to the list.

"Dusting?" I search the group before me. "Who can dust and reposition and refill all the necessities? This may require a few trips to the basement for supplies." I list those maids' names and add, "I think it will be most efficient if the dusters communicate with everyone else and do the running for all necessary supplies. I hope you brought your strong legs with you today, ladies." This garners a few laughs and reduces the tension, if not the heat, building in the small room.

I scan the faces before me and note who and what is left to assign. "Louisa, Hazel, Jane, and I will strip and remake all the beds. Dusters?" I say, scanning the shelves. "We may need more linens brought up, so as soon as we clear out, count what we have and fetch the rest that we will need." I run my finger down the list of guest rooms. "We have . . . Oh goodness, we have all but three rooms to set straight. So you might as well bring enough for the entire floor. Linens, towels, soap, notepads, pens, and the rest.

"Ladies, we have a very big task ahead of us, and unfortunately, none of us will be able to take a break until everything is done. Here is what we will do." The maids gather closer as I explain our plan of attack. Splitting the fifth floor in half, we separate into two teams. We move between the rooms like a troupe of ballet dancers, each of us with our own role and responsibility, yet dependent on the rest for the success of the performance.

Sweat trickles down the sides of my face as I strip my twelfth bed in two hours. Louisa is right behind me with a fresh set of linens to spread and tuck. I run the soiled linens to the laundry cart in the hall, scooping up the discarded towels from the washroom as I go. I dodge a moving vacuum in the hallway before returning to help Louisa situate the bedding.

There is little chatter aside from a direction or a request, and though my arms are aching, I am enthused to see all of us working together toward one goal. The sound of the vacuum grows louder as we place the final pillows atop the taut bedding. A recent addition to the fifth floor, Rosemary steps out from the washroom, cradling cleaning supplies in her arms. "Done," she says as she glances about the room, her cheeks glistening with perspiration.

"On to the next one." I muster an encouraging smile, and the three us vacate the room just as the maid tasked with vacuuming appears at the door. We have found a rhythm of sorts, each of us a cog in our efficient machine. With each run I make to the laundry cart with linens and towels, I do a final sweep of the previous room to ensure the vacuuming is complete and all is in place before checking it off my list and locking the door behind me.

The usual check-in time is three in the afternoon, but word from the bellboys is that an overzealous crowd has taken up residence in the lobby lounge. The group is apparently hosting a banquet this evening in the hotel's largest ballroom and is eager for their rooms to be ready. I can only imagine the standing-room-only situation in the lounge. The furniture is lovely but certainly not sufficient to house an entire hotel's guest list within its ornately decorated walls.

In our thirteenth room of the day, Louisa's weariness is beginning to show. Today's harried events would be a sufficient reason for such a state of fatigue, but I know she is juggling far more than most. Between the hotel and the play, she is the new definition of burning the candle at both ends.

A stab of sisterly concern pierces me, prompting me to check my watch. Half past one. We could all use a break, some water, and a bite of lunch. I do a mental tally of the remaining rooms, estimating the length of time each room will take. With seven more rooms to prepare and guests clamouring for them from the lobby, my spirits sink at the realization of how short on time we truly are.

We are likely to need the full hour and a half remaining before the official check-in time. Though the busyness of the hotel is surely a favourable sign for Mr. Hamilton, it means that we fifth-floor maids will be down to the wire on this particular Friday afternoon.

We float the top sheet into the air before tucking its corners and smoothing its surface. Glancing again at Louisa as we move to room number fourteen on our list, I decide to check on the other team's progress before updating Ms. Thompson. Perhaps a spare maid or two from another floor could help us with the final push.

I gather the used sheets and bed coverings in my arms and dash from the room, knowing time is short.

"Miss Wilson." George, one of Louisa's many admirers, pushes a luggage cart loaded with suitcases through the hallway.

"Hello, George." I rush past him to the laundry cart, intent to move as quickly as my short legs will carry me. "How are things going downstairs?"

"They all seem jovial enough." George stops in front of a room, cleaned and ready for guests, and checks the name tags on a few suitcases before unloading them in front of the door. "It seems Cookie has a few tricks up her sleeve. She's plated silver trays with finger sandwiches and sweets and has got the other boys serving them round like waiters." George chuckles. "Course, I think the merriment might be more due to the bottle of schnapps I saw one of the guests open as I passed by."

I sidestep the mention of alcohol in such an unsuitable public space. "How did you manage to escape serving duties?" I tease him as I dump the linens into the nearly full cart, shoving them down in the hopes of adding one more load before the cart descends to the basement laundry.

"Mr. Olson agrees that I am more suited to dealing with the baggage, given my lack of . . ." George taps a finger on his chin, searching for the right word. "Agility. Yeah, that's right."

I can't help but laugh at George's joke, made at his own expense. "Have you seen Ms. Thompson lately?"

"Just passed her in the service lift. She was heading back up to the eighth floor." George's cheeks flush with colour, a giveaway that he is holding gossip. "She didn't seem too pleased about returning to the penthouse though." The bellboys' nickname for the eighth floor is a nod to more than the accommodations. The demands of those who stay in the eighth-floor suites often extend beyond the reasonable, and the boys must go above and beyond to tend to their every desire.

"Thanks, George." I wave a hasty goodbye and run toward the opposite side of the fifth floor for a status update from the other team.

I catch up with a maid pushing her own full and slightly unstable laundry cart toward the service lift and confirm their numbers. They are one guest room behind us. Thankfully, I already thought to take on the extra room. This will be close, and we will all be spent for the day by three, but I remain hopeful that our cleaning carts and vacuums will be out of sight by the time the guests reach the fifth floor.

I sprint up the back-of-house stairs and collect myself with a deep breath before stepping onto the luxuriously plush eighth-floor carpet. I would like nothing more than to relish the cloud-like feeling beneath my feet but haven't a spare moment.

I look one way then the other down the long hall, it's deep red colours oozing affluence. Ms. Thompson's voice, clipped and direct, steers me in her direction. She is frowning and clearly not pleased with the maid standing before her, but given the looming deadline, I barely hesitate to clear my throat and make myself known.

"Ma'am, I am here with an update."

"Yes, Miss Wilson. I do apologize. I was on my way to lend the fifth floor a hand when other things required my attention."

The way she says "other things" with her nose pointing down at the maid sends a shiver down my spine, as though I myself were on the receiving end of her displeasure.

"We are well on our way, ma'am, but if you have a maid to spare, we could certainly use the help. Not one of us has paused all day, and I fear we are losing momentum as tiredness and hunger sets in."

Ms. Thompson's face softens. "Of course. Rest assured, Miss Wilson, I will be discussing today's events with Mr. Olson. We must do our best to help our staff succeed, after all."

"Yes, ma'am."

"I am done here." Ms. Thompson sniffs the air and dismisses the maid from the room with a wave of her hand. The petite girl with red-rimmed eyes scurries past me. She's in a hurry to disappear, I imagine. "I will meet you on the fifth floor, and I will gather reinforcements as I go. We have all been swept off our feet today, but I believe the ladies from the seventh floor can spare a hand or two."

"Thank you, ma'am." I nod my appreciation before turning on my heel. "I best be getting back. We have a system in place, and I wouldn't want to burden anyone with my absence."

"I will be there shortly." Ms. Thompson calls after me, her words barely reaching my ears as I resume a running pace back to the fifth floor.

Louisa has managed to move on to the next guest room, leaving a heap of linens outside the door. I join her at the bed and fill her in on my brief chat with Ms. Thompson. The news of reinforcements bolsters both of us, and we head to our sixteenth bed of the day in record time. As promised, Ms. Thompson arrives with four seventh-floor maids in tow.

I direct two of the maids to join the other team and two to assist Rosemary with the washrooms, the most labour-intensive task. I can't help but worry that poor Rosemary has seen the brunt of the workload today. With the additional help, I feel us approaching the end.

I arrive at the laundry cart with another load only to find a new, empty cart in its place. Thankful for someone's foresight, I open my arms and release everything in one motion before running back to help Louisa with the final few beds. A vacuum comes to life outside room 518, and I catch sight of Ms. Thompson swiftly pushing the vacuum, making nearly perfect designs in the hall carpet.

By five minutes to three, all fifth-floor maids have returned their less than tidy cleaning carts to the linen closet. Our damp hair sticks to our even damper foreheads. All rooms have been thoroughly cleaned and situated and now await the onslaught of guests.

Ms. Thompson and the four seventh-floor maids join us in the crowded cupboard as we huddle together, linking our arms and rejoicing in the day's success. I wait for the chatter to die down, expecting Ms. Thompson to offer a few words. Her eyes meet mine. With a slow nod, she invites me to address the others.

I clear my throat. Now that the urgency of the day has vanished, I find myself shy and uncertain. "I want to tell you how proud I am to be working with each of you. We were faced with many challenges today, yet every single one of you stepped up and made us better. We worked as a team, and we should all be proud of what we accomplished today."

Ms. Thompson's expression softens, fuelling a sense of pride within me. We pull one another closer into the circle, sweaty, exhausted, and beaming with delight. We remain in one another's embrace until a stomach rumbles, echoing in the small space and sending us into a fit of giggles. We stream two by two from the linen cupboard, making our way to a well-deserved and overdue lunch break.

Louisa links her arm through mine and bumps my hip with hers. "I told you."

"Told me what?" I tuck a rogue strand of damp hair behind my ear.

Louisa lowers her chin to look me straight in the eyes. "You are meant for greater things, Clara."

CHAPTER 21

*W*ednesday, October 19, 1927
Louisa

The entire cast is gathered on stage, finding our marks and working through our lines together. I've done my best to prop up Sarah with words of encouragement. The gloom she's carrying, though, is hard to ignore. It hangs over her head like a dark storm cloud. Gerald is, of course, late again, forcing Thomas to rework the scene schedule.

We are well into a scene that takes place on a train. Sarah is seated across from me, in character as Harriet Craig, as I portray Mrs. Craig's niece, Ethel Landreth. The banter between us comes easily as our characters discuss the value of love in the decision to marry. From the corner of my eye, I see Gerald saunter down the aisle. His smirk leaves no confusion as to his intent as he climbs the steps to the stage.

Like a horse with a bit between its teeth, I chomp down with determination, intent to keep his comments at bay until we've finished the scene. I give him a long glance, noticing a bruise emerging near his right eye. The purple tinge shines in the stage lights, despite what appears to be a smear of makeup over the point of impact.

His mouth begins to open, and I raise my voice to drown out his words. I keep talking, purposefully louder than the scene requires. Sarah needs to get through this scene without interruption to bolster her confidence. The cast is in desperate need of forward momentum, and if Gerald would be quiet for three little minutes, poor Thomas could do his job as director.

I keep Gerald in my sights until the scene is complete, daring him with narrowed eyes to be so bold as to interrupt the work in progress. Sarah is none the wiser, with her back to him. She squeezes my hand and beams as Thomas strides forward to offer a few notes.

A single pair of clapping hands turns every head in the theatre toward Gerald. "Well, well, well, it appears she can string together more than three sentences, after all."

I cringe at his cold words and steal a glance at Sarah, only to watch her shrink deeper into herself. I try to catch her attention, but she is doing her best to avoid looking at anyone.

"It was nice while it lasted," Thomas says under his breath as he steps forward, offering Sarah an apologetic expression.

"I assume you are ready for me, then." Gerald moves to centre stage as though a spotlight is waiting for him there.

"Actually, I was thinking we would move on to the scene with the maids in the kitchen." Thomas pauses, apparently for effect, motioning an arm toward the theatre seating. "Why don't you take a seat in the audience. I'll call you when we are ready for you." Thomas doesn't wait for a reply. He simply turns his back on Gerald and signals for the actresses playing the maids to join him on stage. A few of the cast members move the sets around, transforming the stage from a train car into the Craigs' kitchen.

I tug Sarah's hand, lifting her to her feet, and guide her to two chairs positioned off stage. We sit hidden behind the immense red velvet curtain but within earshot of the action taking place beyond.

"You were wonderful," I whisper. "I am so pleased we are working together."

"Thank you"—Sarah glances toward the stage—"for keeping things going, even when he showed up. I am not sure I could have continued if I had known he was lurking there."

"Sure, you would have." I bump my shoulder into hers. "You are a professional."

Sarah shrugs. "So is he."

"I hate to disagree, but his behaviour is nowhere close to professional." I point my chin toward the rows of theatre seats, ignoring the fact that Thomas chose Gerald because of his accolades from previous productions. "He is merely a loudmouth with a pretty face." I cringe at my own words, their sentiment hitting a little too close to home. At least I know how to be pleasant and easy to work with, I think to myself. "He probably has some highfalutin Hollywood connection that has positioned him as a must-have actor."

"You think?" Sarah perks up at the thought.

"Trust me, this guy is only as good as his last offensive, unprompted interruption. Nobody is going to want anything to do with him once he is known as a difficult actor."

"Thanks, Louisa. You are always at the ready with a pep talk. I do appreciate it." Sarah squeezes my hand lightly before straightening in her chair and turning her attention to the scene unfolding on stage.

With another scene rehearsed without interruption, I am uplifted. We may very well get through an entire day of rehearsals without any unfortunate incidents. Thomas calls

Sarah and Gerald to the stage, and I take the opportunity to join the rest of the cast in the audience.

My bottom has barely graced the plush velvet of the theatre chair when Gerald bursts into a rant, waving his hands wildly as he announces that he simply cannot work with someone so clueless. Sarah twitches at his words as a hush falls over the theatre. Fury burns behind my eyes, and before I can think twice about it, I bolt out of my seat.

Thomas stops me short with a slight raise of his hand. "That's a break," he hollers to the cast and crew. "Everyone, take lunch and meet back here in thirty minutes."

My instinct tells me to steer Sarah straight out of the theatre, but again Thomas beats me to it. "Sarah, Gerald," he says in a lowered tone as the others shuffle up the aisle. "I'd like you both to stay. Clearly, we have a few things to work through, and I think it is best if we do so without an audience."

Sensing my reluctance to leave, Thomas turns toward me. "Louisa?" He reaches into his pocket for his wallet. "Can you pick us up three sandwiches from the deli on your way back?"

I step forward and take the bills he is handing my way. "Anything in particular?"

"Whatever the special of the day is will be fine." Thomas winks at me conspiratorially, and I feel my anger at the situation subside a touch. "Perhaps a bottle of soda too. I could use a little pick-me-up."

I swing my bag over my shoulder and leave the theatre, optimistic that Thomas has everything well in hand and that we will be back on track in no time at all.

With thirty minutes to spend, I walk toward the library. I approach the steps and spot a familiar figure. Masao is tucked against one of the pillars, his face set in a disappointed pout.

"Masao," I call before stepping in his direction. The boy

looks up, his eyes squinting against the bright sun. "What are you doing out here?" I smile, lifting my words into a teasing tone. "The books inside the library are much more entertaining than the cold, hard steps."

Masao shrugs, disappointment evident in his every movement. "Hello, Miss Louisa."

I tuck my skirt against my backside as I take a seat beside him. "What's got you so down?" He glances up at me with soft, dark eyes. "Shouldn't a boy your age be in school right about now?"

Masao's expression erupts into one of worry. "Please don't tell, Miss Louisa. I came to the library for a book. It's lunchtime at school, and I thought I would be fast."

"Why wasn't it fast?" I tilt my head back, trying to assess the boy's concern.

"The library won't borrow me the book I want." Masao pinches his cheek and pulls his skin out to show me. "Because of this."

"The library won't lend you a book," I correct him. "What do you mean by *this*?" I gently brush his cheek.

"Because of my skin colour. Because I am Japanese."

"I see." I pause for a moment, choosing my words with care. "So, you think the library—this public library that is open to everyone, in all of Vancouver—won't lend you a book because of your skin colour?"

"Yes, Miss Louisa. I know this." Masao shakes his head. "I am Japanese. You are not. You do not understand."

"What book were you looking to borrow?"

"The red book. The one about growing apples." Masao's eyes light up with excitement. "There are pictures and words, and it will tell me how to grow an apple tree."

"Ah, so you are looking for a horticulture book." I tap a finger against my chin. "I understand now."

"Yes, it is because I am Japanese." Masao repeats his belief, and I flinch inwardly at this young boy's awareness.

I want to disagree with him, but I know in my heart that his view into the world of racial superiority is like looking through a magnifying glass when compared to my own limited experience. Not wishing to dampen his mood any further, I change tracks, seeking a solution that will put his mind at ease.

"The book you are seeking is intended for adults." I soften my words in an effort to convince him of my logic. "I imagine the librarian didn't think that you were a suitable reader for such a big topic. Do you think many boys your age want to learn how to grow an apple tree?"

Masao laughs at my question, but his laughter is short-lived. "Maybe it is funny. But if I want to learn about apple trees, I should be able to. Adults are not the only ones who can plant a seed and watch it grow."

"You do have a point there." I nod in agreement. "Sometimes all it takes is another approach." Masao lifts his head in interest. "A polite request by an age-appropriate patron might be the solution to your problem."

"What do you mean?" Masao stops fidgeting and gives me his full attention.

"What if I were to check out the apple book with my library card?"

Masao nods enthusiastically.

"Now, you must promise to take very good care of this book and return it before the due date." I smooth my expression into one of a seriousness nature. "My reputation as a library patron will be on the line." I lift one eyebrow to convey the importance of my message.

"Oh, I will, Miss Louisa. I promise I will." Masao reaches for my hands, squeezing them with gratitude.

"What is the title of the book?" I return his squeeze.

"*Apple Growing in the Pacific Northwest.*" Masao beams as he recites the book's title, clearly proud of himself for knowing the correct answer.

"All right, then. You run along back to school, and I will go in and borrow the book." I stand, brushing off the back of my skirt. "I am rehearsing at the theatre for a play." I point toward the large theatre sign, and Masao's eyes follow. "Why don't you meet me there after school. About four o'clock?"

"Yes, Miss Louisa. I will come at four o'clock." Masao is about to dash off when he stops abruptly, turns back to face me, and steps in with a fleeting hug around my waist.

I smother a laugh as I watch him speed away, shouting a thank you over his shoulder. Once he is out of sight, I climb the steps and enter the library, heading straight for the horticulture section. Having retrieved several books over the years for Papa, I am familiar with this area of the library. I locate the red book about growing apple trees and proceed to the librarian's desk.

I squint in response to the brightness of the day as I leave the library, with the book stowed in my bag. Chuckling to myself, I am both amused and relieved. The librarian confirmed my suspicion that it was Masao's age and not his heritage that kept her from lending him the book.

I stop by the deli and purchase three sandwiches and a bottle of soda, as Thomas requested. My stomach grumbles as the employee wraps the freshly made sandwiches in brown paper. I remember the somewhat squished peanut butter sandwich waiting for me at the bottom of my bag. Clara's voice pops into my head with a reminder to be thankful for what I do have, not to covet that which I do not.

I pay the clerk and tuck the sandwiches and soda into my bag. Holding Thomas' change tightly in my grasp, I look both ways and dart across the street, the theatre's large neon sign guiding my way, although it is unlit this early in the day.

As I reach for the theatre door, it swings open wide and forcefully. I open my hand to stop the door from hitting me square in the face, and Thomas' change scatters to the sidewalk in a jingle of coins.

Sarah steps through the door, her face mottled by fresh tears and black mascara. "Oh, Louisa. I didn't see you there." Sarah brushes past me, apparently in a hurry to leave.

"Sarah, where are you going? I have your lunch." My words are inadequate for the emotion contorting her face. "What about the play?"

"I can't do it, Louisa." Sarah shakes her head. "No, I won't do it."

"What are you talking about? You are Mrs. Craig." I step over the spilled coins and reach out a hand.

Sarah takes a step back, unwilling to be drawn back in. "If you think you can tolerate him, then I dare you to try. He is an oaf and a fool and one of the meanest men I have ever met."

My shoulders sink. Sarah has found her gumption at last. Unfortunately, it isn't the sort she plans to leverage for the benefit of the play. "But if you aren't the lead, there will be no show at all." My voice breaks with swirling emotions. My plan to build a career, supporting role by supporting role, is crashing down in front of me. The decision to pass on the lead of Mrs. Craig, though difficult, was sound. It allowed me to focus on my smaller role without the unsettling question of whether my success should be attributed to my talent or my looks.

"I am sorry, Louisa. Truly, I am." Sarah's voice softens for a moment as our eyes meet. "You've been kind, and I am grateful to have met you." Tightening up her posture, she squares her shoulders, the defiance running through her taking control once more. "But I am through."

Without another word, Sarah turns on her heel and scurries away as though the theatre is on fire.

Maybe it is, I think to myself as I pick up the loose change and tug on the heavy door, uncertain of what I will find inside.

CHAPTER 22

*W*ednesday, October 19, 1927
Clara

I am still ruminating on Louisa's remark about me being meant for greater things. It's true that I stepped up and helped organize our team of fifth-floor maids, but I can't quite convince myself that I was responsible for our success last Friday. I didn't really take charge. I simply did as Ms. Thompson instructed.

I am no more special or capable than any other maid here. I scan the locker room as the ladies I've come to respect from their work ethic prepare for the day ahead. My eyes land on Jane Morgan primping in front of the small mirror. Even Jane has stepped into the position, albeit with a little protesting along the way. Still, over the past several months, she has shown herself to be a competent maid.

When we are here, at The Hamilton, we are all on equal footing. We are maids. We clean, scrub, and tidy for the benefit of those who can afford the luxury of extended travel. No matter where our paths began, we are quite simply working-class women. Louisa may strive for greater aspirations, but I feel fortunate to be working in this fine hotel with these women who value a good day's work as much as I do.

I tie my hair into a low bun at the nape of my neck and secure my cap with hair pins. A shiver runs the length of my spine as I recall the last time I showed the slightest interest in a life among higher society. One minute, Louisa and I were sharing a carefree moment, strolling behind a flapper couple out on the town, me imagining what their life might be like. The next minute, we were caught up in an ugly scene, with Louisa going toe to toe with a complete stranger over an incident that had nothing to do with us.

Even as the scene plays in my mind's eye, I am disappointed with myself for making a bad situation worse by intervening. I had no authority to step in, and doing so only made the situation spiral further out of control. I don't know how Louisa manages to assert herself when provoked without batting an eye.

I shouldn't have gotten involved at all, even though I felt immensely sad for the man with the groceries. Embarrassed for him. Even scared for him.

I've always thought it prudent to keep my head down and do my bit to contribute to my family and those around me. When faced with the harsh reality that not everyone is treated fairly in this city, I can't help but wonder where I fit into that equation. And do I have any role in finding a solution?

"A penny for your thoughts." Rebecca Smythe leans in and whispers, "You seem deep in thought. Is everything all right?"

"Yes." I glance up at Rebecca, her eighth-floor maid's uniform crisp and vibrant. "No," I concede with the gentle encouragement of her kind smile.

"What seems to be the trouble?" Rebecca steers me away from the group, to a quieter corner of the locker room.

"I am not sure." I pause, my face twisting in concentration. "Have you ever felt like you should do more? Like life might be calling you to step beyond what you are comfortable with?"

Rebecca's head tilts as she considers my question. "Planning on joining the circus, are we?"

A laugh erupts from within me. "Not exactly. Oh, I don't know. Feel free to ignore my rambling. I was only considering something Louisa said. I suppose I've let my free-thinking, ambitious sister get under my skin."

Ms. Thompson enters the locker room, clearing her throat to draw our attention.

As we shuffle into place, with all eyes on Ms. Thompson, Rebecca whispers in my ear. "You know, not all of Louisa's ideas are ill-advised."

"Ladies, I have an announcement to make." Ms. Thompson's voice echoes through the cavernous room. "I'd like us all to come together to congratulate Miss Perkins on her recent engagement."

The room comes alive with chatter and well wishes as Miss Perkins blushes and smiles.

"We wish you well, Miss Perkins, and may you have many years of happiness." Ms. Thompson's faint smile indicates her sincerity. "Now, ladies." Ms. Thompson lowers her hands in front of her, palms flat, signalling for us to quiet. "What this means for all of you is that a position as an eighth-floor maid will be coming available in a matter of weeks."

The noise level rises again, with high-pitched chatter over the deeply coveted position.

Rebecca reaches out a hand to clasp mine. "God works in mysterious ways, Clara, but I can't think of a time when I saw Him work so very fast."

I glance sideways at Rebecca, a question forming on my lips.

"You just told me that life might be calling you to step beyond what you are comfortable with. I didn't think your wondering would be answered with such speed."

I open my mouth to respond, but no words come out.

Rebecca shakes her head. "Don't even think about letting this opportunity pass you by. Even if only to save yourself from Louisa's wrath, should she hear you didn't apply for the position when you had the chance."

Ms. Thompson interrupts my thoughts. She goes over the process for those wishing to be considered for the position on the eighth floor. A numb feeling grips my body, and my worry shifts from the position to my current inability to move at all.

Fifteen minutes later, I am in a fifth-floor guest room, bent over a porcelain tub, with a cloth in hand. Though I have no idea how I've managed to get myself here, I have a vague recollection of Rebecca steering me toward my cleaning cart before climbing the remaining three floors to her station on the eighth floor.

I rinse the tub free of my baking soda scrubbing agent. The water swirls down the drain, making a gurgling sound that reminds me of the tut-tutting of two older ladies last summer. Louisa and I were leaving the apartment with a list of errands to complete on our day off from the hotel. The ladies were sitting, blocking the steps down to the sidewalk, and appeared less than eager to move in order to allow us to pass.

Louisa greeted them in her cheeriest of voices, with warm words about the lovely day ahead. We were a few strides away from the front door when I heard one of them say to the other in her most condescending tone, "Renters."

I might have stopped in my tracks, but Louisa kept moving forward, unfazed. I still don't know whether she heard. All I remember is feeling put in my place.

This, I think to myself, is what I must call upon the next

time Louisa tries to coerce me into stepping beyond my station. These little slights remind me that advancement is beyond my opportunities.

Others see me as a girl from a poor family or a girl who lost her mother—labelling me as orphaned, although my father remains the head of our household. The woman from The Newbury marked me as a renter, her disgust evident. In the eyes of some, I am just a girl. A girl without a voice or social standing. Invisible, like to the clerks in the dress shop. How does anyone rise above their station when others are intent to keep them down?

By lunchtime, I have convinced myself that applying for the eighth-floor maid's position is a bad idea and would surely lead to disappointment. If I were to apply, I would wind up making a nuisance of myself, trying to be something I am not. I would rather face an angry Louisa. Rebecca is waiting for me at the entrance to the lunchroom, and for once I am not keen to see my friend at the midday break.

"Sooo . . ." She draws out the word. "Have you given any more thought to applying for the position?"

"I have."

Rebecca cuts me off with her exuberance. "I am so happy to hear it. I just know you will make a fantastic addition to the eighth floor." We slide into chairs, placing our lunches on the table. "To think that we will be able to work together. I can't tell you how excited that makes me."

Rebecca is unwrapping her sandwich when I burst her bubble. "Actually, I have decided not to apply."

"What? Why?" Rebecca's disappointment creases her forehead.

"If you must know, I do not feel I am qualified for the position." I scrub the word "deserving" from my mind as I infuse my posture with a false stoicism.

"Clara, you can't be serious. You are the most qualified maid here." Rebecca lowers her voice and gestures to those chatting animatedly around us. "Have you considered the raise in pay?"

"I have, but——"

"But nothing." Rebecca pushes forward. "Let me see if I understand where you are coming from."

I shrug and bite into my sandwich.

"You somehow think you are unworthy of a higher position. I truly don't understand this, but let's say I do. Have you considered that one of the ways to become worthy of a higher position is to work in one? The more challenging the position, the more opportunity there is to learn and grow."

I concede Rebecca's logic with a slight incline of my head.

"Besides, the higher wage would surely allow a little more room to breathe in that suffocating, worrisome brain of yours. You hardly spend a dime on yourself. Louisa had to browbeat you into shopping for new dresses, and even then you only purchased the one. Have you thought of what a higher wage would do for your family?" Rebecca pauses a moment, eyeing me warily. "Further," she says, lowering her voice, "what if Louisa doesn't keep her position at The Hamilton? She could leave to follow her theatre dreams. Have you considered how you and your father will afford to remain in the same apartment without Louisa's income as a maid?"

Rebecca's last question strikes fear into my heart. Once you've experienced poverty, it is impossible to ignore the effects it can have on your life. The threat of going without necessities filters into every decision I make, from what I buy at the market to the time I spend repurposing and making do. I have yet to find comfort in the financial security Papa, Louisa, and I have recently acquired.

"Don't let this opportunity slide through your fingers,

Clara. I believe you are more than capable of doing a wonderful job in this position. The only thing holding you back is a lack of belief in yourself."

We eat the remainder of our lunch in silence, Rebecca giving me the space I need to sift through her advice. Even my oatmeal cookie is far less appealing than I expect it to be. As I chew, I think back to the forthright customer in the dress shop, who warned me against being a wallflower.

Maybe it is time for me to locate some courage. I sneak a glimpse at Rebecca, feeling my cheeks warm as I realize that the last risk I took of this magnitude was applying for my current position as a maid at the hotel. I can't help but acknowledge the success of that decision, chuckling at the irony. I suppose I became comfortable after all.

Louisa has been telling me for months to find something that excites me. Rebecca is convinced I am a worthy applicant for this role. Even Cookie, with her new promotion in hand, tried to open my eyes to the opportunities that might await me.

My courage, it seems, is always in short supply when I need it the most. Mama's voice rings in my memory and stills my nervous heart. She used to tell Louisa and me, whenever nerves got the better of us, that courage didn't mean we would not feel the effects of fear. She said we were to recognize the fear and step forward anyway. She loved to quote Mark Twain, reminding us that *"Courage is resistance to fear, mastery of fear, not absence of fear."*

I cling to my memories of Mama, imagining how she might have seen my current situation. If she were here, she would tell me the same thing Rebecca did. She would tell me to be brave, and she would ask me what I had to lose by simply applying for the position. She would encourage me to go forward, reminding me that the only thing we can count on in life is change itself.

A soft sigh escapes my lips, garnering Rebecca's attention. I keep my voice low, not willing to share my decision with anyone else in the room. "I suppose if I submit my application quietly."

Rebecca's smile grows wide, and her eyes crinkle with delight. "I won't tell a soul."

With a decisive nod, I take in a lungful of air. "I will inform Ms. Thompson tomorrow that I would like to be considered for the position of eighth-floor maid."

CHAPTER 23

*W*ednesday, October 19, 1927
Louisa

"No good coming from in there." Mr. Johnson's voice startles me as I cross the theatre lobby. "No, ma'am. That man has vileness running though his veins, and he sure does know how to spew it."

I spot Mr. Johnson by the ticket booth, wiping a damp cloth the length of the dark wood. "Is it really that bad?" I ask, the hitch in my delivery betraying my concern.

"Miss Wilson, I've seen a lot of actors who think themselves better than others, but I ain't never seen one so mean to the bone. He's like a dog who's only been taught to fight." Mr. Johnson makes another swipe with his cloth. "I feel sorry for that little thing who ran out of here. Don't expect we'll see the likes of her anytime soon."

"No, I don't suppose so." I can't help but wonder if Sarah was part of the reason Gerald has been so difficult. Perhaps she wasn't appeasing enough for his liking. Or maybe the two simply did not get along, although she did seem rather easy to get on with.

I shake my head and glance over my shoulder, toward the theatre entrance. Biting my bottom lip, I ready myself to face the unavoidable news that the play has been cancelled. "Well, I suppose there is no point in delaying the inevitable."

"Walk tall, Miss Wilson. Walk tall." Mr. Johnson bids me good luck with a friendly wave.

I pull on the heavy door and find the stage empty, save for a partially dismantled set from the scene in the Craigs' living room. I tread softly down the aisle, breathing a sigh of relief that I'll have a moment to gather myself before Thomas breaks the news.

My eyes adjust to the darkness, the low stage lights casting soft shadows. I almost miss Thomas entirely as I prepare to sit in a theatre chair.

"Lou." Thomas is sitting on the floor, with his back against the elevated stage. He gestures for me to join him, appearing much smaller than the man I know him to be.

"What are you doing sitting on the floor?" I cross the theatre but stand before him, reluctant to sit on the floor when there is a theatre full of comfortable fold-down chairs.

Even in the low light, I can see his cheeks flush with colour. "Hiding."

"Hiding?" A teasing tone edges into my question. "Hiding from who?"

Thomas pats the floor beside him once more. Reluctantly, I place my bag next to the stage and lower myself to the ground.

A long, slow sigh eases past his lips. "Well, it seems we are without a Mrs. Craig." His strangled laugh does little to lighten the words. "How does one produce a play called *Craig's Wife* without the wife of Mr. Craig?"

"I'm so sorry, Thomas." I place a hand on his forearm and feel the warmth of his skin through his shirt sleeve.

Thomas places his other hand on top of mine and a jolt of electricity rushes through me, heading straight for my heart.

A moment passes, each of us looking in the other's eyes. My breath hitches as I break our connection. "I wish there was something I could do."

Thomas swivels to face me, excitement blossoming on his face. "There is, Louisa. You can agree to play Mrs. Craig."

"Oh Thomas, you know I can't." I stammer my put-upon excuses. "I don't have the time. I am already exhausted between my work here and at the hotel." I tuck the true reason for my resistance behind invented stoicism.

"What if I could arrange it so that you could still work and rehearse?" Thomas' eyes grow wide with anticipation, like a puppy dog hoping for a reward.

I narrow my eyes, letting him see my doubt on full display. "We are only three weeks away from full dress rehearsals. I can't possibly learn the lines in such a short time."

Thomas is more than ready to catch me in a lie. "You forget, Lou. I've seen you take an entire play home for a weekend, only to return on Monday with every line memorized."

"I—I don't think that is true." I try to argue, but he cuts me off with a boisterous laugh.

"You don't remember?" Thomas's expression bursts with joy. "How can you not remember? Louisa, you didn't just memorize one character's lines. You memorized the entire play, right down to the stage directions. Every character. Every scene. All of it."

Apparently, it is my turn to blush, as I realize Thomas has been paying attention to me all these years. Perhaps he does mean what he says. What if Thomas really does consider me a talented actress? "Well, I guess if you count that. But it was a very short play."

"Yeah, except for the main character's monologue that went on for five minutes straight." Thomas suppresses another chuckle. "You were made for the stage, I'm telling you. With your memory, timing, and ability to put on a persona like a hat, this role is for you."

I consider his words. Watching his hopeful expression, I feel myself give ground to the idea. My stomach rumbles, easing the tension between us and reminding me of the sandwiches in my bag.

Thomas' teasing smile expands. "I'll make you a deal. You can have that sandwich you bought for Sarah if . . ."

He pauses, and I catch myself leaning toward him.

"If you agree to pick up the role of Mrs. Craig for the remainder of today's rehearsal."

I eye him skeptically. "Today only?" I reach for my bag to retrieve the sandwiches.

"That's right. The rest of the cast needs to rehearse." Thomas accepts the brown paper-wrapped sandwich and the bottle of cola. "And I think I can change your mind by the end of the day."

The wink he delivers makes my stomach flip. I unwrap one of the sandwiches as I contemplate my next words. "I agree to play Mrs. Craig"—I raise my voice emphatically, making certain he hears me—"for this afternoon only. After that, you will need to find another solution."

"Unless I can convince you otherwise."

"This afternoon only. For the sake of the rest of the cast." I lift an eyebrow, determined to make myself clear.

"Okay," Thomas says, before bumping his sandwich against mine in a celebratory toast. "You've got yourself a deal."

We spend the last ten minutes of our break devouring our sandwiches and reviewing the scenes Thomas plans to rehearse this afternoon. As the rest of the cast trickles in, Thomas stands to announce the change of plans, assuring everyone that the show will go on.

When Gerald finally appears from wherever he's been lurking, Thomas tosses him the other sandwich. He waits until Gerald's mouth is full before informing him that he has a new leading lady for the day. I stifle a giggle as Gerald's face falls. For the first time, I wonder if Gerald is even interested in seeing this production succeed.

As we move through the afternoon, Thomas keeps me busy working through scenes with every actor except Gerald. While I'm on stage, it is easy to forget he is even in the theatre. During a quick water break, I scan the room to make sure he hasn't abandoned us altogether. Sure enough, he is slouched in the back row with his hat pulled down over his face, apparently taking a nap.

I consider us fortunate to have had a few hours of uninterrupted rehearsal, and I feel Thomas' confidence returning as we run scene after scene. The momentum is pushing us all to do our best, and as if by magic, the play begins to take shape.

As three o'clock nears, Thomas takes a lungful of air and calls Gerald to the stage. The rest of the cast clears off, hiding in the darkest corners of the theatre, intent to watch without being observed themselves. A warning chill runs down my spine.

Deciding that determination is the best approach, I paste on a smile and toss my hair over one shoulder, greeting Gerald as he climbs the final step onto the stage. "I am delighted to have the opportunity to work with you today."

Though his dark eyes do not lend themselves to

friendliness, he surveys me quietly. I take his silence as a win and hold inside a squeal of delight. I have managed to sway him a little my way, or at the very least confound him for a moment.

Thomas directs us to begin, and we fall into our roles with relative ease. Being opposite Gerald as he plays Mr. Craig, I am surprised to see his talent shine through. This is the first time I have seen him truly act. He has been so preoccupied with ensuring poor Sarah was receiving a lashing that he never put himself into his own role. He is good, I think to myself as the oblivious Mr. Craig dotes on his wife with kind words she doesn't deserve.

The moment I pay him the compliment in my mind is the same moment Gerald turns from Dr. Jekyll to Mr. Hyde. The change is as abrupt as it is obvious, and I can't understand the cause.

"You see there," Gerald shouts toward Thomas, who is standing off to the side of the stage. "This is what I am talking about. She came out of character."

Thomas steps forward, twisting the pages in his hand into a tight cone. "This is the first time Louisa has read the scene. I wouldn't expect anyone to remain in character without first having had the opportunity to get to know the character."

"Well, this won't work for me." Gerald huffs and stomps to the opposite side of the stage. "Either she either stays in character or we call it a day."

Thomas runs his fingers through his hair, preparing what I expect to be another attempt at reason.

I stop him with a subtle wave of my hand and move toward Gerald. "You are absolutely right. I broke from character. Thank you for being so kind as to point that out to me. I will aim to stay in character, despite having to read from the script." The words taste like bitter melon on my tongue, but I am convinced I can persuade Gerald with a touch a charm. That is, after all, how I've managed to move through life thus far. "Shall we try again?"

I invite Gerald back to centre stage. He joins me, but I feel his reluctance. I assess him as his mood shifts to that of a toddler about to pitch a fit, aware that the situation is precarious at best. Five minutes later, Gerald has found another issue, this time with the lighting. He rants for a few minutes, blaming the subtle flicker of lights for distracting him from his lines. Thomas instructs a member of the crew to fix the light while we take another short break.

"You are doing great," Thomas whispers as he passes by me.

I am unable to smother the smile lit by his words. I realize a moment too late that Gerald has witnessed our exchange. His taut lips elicit a drop of perspiration that snakes its way down my back. Unease washes over me.

As though energized by our interaction, Gerald begins his attacks anew. He assaults everyone in earshot without pause, without reason, and most certainly without logic of any kind. I feel as though I've entered a boxing ring without the benefit of gloves or a referee.

Gerald lodges complaint after complaint, delaying our progress into oblivion. My patience withers, and I resist the urge to raise a white flag in defeat. A whispered notion rattles me more than I'd like. Maybe this is my penance for fancying to play a lead role I don't deserve. Gerald has beaten me, and from his smug expression, he knows so. My cheerfulness and kind words have the opposite of their intended effect. A last resort of batting my eyelashes garners me a face full of spittle as he laughs.

The theatre door lets in a shaft of light from outside, catching my attention as I try to regain my footing in the scene we are struggling through. Masao steps inside. Quiet and respectful of the space, he tucks himself into a fold-down theatre chair and watches with a closed mouth and wide eyes.

Masao's presence in the theatre does not go unnoticed for long. Gerald is chomping at the bit as Thomas offers direction, and as soon as he has finished, Gerald lunges toward the audience. He nearly stumbles off the stage, and I am stifling a laugh when awareness dawns on me: he is pointing at Masao. The hairs on the back of my neck stand on end, warning me of imminent danger.

"What is he doing here?" Gerald swings his arm wide, an accusatory finger pointing directly at Masao. "This is a closed rehearsal," he shouts from the edge of the stage.

Masao is already standing to leave, a frightened expression contorting his face, when I find my voice. "He is here to see me." I hurry down the steps. "I hardly think a child will pose any threat to your stellar performance here today." I shoot the words over my shoulder as I stride quickly to Masao's side, my agitation over the afternoon's events building steam.

"What kind of a woman are you, anyway?" Gerald hisses from afar. "Consorting with the likes of——"

Thomas holds up his hand. "Enough. This is uncalled for."

I wrap a protective arm around Masao's shoulders, whispering close to his ear, "I apologize for him. I wish I could say he knows better, but to be honest, I haven't seen him be kind to anyone."

Masao's head bobs, but his face remains solemn. I give his shoulders a gentle squeeze. "This has nothing to do with you. Please try not to take it personally. He is just an angry man."

Thomas crosses the theatre and stops beside me, a genuine smile lifting his cheeks. "Who have we got here?"

"Thomas, this is my friend Masao." Gratitude for Thomas

overwhelms me, bringing moisture to my eyes. "Masao, this is Thomas. He is the director of the play."

Thomas extends a hand, and Masao shakes it. "Firm grip you've got there. I can see why Louisa has chosen you as a friend. You've got integrity in that handshake of yours."

Masao beams at Thomas.

"Are we done playing house yet?" Gerald hollers, his frustration evident in the creases of his brow.

"Masao, we are running behind schedule today. Can I meet you on Friday?" I turn my back to Gerald, blocking Masao from his view as best I can.

"Yes, Miss Louisa." Masao nods, but I can see he is disappointed at not having the library book immediately.

"I have a very long day tomorrow, with work at the hotel and then rehearsal here afterward." I try to help him understand as quickly as I can, not wishing to add to the tension in the theatre. "I can bring you the book Friday though. I am meeting Clara at the clock after she's done at the hotel."

"Yes, Miss Louisa. I understand." Masao's eyes flash with fear as a commotion rushes forward from behind me.

"I will not stand for this kind of interruption." Gerald seethes, his steely gaze fixed on Masao. "Especially when it involves——"

I step between them, coaxing Masao toward the door. "Go, Masao. Meet me at the clock. Friday at five."

I hear the whoosh of the door closing behind Masao before I launch into Gerald. "How dare you?" I am in Gerald's face before he has a chance to react. "How dare you bully a little boy. For that matter, how dare you bully anyone at all. I don't know where you got the idea that you could walk all over people without a single repercussion, but let me tell you something."

Thomas and Gerald step back in unison. My frustration bubbling over is clearly more than either of them expected.

Thomas approaches me slowly, reaching for my arm. "Lou."

"Well now, it seems you are not as nice as you pretend to be," Gerald mocks, still out of striking distance.

A moment passes as I tamp down my emotions before I can regain eye contact with Thomas.

"Louisa," Thomas says, looking directly at Gerald, "this has been quite the day." He sends Gerald back to the stage with a wave of his hand before returning his attention to me, "I think we are all exhausted. Why don't we finish this scene and then meet back here tomorrow? Can you give me one more day to convince you to stay the course? One more day as Mrs. Craig, and if you still decide you don't want the role, I'll figure it out."

Resignation trickles past my pursed lips. "Fine." I feel the compounding pressure of rehearsing the role of Mrs. Craig, managing my overly packed schedule, and looking at Gerald's sour expression. I have in a matter of hours proven to myself that not everything in life is made easier by being appeasing, nice, flattering, or charming. Sarah wasn't at fault for her struggle portraying Mrs. Craig. No, all the blame for our lack of progress rests squarely on Gerald's shoulders.

An hour later, I leave the theatre, deciding to take the long way home and hopefully create some distance between myself and my unsettled emotions. My thoughts swirl like a vast eddy in the middle of the ocean. I am angry with myself for losing my temper with Gerald.

On the one hand, I scold myself for not having stayed the course in my attempts to cajole him into being agreeable. Surely, I would have won him over in the end, a little voice argues. But on the other hand, the rehearsal had already begun to disintegrate before Masao appeared.

The truth slaps me in the face, and I've no way to dodge it. Clearly, Gerald recognizes my lack of talent, and given his hostile attitude toward me, he isn't about to be swayed by my charms. Thomas said he was an exceptional actor, and from what I saw today, he was right. I suppose Gerald is simply calling me out, and I have no choice but to decline the role Thomas so desperately wants me to play.

CHAPTER 24

Thursday, October 20, 1927
Clara

Louisa and I walk to the hotel. Her quiet mood, which I assume is due to her long days at the hotel and the theatre, gives me time to run through what I plan to say to Ms. Thompson. I've been over the imaginary conversation a dozen times and have decided I should complete my list of duties before locating the hotel matron in her basement office later in the day.

As we cross the street toward The Hotel Vancouver, Louisa's head swivels to look through the windows into the warmly lit lobby. "I'm heading straight to the theatre after work." She sniffs. The cool, damp air has been causing both of our noses to run.

"I remember," I say, wondering if my sister actually believes I don't know the schedule she is keeping. "I packed you an extra sandwich and an apple for later."

"Thank you." Louisa's mouth lifts, but the smile doesn't

quite reach her eyes, leaving me to wonder if more than fatigue has got her down this morning.

I pull on the heavy back door of The Hamilton and step inside. Warm air and the scent of fresh-baked bread welcomes us.

"Well, good morning to you both." Cookie bustles from the pastry kitchen, through the swinging doors into the kitchen, and back again before we've even stepped fully into the hall. "Come with me, ladies." Cookie gestures to us with a wave of her arm. "I've got just the thing to warm the chill away."

As if on cue, a shiver takes hold of me. I tuck my toque and mittens into my shoulder bag and follow her into her pastry kitchen. "The days are getting colder," I agree as a warm, sweet scent draws my attention toward the freshly iced pastry resting on Cookie's trolley.

"Fresh from the oven." Cookie winks conspiratorially. "But cool enough to eat."

"Oh heavens, those look amazing." Louisa reaches for one. "What kind of treat are they?"

"Back in Ireland, we call them cinnamon buns, but I've seen them elsewhere with different names." Cookie points to the tray of sticky rolls. "They get their name from the cinnamon wrapped up in the centre."

Cookie offers me a pastry from the tray, and I bite into the warm, soft bread, its gooey middle delighting my tongue. "Oh, my. This is delicious."

Our enjoyment of her latest creation inspires our friend to do a short hop about her kitchen. She catches our open-mouthed stares from over her shoulder. "This is what we Irish call a jig."

Despite her stout build, Cookie's legs dance with ease as she moves to a tune inside her head.

Louisa and I clap in unison. "Wonderful," I call out.

"Bravo," Louisa chimes in.

Cookie bows slightly at the waist, her face aglow. "You best be off, now that you've had your sweet. I wouldn't want to be the reason you're late."

"Thank you for the bun," I say, giving my friend a quick embrace.

Louisa and I change into our uniforms, helping one another with our apron ties and hair pins as we hurry to make it to the fifth floor in time for roll call. I fight the nerves gathering in the pit of my stomach, thankful Louisa is none the wiser about my plans. Despite my quiet mood this morning, she doesn't seem to suspect that I have anything but our typical responsibilities on my mind.

With my roster of duties in hand, I push my cleaning cart to room 503 and knock lightly on the door. "Maid service," I call, with my head bent close to the door. I wait a few moments, listening for sounds from inside the guest room, before knocking again. Finally, I announce myself once more as I enter the room using my master key. I've been diligent about making my presence known since a maid on the third floor inadvertently walked in on a guest exiting their washroom without a stitch of clothing. I have no desire to cause either party such embarrassment.

Today, my list of tasks includes cleaning the fifth-floor lift's exterior. The brass surrounding the modern contraption seems to be in constant need of polishing. We buff it to a shine daily, only to have the call button covered in fingerprints within the hour. I push aside thoughts of the dreaded task as I set to straightening the guest room.

Even after all this time as a maid, moving about an occupied room continues to unnerve me. I feel as though I am treading on someone else's space as I move personal items out of the way in order to dust and vacuum. I always prefer to clean a room once a guest has vacated, making it fresh and new for the next guest.

This morning, though, my mind is occupied with rehearsing the words I intend to deliver to Ms. Thompson. Hopefully my practice will keep me from stumbling over myself as I ask to be considered for the eighth-floor position. I bolster myself with knowledge of Rebecca's support, while simultaneously attempting to temper my desire.

Papa always says, usually to the ever-eager Louisa, *You can't ride two horses at one time.* I never really understood the phrase. But this morning, I am beginning to see what he means. I can't hope for something with all my heart while at the same time bracing myself for utter disappointment.

I shake the cobwebs from my head and stiffen my posture. "If I am going to do this, I am going to do this right. I will go in and tell Ms. Thompson I would like to be considered. I must believe I will be successful." I say the words out loud in an effort to convince myself.

"Well, I dare say it certainly seems you will."

I whirl around, startled by another's presence. Mortified, I feel my cheeks flame. "My apologies, sir." I curtsy uneasily.

"No, it's I who should apologize." The man's handsome face is friendly and kind. "I didn't mean to intrude." He gestures to the end of the unmade bed. "I came back for my hat is all."

"Of course." I step toward the bed and retrieve his hat, holding it gently by the brim so as not to crush the soft, brushed fabric.

"Thank you." He lifts the hat to his head, casting a shadow over his grey-blue eyes. "I don't mean to pry . . ."

"Sir?" I twist the feather duster in my hands.

"I am a pretty good listener." He removes his hat with a

smile, and I find myself unable to take my eyes off his. "If you want, you can practice on me."

"Oh." I tuck my chin in an attempt to hide my humiliation. "That isn't necessary. I don't expect you to—"

"Nonsense. This is the least I can do. For interrupting you in the first place." He sits on the bench at the foot of the bed. "Go ahead and tell me, just like you plan to say it to—who was it again? Ms. Thompson?"

A small laugh breaks the hold my teeth have on my bottom lip. "Yes, Ms. Thompson is the matron of the hotel."

"Ah, the plot thickens." He teases me with a wink and gestures for me to continue.

Sensing he is keen to see this charade through, I position myself in the centre of the room. "Very well." I glance toward the half-open door. Wary of being discovered, I push out the words as quickly as I can. "Ms. Thompson, I would like to be considered for the eighth-floor maid's position. I am a hard worker, and I would like the opportunity to prove myself in this most esteemed role at The Hamilton."

He nods approvingly. "Very well done, Miss . . .?"

"Wilson. Clara Wilson."

"Well, Miss Wilson. I think this Ms. Thompson would be a fool not to promote you immediately." He stands, placing his hat back on his head. "Though, as a guest of the fifth floor, I must say that I will be sad to see you go."

"Thank you, sir. That is very kind of you to say."

He tugs on the bottom of his suit jacket, straightening it as he strides toward the door. "I wish you all the best, Miss Wilson."

"Thank you." I am reluctant to let our interaction come to a close. "I plan to speak with Ms. Thompson this afternoon."

"Well then, this afternoon it will be." He lifts the hat from his head, signalling his farewell, and then slips out the door.

I silently count to five, allowing enough time to ensure I am once again alone before I let out a restrained giggle of relief and joy. A complete stranger just gave me the confidence boost I needed, and for that I am grateful.

A song dances through my mind as I strip and remake the bed. As a thank you, I place a wrapped mint on the pillow, though they are usually reserved for the children of hotel guests. I complete room 503, along with the rest of the rooms on my list, with a lightness I had forgotten I had within me.

By the time I have finished polishing the brass surrounding the call button of the lift, I feel buoyed by the opportunity before me. I tuck my cleaning cart into its cubby in the linen closet and descend the stairs to the locker room. I check my appearance in the mirror, tucking my hair back into a neat bun before pinching some colour into my cheeks.

Cool air greets me as my feet reach the bottom stair in the basement. I say hello to two bellboys who are moving a guest's luggage into the storage room. Passing by Mr. Olson's closed office door, I hear him in animated conversation with another person. Both male voices rise and fall as they share a jovial exchange.

Ms. Thompson's door is slightly ajar. I hesitate, taking a deep breath before knocking lightly.

"Yes. Come in." Ms. Thompson is seated behind her desk, her rarely worn spectacles perched lightly on the tip of her nose.

"Ms. Thompson, I was hoping to have a word with you." I step into the small room, barely large enough for the desk, two chairs, and bookshelf.

"Ah, Miss Wilson." Ms. Thompson peers up at me. "Please have a seat."

I sit in the chair opposite the matron's desk and do my best not to fidget.

"Well, Miss Wilson." Ms. Thompson gives me an encouraging look. "What is it I can do for you?"

Before I lose nerve or momentum, I let the purpose for my visit tumble out. "I would like to be considered for the eighth-floor maid's position. I am a hard worker, and I would like the opportunity to prove myself in this most esteemed role at The Hamilton."

Ms. Thompson's expression lifts a fraction, into what I am hopeful is a smile. "I see." She folds her hands on the desk. "What would you say is your most valuable asset as a Hamilton maid?"

"Ma'am?"

"I am asking, Miss Wilson, what will you bring to the role of an eighth-floor maid? You know the position is a demanding one. The guests of the eighth floor have high expectations."

"Yes, ma'am. I will bring a courteous attitude and a solid work ethic to the position. I am quite confident in my ability to prepare guest rooms—I mean, suites. Above all else, I am willing to learn whatever skills necessary to become a most accomplished maid on the eighth floor."

"I am very pleased you thought to apply for the position, Miss Wilson. I worried you might not."

I am about to reply when the door opens abruptly, preceded by a quick knock. "Oh, sorry to disturb. I didn't realize you had company."

"It's quite fine, William. I'll only be a minute longer, and then we can go." Ms. Thompson stands behind her desk, extending an arm toward the door. "Miss Wilson, I'd like you to meet my brother, William Thompson."

I turn to greet Ms. Thompson's brother. The colour drains from my face when I recognize the man from room 503. "You?"

"Hello again, Miss Wilson." This time it is Mr. Thompson's turn to blush. "I see you made it to your intended destination this afternoon."

"I'm sorry," Ms. Thompson cuts in, "have you two met?"

"I—I didn't . . ." My voice hitches with embarrassment.

Mr. Thompson spreads his hands, palms up. "In my defence, I didn't know what you were going to say when I asked you." He defends his actions like a schoolboy who's been caught dipping a girl's ponytail in the ink jar, as if my standing in this hotel is of no importance.

Humiliation at having shown so much of myself to Ms. Thompson's brother steals my ability to speak.

"I promise you, Miss Wilson, I had no intention of calling you out on anything." Mr. Thompson sneaks a boyish glance at his sister. "I am quite sure even my sister would attest that I am not the malicious sort, in any sense of the word."

I stand, the abruptness of my motion causing the chair to squeal against the hard floor. "I am sorry, sir, but I do not see the humour in any of this." I move to step past him, but the lack of space in the room stops me. "You must let me pass, sir." My voice is pitched high as I try to gather my emotions, so as not to heap more shame upon myself by bursting into tears.

"Miss Wilson." Ms. Thompson's voice slices through my distress. "Pull yourself together. I am sure there is some sort of an explanation as to"—she waves her arms in the air—"whatever this may be."

"Yes, ma'am. If you would excuse me." I bow my head, willing her to understand that I do not wish to come completely undone in the presence of her and her brother.

"You may go, Miss Wilson, but might I remind you that this type of outburst is far from the behaviour expected of a fifth-floor maid, let alone one on the eighth floor."

Ms. Thompson's eyebrows lift toward her hairline, and my

heart sinks with the knowledge that I've disappointed her. "Thank you, ma'am."

Mr. Thompson steps into the hall, allowing me to pass. He begins to apologize again, but I wave him off before dashing down the hall toward the locker room, wondering how in the world I managed to ruin my chance at the promotion so quickly.

CHAPTER 25

Thursday, October 20, 1927
Louisa

The clock is nearing nine thirty when I slip from the hall into our apartment. My eyes take a moment to adjust to the low light before I notice Clara sitting in near darkness at the kitchen table, her hands wrapped around a cup of tea. "What are you still doing up?" I keep my voice low so as not to disturb Papa, whom I assume is sound asleep, given how early he starts the day.

"I thought you'd be hungry." Clara stands and moves to the kitchen. "I'll heat you up a plate."

I drop my bag in our bedroom and slide off my shoes, letting the cool wood floor knead my feet as I walk to the kitchen. "You didn't have to wait up, but thanks."

"I didn't feel much like reading, and sleep is elusive tonight." Clara's shoulders lift then fall, and I sense a touch of defeat in her movements.

"Everything all right?" I lean my hip against the counter's

edge as Clara takes a plate from the cupboard and begins reheating a serving of dinner on the stovetop.

Clara shrugs again, confirming my suspicion that all is not well with my sister.

I try to coax her out with idle chatter. "Did you and Papa have a nice evening?"

"Mm-hmm." Clara pulls a fork from the drawer, placing it beside the waiting plate.

"Well, I had an exhausting day," I announce before lowering my voice to a murmur, "again." My sigh is laced with frustration.

Clara looks up from the skillet. "I worried the play would take up too much of your time." Clara steps toward me, hand poised to check the temperature of my forehead. "You aren't feeling ill, are you?"

"No, nothing like that." I wave my hand in the air, as though warding off any potential illness. Getting sick now might stretch me one step too far.

The beef-and-potato hash pops and sizzles in the skillet, drawing Clara's attention back to the stove. With a wooden spoon, she plops the steaming hash onto the plate.

"Here." Clara hands me the plate and fork. "I'll get you some water."

"Thanks." I move toward the table and settle myself at my usual spot.

Placing two glasses of water on the table, Clara sits down opposite me, her gloom turning the corners of her mouth into a frown.

I blow the steam from my forkful of hash. "Are you going to tell me what is troubling you, or are you going to sit there and pout?"

"I'm not pouting." The defiance molded into her expression does little to convince me.

I smother a harumph with a large bite. "Well, I have found myself in a bit of a situation." Exhaustion from the week invites my mask to fall. If there is anywhere I can be completely myself, it is here: within these walls, with my sister.

Clara leans forward, her interest piqued. "What kind of a situation?"

"It seems I am not quite as charming as I thought myself to be." I follow another bite with a sip of water. "The actor who is portraying Mr. Craig is . . . difficult, to say the least."

"Difficult? In what way?" Clara's eyebrows converge in question.

Clara sits quietly as I offer a litany of grievances about Gerald, barely pausing to eat or even take a breath.

I do my best to lighten the mood with a forced smile. "You know me. If someone is being difficult, I can usually charm them into a better disposition." I slouch back in my chair, the truth I am afraid to speak resting on the tip of my tongue.

"What are you not saying?" Clara attempts to raise one eyebrow, an expression of mine she's been trying to master since we were little.

I tug my bottom lip between my teeth and consider the words that I know need sharing. "I know he is rude and quite likely the most difficult person I've ever had to work with, but what if Gerald is right? What if Thomas only gave me this role because of my looks?" My last sentence squeaks out past tensely stretched lips. "What if I don't have any talent for the stage at all?"

Clara reaches a hand forward, squeezing my own. "That isn't true, Lou. You can't believe it is true. Yes, you are beautiful, but Thomas said you'd be the perfect Mrs. Craig. From what you've told me, he doesn't seem like one to lie. Honestly, I don't understand why you are suddenly shying away from being the star of the show."

I cringe at the sentiment, my visible discomfort eliciting another squeeze from Clara's hand. "Is there something else you are not telling me?"

My mouth twists in resistance. "Do you remember after we arrived in the city?" I pause to gather myself.

Clara nods and waits for me to continue.

"One day, shortly after we moved in, I left the apartment early and spent the day auditioning for a role."

"I didn't know that." Clara pivots in her chair and leans in.

"I was intent on making the most of our new situation. I was determined to do everything I could to make my mark on Vancouver's theatre scene. I was on my way too. After three rounds of auditions, the director asked me to be the production's female lead."

"How did we never hear anything about this?" Clara's face crumples in question.

"Because after he offered me the role, I overheard some of the other actors saying I didn't get the role because of my talent. I got it because of my looks." A long sigh passes through my lips, like air leaking from my deflated mood. "Apparently, the director is known for casting only pretty girls in his plays, and though I can't confirm much more than that, the chatter indicated he had reasons other than an appreciation for good looks." I raise an eyebrow, hoping to convey the sentiment without having to spell it out for her.

"You don't mean . . . ?" Clara's hand flies to her mouth. "Do you think he would have made advances toward you?"

I shrug, unsure of what might have happened. "I never gave him the chance. I didn't even tell them I wasn't accepting the role. I simply never showed up again."

"Oh Lou, I am so sorry." Clara squeezes my hand in hers. "Is that why you moped about the apartment for so long? I thought you were low because of our relocation. It all makes much more sense now."

"I thought I'd lost my chance. I don't want to get a role because of how I look. I want to earn one with my acting ability."

"Of course you do. Though, I do think it may be difficult to separate your beauty from your talent. At first glance, anyway. You may have to persevere to prove yourself is all. Don't let anyone underestimate you, Lou." Clara's gaze falls to the table, a sheepish smile pulling at the corners of her lips. "Even me."

I appreciate the sisterly support. "I haven't managed to drag myself to another audition since. Until Thomas cajoled me into one, that is. I don't know what to do now. I thought it was safe to play a smaller part, but now—" I drop my head into my hands. "Now, if I don't play Mrs. Craig, there is no guarantee there will even be a show, and that might end Thomas' career too."

Clara leans closer, determination settling on her face. "Thomas said you were the one he thought of to play the lead. You can't dismiss his eye for talent." Clara pushes forward. "Besides, you already are Mrs. Craig. Why in the world would you give up this opportunity? You've dreamed about being a famous actress for as long as I can remember. You can't let one nasty director ruin your dreams. If you want to know whether you are being cast because of your looks, maybe next time audition for a lead role playing an unattractive character. Then you'll know for certain."

I can't help but laugh at Clara's logic. "I can see your point. But—"

"No buts, Louisa. Thomas hasn't given you any reason to mistrust him, has he?"

"No. He has been kind to everyone in the cast, even Gerald, and that is saying something."

"Then I'd say it's about time you started following your own advice."

I raise an agitated eyebrow in Clara's direction. "What advice would that be?"

"How many times have you told me that I will never succeed if I don't at least try?" Clara straightens her spine, knowing all too well that she has caught me with own words.

I hold back the smile that is edging forward. "I really do want to play Mrs. Craig."

"And so you shall. What is it you are always telling me? If you don't dream beyond your lot in life, how will you ever improve upon it?" Clara's eyes twinkle in the low light as moisture gathers on her lower lids.

"You have been listening. I would never have guessed." I tease her with a gentle nudge of her arm.

I push my dinner plate away, my appetite replaced with nervous bubbles. "What about Gerald though?" I tap a finger to my lip. "I am already clawing my way through rehearsals. I definitely don't trust him. Something isn't right about the situation, but I don't know what it is."

"I know you are worried, Lou. I can't tell you what to do about Gerald. All I can say is that you shouldn't let him get in the way of your dreams. You've worked too hard to allow that to happen."

"That sounds like something I might say." Clara blushes, clearly pleased by my appreciation of her insight. "Are you ready to tell me what's been troubling you?"

Clara's gaze finds the kitchen table. "I took your advice and applied for the eighth-floor maid's position."

"You did! That is fantastic. You will shine on the eighth

floor. I am certain of it." I can't hide my enthusiasm for my sister's leap of faith toward her future.

"But I think I've ruined my chances." Clara runs a finger over a scratch in the tabletop.

"What do you mean? How could you have ruined your chances at something you've only just applied for?" I place my hand over hers, quelling her nervous, repetitive motion.

"I finally got up the courage to consider an opportunity, something beyond my station and what I know. Then Ms. Thompson's brother—and oh, she was not pleased with me." Clara is babbling, making no sense at all.

I listen patiently for a few minutes before interrupting to ask her to start from the beginning. I move to the kitchen to make tea and give my sister some space as she tells me about meeting Ms. Thompson's brother and his role in what she assumes is her certain demise.

Settling in at the table again, I consider Clara's dilemma. "I am not sure I understand why Ms. Thompson wouldn't still consider you for the position. You are clearly the best maid on the fifth floor. She gives you extra duties because she is aware you can handle them."

Clara shakes her head. "I never should have stepped beyond my station. I am a simple girl." Clara lifts her head, and I read fear in her eyes. "This is what happens, Lou. This is what happens when I venture beyond my place in society. A girl like me is meant to be invisible, to stay out of the way of those who are more important. That is why I am so good at disappearing into the walls at the hotel. I am already invisible to them. I am not meant to rise through the ranks. I am not like you. I did what you asked of me. I tried. But now it is time for me to step back and find comfort in my position in this world."

"Don't be silly. You have every right to expand your

horizons." After being on the receiving end of Clara's advice over the past hour, I am dumbfounded that she can entirely ignore it where her own problems are concerned. Fear is the only reason that makes sense. Though she is often more timid than I, she is capable of wanting more in life. I don't believe for one second she isn't.

"I don't think I have what it takes. I don't have the stomach for adventure like you do. They might not even want me on the eighth floor. Have you considered that?"

I sigh, knowing she may not hear what I have to say, despite having said the same thing herself only moments ago. "I think they would be lucky to have you on the eighth floor. You will never know what you are capable of until you try. You don't need to be adventurous to have dreams, Clara. Nor do you need a bucketful of courage to do what you believe to be right. You do, however, require an understanding of what you believe to be true."

Clara avoids my eyes, showing more interest in the floor. I wait a few minutes, letting her consider what is before her. "What if we both agree to step toward what we are frightened of?"

She catches my gaze with a quick glance. I can almost hear the gears in her head turning. I give her one more thought to consider. "Wouldn't you rather be someone you could look up to?"

Clara's head lifts. "Yes. Yes, I would."

I reach out my hand, palm up. "Then why don't we do this together?"

As she hesitantly places her hand in mine, Clara's mouth twitches with a nervous smile. "Together," she whispers.

CHAPTER 26

$\mathcal{F}$riday, October 21, 1927
Clara

Louisa and I part ways at the corner of Georgia and Howe. She is headed to the theatre for a full day of rehearsal, the time afforded to her because another maid was willing to work her shift. I meander toward the hotel, dawdling at the pace of a small child.

A gust of wind surprises me as I pass the open space between the cornerstones of The Hotel Vancouver and The Hamilton. Clutching my jacket collar with a clenched fist, I duck my head and brace myself against the weather. This morning, apologizing to Ms. Thompson is at the top of my list, but I am not relishing the task of schlepping down to the basement with my tail between my legs.

The heavy exterior back door flies open as I round the corner of the alleyway. Cookie, fanning herself with both hands, waddles down the few steps before turning to greet me. "Top of the morning to you, Miss Wilson."

"Good morning." I raise a gloved hand. "Cookie, it's

freezing out here." A chill runs through me and emphasizes my words. "Aren't you cold without your coat?"

Cookie inhales slowly. "Needed me some fresh air, and there is nothing crisper than Vancouver's sea-laced autumn air. I hope the young'uns are prepared to wear layers over those Halloween costumes."

"I suspect we may differ on our appreciation of the cold weather," I tease. "I'm not sure I own enough clothing for the wet winter ahead. The damp gets into my bones and stays there until June rolls around again."

Cookie laughs good-naturedly. "Spend some time with me in the pastry kitchen, with both ovens running and a whisk in your hand. I promise, you'll be warm in no time at all."

"I might just take you up on that offer." I start to squeeze past her, but she places her hand on top of my arm.

"A little bird told me you put your name in for a promotion." Cookie's eyes dance. "Maybe it's not my place to say, but I wanted you know how proud I am of you, no matter the outcome. I know it took a might bit of courage to do so."

My cheeks burn. "Thank you. That is kind of you to say. Though I suppose you don't know about the embarrassment I made of myself yesterday."

Cookie eyes me, her head cocked to the side. "Do you mean your interaction with Mr. Thompson? Isn't he a fine fellow? And handsome too. Did you know he is staying at the hotel?"

My strained sigh creates a cloud-like puff of air. "Yes, I cleaned his room yesterday, though I didn't know who he was at the time."

"I tell you, if I were your age, I'd be inclined to get to know Mr. Thompson a little better while he is visiting." Cookie bumps my arm with her elbow. "He seems like the right kind of man for someone looking for a fine husband."

"Cookie." My embarrassment is at full height. "I am not looking for a husband. Fine or otherwise." I nudge a stone off the step with the toe of my shoe. "Besides, I've already made enough of a scene in front of the man. He is Ms. Thompson's brother, after all. The best thing I can do now is try to avoid him altogether."

Cookie's expression becomes serious. "Clara, you shouldn't carry a single worry. You've done nothing to offend the man. He told me himself this morning as he was sampling a fresh batch of pastries. He said he found you . . . what was the word he used? Intriguing. That's it. He found you intriguing."

I didn't think myself capable of blushing a deeper shade of red, but at the thought of Mr. Thompson having anything to say about me at all, a new heat warms me through and through. "Oh, Cookie." I place a hand on her arm as I step past her. "I am sure Mr. Thompson has many things to do while visiting Vancouver. He most certainly won't be concerning himself with what I am up to. At least not if I can help it."

Cookie's last words echo in my mind as the door closes behind me. "I wouldn't be so certain about that."

I dismiss my friend's murmurings and decide the most prudent course of action is to speak with Ms. Thompson first thing. Not wishing to delay the apology, I don't even stop at the locker room to change into my uniform. Instead, I head directly to her basement office. I hesitate in front of the closed office door, believing the frosted glass window is disguising my presence. I lift my hand to knock before dropping it to my side.

The matron's voice from beyond the door startles me. "Come in, Miss Wilson. There is no need to lurk."

"Yes, ma'am." I turn the doorknob and step inside the small office. "I didn't mean to disturb you, ma'am."

"You haven't. The morning is only getting started, and I

had an inkling you might be stopping by before roll call." Ms. Thompson stands, placing both hands on her desk as she leans forward. "There is nothing to be timid about. William filled me in last night over dinner. I would apologize for my brother's rather forward behaviour, but if I made a habit of that, I am afraid I would have time for little else."

"Yes, ma'am." My hands twist together nervously. "I thought that perhaps, well, that you might wish me to retract my application for the position on the eighth floor, and I—"

"Why ever would you think such a thing?" Ms. Thompson steps around the desk. "You are a fine candidate for the position, Miss Wilson."

"I suppose I wondered if I were the right caliber of applicant. As you know, I come from a working-class family, and I don't have the same pedigree as some of the other eighth-floor maids. I don't have years of experience as a maid, nor do I possess a family name that might warrant such consideration."

"Miss Wilson, are you under the impression that you have somehow stepped beyond your station here?"

A slight incline of my head is my timid response.

"I can tell you with great authority that you have not. The only thing you have stepped outside of is the ability to keep your emotions in check. And that, I must admit, is partly the fault of my dear brother."

"Yes, ma'am." I dip into a curtsey, compelled to show the hotel matron the utmost respect.

"I am being honest with you when I say that The Hotel Hamilton management prides ourselves on discovering the talents and skills of our staff. When we recognize such achievements, we aim to help those employees showcase their talents. You shouldn't sell yourself short. You have much to offer." As Ms. Thompson's chin dips, her eyes look beyond her slender nose and lock on mine. "You will be considered for the position, Miss Wilson. Am I clear?"

"Yes, ma'am."

A soft knock at the partially open office door garners our attention. "Here are the papers you asked for, ma'am." Rebecca waits at the threshold. Her smile sets me at ease, warming me with her friendship. I feel heat rise within me and realize I am still wearing my heavy coat.

"Thank you." Ms. Thompson takes the pages from Rebecca and places them on the corner of her desk. "Serendipitous timing, Miss Smythe." Ms. Thompson's eyes twinkle in the dim light of the cramped office. "Would you be so kind as to share with Miss Wilson what I told you when you came to me, worried you were ill-suited for your current position on the eighth floor?"

"Of course, ma'am." Rebecca stands tall, her hands clasped in front of her as she directs her attention toward me and clears her throat. "The only things that can lower one's standing are a bad temper, a poor disposition, and an unwillingness to learn."

"Excellent. Thank you, Miss Smythe." Ms. Thompson returns her attention to me. "As you can see, Miss Wilson, I do not judge a maid by her family name. I judge her by her attitude and her effort." Ms. Thompson returns to her desk. "Why don't you two be off and ready yourselves for the day. I am sure there is more Miss Smythe can share with you along the way."

"Thank you, ma'am." We say in unison before turning to leave.

"Oh, and Miss Wilson." Ms. Thompson holds a finger in the air. "If you truly want to show me what you are capable of, you may find it best to follow what you already know to be right. A strong moral compass is sure to steer you in the best of directions."

"Yes, ma'am." I am still pondering Ms. Thompson's last words as Rebecca tugs me down the corridor.

"I am not sure what that was all about, but Clara, I certainly hope you haven't changed your mind about working on the eighth floor."

"No, I suppose I was only struggling with how I might fit in there." I clasp Rebecca's hand. "I want to work alongside you. Truly, I do. I am just not sure." I shake my head, embarrassment creeping in again. "I made a complete fool of myself yesterday, and I—"

Rebecca cuts me off before I can explain. "I am sure that whatever happened, the situation isn't nearly as dastardly as you suppose it to be. Besides, you must remember that I too have humble beginnings. Yes, there are a few maids who come from wealthier families, but their time here is limited. They have other obligations to fill. Marriage, schooling, and even travel await them. Besides, they aren't a nasty bunch." Rebecca jostles me as she pulls me into a sideways embrace. "They are nice girls. Hard workers and, I can assure you, very welcoming."

"But—do they warm to new people, or does adding a new maid to the mix upset the apple cart, so to speak? I worry that I may cause more disruption than help if I don't fit in with your tight group. And what if my skills are not up to snuff? Will they be disappointed by me?"

"Has anyone ever told you that you worry too much?" Rebecca links her arm through mine, pulling me up the stairs and toward the locker room.

"Maybe a time or two." My sheepish smile gives me away.

"Why do you automatically assume you have less to offer

than everyone else in the room? I know Louisa can be a whirlwind, so perhaps you are used to taking a back seat."

I shrug, uncertain of how to respond.

"We are meant to strive for greater things. I believe it is in our nature to do so."

"Louisa tells me the same thing, all the time." I roll my eyes in mock annoyance of my sister.

"When you allow your own light to shine, you aren't dimming another's." Rebecca stops and faces me straight on. I imagine she is willing the words to make a dent in my thick skull.

"Yes . . ." I feel my breath catch in my chest as I wait for her to continue.

"When you allow your light to shine, you are giving others permission to let theirs shine as well."

"I've never thought of it that way."

"There is room enough for all of us to light up the world, Clara. Won't you be a shining star with me?" Rebecca giggles and pulls me into the locker room.

We are still linked together and laughing as we enter the nearly empty room. "We'd better get a move on or we'll be late to roll call."

CHAPTER 27

Friday, October 21, 1927
Louisa

"Lou." Thomas calls to me from across the street, his arm raised to grab my attention. He dashes toward me, weaving between a few cars and a bicycle. "I'm glad I caught you."

"I wasn't too hard to catch," I tease, just so I can watch his cheeks flush with colour.

"A target standing still. My favourite kind." Thomas chuckles, then gently guides me by the elbow to the other side of the theatre door. "I wanted to tell you what a great job you are doing. I knew I was right to cast you as Mrs. Craig."

I give an unladylike snort at his comment, and I raise a palm to cover my nose and mouth in as demure a fashion as I can muster.

Thomas' expression turns serious. "I would never tell an untruth, Louisa. Not to you."

"Thank you for your kind words, then." I recover myself by delivering a sincere smile. Hardly a moment passes before my smile drops into a scowl. Thomas' eyes follow my own.

Gerald is standing on the corner, having what appears to be a heated discussion with a squat man who looks more like a ruffian than a theatregoer.

Their conversation breaks off, and the man darts across the street and out of sight. Noticing us watching him, Gerald saunters toward us with more confidence than any one person should carry.

"If only more of us believed I was capable of carrying the role. He certainly doesn't think so." I push the words out in hurry so Thomas can hear them before Gerald reaches us.

"I said he was a talented actor. Not that he was pleasant." Thomas winks at me as Gerald steps in front of us, inserting himself into our conversation without requiring the slightest hint of an invitation.

"Blooming cold out here this morning." Gerald looks the theatre door up and down. "Has the old man not unlocked the door for us yet? I'll have a word with the owner. That janitor doesn't move fast enough to handle a theatre of this size."

I consider biting my lip but decide otherwise, the advice I shared with Clara last night still ringing in my ears. "His name is Mr. Johnson, and he is spry enough to do this job and others, if you ask me."

Gerald eyes me warily. "Ah, I should have known that *you* would have taken the time to get friendly with the help."

Thomas puts a hand on my forearm. "Doors are open. I only popped out for an errand. Let's get out of this cold, shall we?" He opens the door and waves me forward. "Ladies first."

The smell of freshly brewed coffee fills the lobby as Mr. Johnson greets us. "Just as you asked, Mr. Thomas. Hot coffee to warm the bones, and my wife dropped by with some fresh-baked biscuits as well." Mr. Johnson's smile is wide and bright against his dark complexion, prompting my own grin.

"Please, it's just Thomas. No 'mister' necessary among

colleagues." Thomas shakes Mr. Johnson's hand and slaps him on the back in a friendly gesture.

"Colleagues. Humph." Gerald's comment lands on an inattentive audience.

"Those biscuits look heavenly." I lift one from the basket, the soft, flaky dough eliciting a gurgle in my already well-fed stomach. "Almost makes me want to try my hand at baking something like that. Please tell Mrs. Johnson thank you from us."

"Any time you want to learn, Miss Wilson, you just say the word. Mrs. Johnson will be more than happy to give you a lesson." The sincerity and openness Mr. Johnson presents to the world continues to astonish me. A man who has certainly been on the receiving end of unkind words and actions, due to the colour of his skin, has not an ill-mannered bone in his body.

"I am afraid she may be biting off more than she can chew with me." I laugh. "I am not one for the kitchen, Mr. Johnson. My sister reminds me so on a regular basis."

"By the talent you possess on that stage, Miss Wilson, I don't expect you will ever have the need to bake your own biscuits." Mr. Johnson delivers a playful wink before informing Thomas of where he can find more sugar and cream for the rest of the cast.

Each with coffee and a biscuit in hand, we head into the auditorium. The doors open every few minutes, spreading light into the darkened theatre as the rest of the cast enters. Thomas directs the stage crew to organize the set as the rest of us wait, contentedly sipping and chatting. I sit with the actress who has taken on my previous role of Ethel and listen as she runs through lines, seeking my input.

As the stage crew moves furniture and props, Thomas addresses the room. "Opening night is only four weeks away.

Dress rehearsals begin in two weeks' time, and we have plenty to cover before then. Today, I thought we'd split into groups so that everyone has a chance to really feel their roles. I will move between the groups and assess as we go. We are on the cusp of seeing all our hard work come together."

A little whoop goes up from the actor playing the maid's beau and is followed by hand clapping and wide smiles. As I scan the cast's faces, I see how tired each of them is. Most of us are part-time actors, who hold down jobs and manage families. When I think of everyone's effort and sacrifice, I am buoyed to give them my best at every turn.

The only sour face in the crowd belongs to Gerald. I steel myself as he and I are called to our corner of the stage to go over our lines. Thankfully, the others are busy with their own work. The lack of an audience lessens the blow of the complaints Gerald hurls in my direction. Receiving a lashing is one thing. Having one handed down to you in front of a crowd is another thing entirely.

Thomas inserts himself whenever he can, but Gerald seems to be in fighting form today. We manage through the morning, finally agreeing that Gerald will never have control over the posture I exhibit while standing by the Craigs' piano. I catch a glimpse of Mr. Johnson standing in the theatre's shadows, shaking his head at Gerald's behaviour.

On more than one occasion, I remind myself of what is at stake. The cast, the crew, and Thomas all have much to lose if I allow Gerald to monopolize the rehearsal with his antics. I take to digging my nails into my palms whenever the urge to speak my mind presents itself. At this rate, I expect my hands to be cut and bleeding in no time at all.

During the lunch break, Thomas pulls me aside. "How are you holding up?" His expression tells me he is bracing himself for my response.

I lift a single eyebrow, challenging his question. "Are you sure you want to know?"

"Yes," he says, but his glance toward the floor gives him away. "No, not really. But I do want to support you, and I want this play to be a success."

"I don't think there is much anyone can do." I tilt my head toward Gerald. "I don't know what it is, but something isn't right about this situation."

"I imagine not. He has been nothing but demanding and rude to everyone. If I could afford to cut him free, I would." Thomas runs a hand through his hair, and I push down the urge to reach up and touch it myself. A whoosh of frustration leaves his lips. "What a fool I was to agree to pay him in full, even if I dismissed him from the role. Honestly, given his talent, I never thought I'd have to consider it."

Understanding of Thomas' predicament dawns on me. Thomas is tied to Gerald whether he likes it or not. My mind whirs with this new information, yet I can't let go of the feeling that something more is at play. I shake my head, not convinced the situation is as it seems. "No, it's more than that. It is almost as if he doesn't want the show to succeed."

Thomas' face clears, like something has revealed itself to him.

"What?" I lean closer to him, the scent of his soap lingering in the space between us. "What did you think of?"

Thomas shakes off my question. "I think I may have an idea of what is going on after all." Taking a step back, Thomas calls out to everyone. "All right, let's pick up where we left off." With a wink in my direction, Thomas climbs the stairs to the stage two at a time.

I am blessedly entrenched in working with other actors for most of the afternoon. Not having to deal with Gerald's constant ridicule is a relief, allowing me to regain my footing and my confidence. The scenes I share with the other actors are smooth and fluid. We listen to one another's cues and move about the stage as though we are one, connected and sure. Not a single line is forgotten or misspoken. We are well-rehearsed and it shows.

Thomas floats between the groups of cast members, offering a few words here and there. But mostly he stands and watches, a silly grin pasted on his face.

As four o'clock nears, Thomas calls us together at stage left while the crew removes and reassembles the final set. "Okay, we are going to run through this one last time with everyone on the stage. Let's end today's rehearsal on a high note."

Thomas brushes past me as I position myself on my mark. "You've got this, Lou. Don't let him push you around."

I nod, a single defiant gesture. Bolstered by the afternoon's levity and progress, I am convinced that both Thomas and Clara knew what they were talking about. I am grateful for their support and their concern for me. I give myself a pep talk, telling myself I am meant to play this role as I slide back into Mrs. Craig's skin. Before I disappear into her entirely, I close my eyes and repeat in my head, I am talented. I have something to offer the theatre. I am Louisa Wilson, and I am an actress.

The scene plays out, with first the maids and then Aunt Ellen delivering their lines. Finally, Gerald moves into the scene as Mr. Craig. His delivery is impeccable, his embodiment of Walter Craig flawless. In the moment, it is easy to forget his prior transgressions. I feel the momentum as the play takes on a life of its own. This is what I long for on the stage, all things clicking into place like a living, breathing jigsaw puzzle. All I want is to remain in this perfect, magical moment, with the entire cast and crew coming together to create a masterpiece.

The experience is so close to being otherworldly that I am stunned when it crashes to the ground.

"No. No. No." Gerald is striding toward me, his hands waving madly in the air. "That isn't right."

My voice is stolen by the surprise of the interruption. I look for Thomas and find him at the side of the stage, wincing as though in pain.

Thomas steps forward, intersecting Gerald before he reaches me. "Gerald, we've been over this a hundred times. You are the actor. I am the director. You do not interrupt a scene or a rehearsal. That is my job."

"Then why don't you do your job?" Gerald's challenge elicits a murmur of discontent from those on stage. "I know she's your girlfriend, but seriously man, you need to show her who's boss."

Thomas sneaks a glance in my direction. "First of all, apologies, Louisa. She is not my girlfriend. Second of all, I was doing my job. Louisa did nothing out of sorts for her character. The only one causing an issue, currently, is you." Thomas glares at Gerald, not backing down as the words settle over the stage.

"Now, can we get back to the scene, please?" Thomas waves Gerald back to his mark. "Let's begin again."

All eyes follow Gerald as he takes a lap around the stage. He ventures close to where I stand, shaken and unnerved, and utters the final blow. "You're nothing but a talentless pageant queen. Know your place."

The breath is knocked out of me. I stumble backward as though I've been struck. All my insecurities rise to the surface. Gerald has uncovered my deepest fear and splashed it about the stage in front of everybody. My face falls slack as I stumble away from centre stage.

"Louisa." I hear Thomas calling after me, but I cannot stop my moving feet.

I grab my bag from the floor and dash toward the lobby. I don't stop when Mr. Johnson calls out to me, concern etched into his voice. I push through the doors and walk as quickly as I can away from everything.

Tears stream down my face as I push through the Friday afternoon crowd on the busy sidewalk. Gerald's words reverberate through my head, pointing out every flaw, every misstep, every insecurity I know to be true. I admonish myself for ever believing I would succeed. What a fool I've been. That man was able to shine a light on all of my flaws, his stinging words putting me in my place once and for all. He could see the truth, that my talent is wanting and only my good looks afforded me the role. Or, I consider, my thoughts taking a darker turn, perhaps he is the only one brave enough to say the truth to my face. My heart shrivels at the magnitude of my ruin as the actress inside me withers and dies.

Clara is right. Staying within our station is the safer way to live. Even as I think it, I chide myself for the self-pitying thought. I could never live in the shadows, but I may never live in the limelight either. My pace slows, the weight of this afternoon's events dragging me down. This is the cost of dreaming. Clara was right about that.

"Clara." I say her name out loud, remembering I was to meet her after the rehearsal. I glance around the street to gain my bearings. A businessman passes by. "Excuse me, sir, do you happen to have the time?"

Lifting his briefcase-carrying hand, he pulls back the sleeve of his long wool coat to peek at his wristwatch. "It's about a quarter to five." He offers me a curt nod and continues on his way.

"Thank you," I call after him in a hoarse whisper, catching

my reflection in a shop window as I turn in the opposite direction. I look a fright, with my face tear-stained and my dress rumpled. All I want is to run straight home and crawl under the covers. Even so, I can't stomach the thought of leaving my sister to worry after me.

I smooth my hair with one hand, attempting to regain a shred of dignity through my appearance. I am rifling through my bag for a hairpin when my hand brushes the hard spine of the red library book. A defeated sigh slips out. Masao is waiting for me too. "Can this day get any longer?" I ask myself under my breath.

I tuck my hair into place and steady my wrought nerves, doing my darnedest to paste a pleasant expression onto my face. I pivot on my heel and retrace my steps toward the clock, pulling the apple-growing book from my bag as I walk.

The saddest thing, I realize as I make my way toward the clock, isn't that I won't be centre stage in front of hundreds of theatregoers come opening night. It is that I will no longer be involved in the daily process of working in the theatre. Despite Gerald's bullish nature, this experience has reminded me of how much I love the process of creation for its own sake. The rehearsals. The camaraderie of the cast. The evolution of the character. I have fallen in love with acting all over again, and in the end, it wasn't about being noticed or beloved by others. It was entirely about being immersed in something greater than myself.

My mind returns to the theatre and to Thomas. Whatever must he think of me now? Not only do I lack the necessary talent for the role, but I behaved like a child by running from the theatre as I did. I have left him and the rest of the production in a lurch, and I can't imagine that he will ever forgive me.

CHAPTER 28

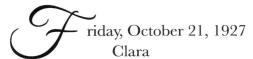 riday, October 21, 1927
Clara

The morning passes quickly as I immerse myself in tidying the fifth-floor common area. I refresh the flowers and give the carpet an attentive vacuum. At the first opportunity, I tuck myself and my cleaning cart discreetly into a nook to check which guest rooms are on my list. I breathe a sigh of relief when I realize Ms. Thompson has not assigned me to her brother's room today. The last thing I wish to do is further embarrass myself in his presence.

As I move about each room, paying careful attention to every detail, I mull over Ms. Thompson's advice. The words *strong moral compass* ring in my ears, and I do my best to decipher her intentions.

It being Friday, a few of the rooms require a rollaway cot for children of guests staying through the weekend. Though the bellboys deliver the portable beds to each room, each maid is responsible for fitting them out with bedding.

I fluff a pillow a few times before placing a wrapped mint

atop its crisp white pillowcase. A smile lifts my cheeks as I imagine the delight on the child's face as they spot the special treat, just for them. Movement at the door draws my attention.

"Don't suppose you have an extra one for me?" Mr. William Thompson leans his head and chest into the room, inclining his head toward the mint I've left on the pillow.

"I am afraid not. These are for the children, sir." I sense his teasing but lower my eyes so as not to encourage him.

"Ah, what I wouldn't give to be eight years old again." Mr. Thompson chuckles.

I move toward the door, since the guest room is now complete and ready for its new occupants. Feeling the inappropriateness of Mr. Thompson's presence in another guest's room, I motion for him to step into the hall. Closing the door behind me, I turn to find his warm, grey-blue eyes upon me. I am unnerved and speechless as his eyes move like storm clouds shrouding out a clear blue sky.

Mr. Thompson breaks the silence by clearing his throat. "I am glad that I found you, Miss Wilson."

"You were looking for me, Mr. Thompson?" If there was ever a moment to wish I had mastered Louisa's single eyebrow lift, this is it.

"Yes, I wanted to apologize for yesterday. I didn't intend to deceive you. I should have spoken up." He shuffles nervously from one foot to the other, and I wonder if he has been coerced into offering this apology. "And please, call me William."

"There is no need to apologize." I step closer to my cart, pretending to busy myself with the items on the top shelf as the hotel matron's words enter my awareness again. *A strong moral compass is sure to steer you in the best of directions.* I tamp down my fascination with his inviting gaze and assert myself. "And I think it would be best if I address you as Mr. Thompson." I steal a quick glance his way. "Your sister is my matron, after all."

"Yes, of course." I hear the edge of disappointment in his voice as he looks past me toward the end of the hall.

"Besides, I imagine we won't be seeing much more of one another, since you will be leaving Vancouver soon, I presume." Though I deliver the words as a statement, I lean forward slightly in anticipation of his answer.

"Yes. I will be returning to Toronto after the weekend."

"Toronto. My, you are a far distance from home." Hazel closes the door on her own completed guest room and catches my eye with a barely disguised grin as she rolls her cart past us.

"Several days travel, indeed, but seldom do I tire of seeing the countryside from the vantage point of a train window. Have you ever been, Miss Wilson?"

"I have been neither to Toronto nor on a train, Mr. Thompson." I feel my cheeks warm at my frank admission of having experienced so little of life, and I admonish myself for my inability to maintain any level of composure. "In fact, I have never left the city. I was planted here, it seems, and here I shall remain."

"You are fortunate. Vancouver is a beautiful place to spend your days." Mr. Thompson smiles sincerely and doesn't appear bothered by my lack of adventure, which I choose to take as an indication of good manners.

"Well, it was nice to see you again." I incline my head, gesturing down the hall. "I best be on my way."

"Of course. My apologies, Miss Wilson. I didn't mean to delay you." With a tip of his hat, Mr. Thompson strolls with a relaxed stride toward the lift.

I let out a slow exhale and wonder what the devil is wrong with me. Babbling on, with Ms. Thompson's brother no less, while I should be focused on my duties. I chide myself with a stern verbal warning. "Goodness gracious, Clara, get hold of yourself."

I push my cleaning cart to the next room on my list and try to prod the interaction with William Thompson from my mind. The vacuum cleaner drowns out all other noise. I only wish it could cancel out the ruckus inside my own head.

I try my best to put on a good-humoured mood, as Louisa has coached me to do, and imagine myself in an eighth-floor maid's uniform. Each time I direct my thoughts to the luxurious eighth floor, an argument erupts inside my head. The voices of Ms. Thompson, Rebecca, Cookie, and Louisa all jump into action, shouting words and directives. I feel as though I am in a foot race, struggling to keep up with the pack. My own voice is timid but insistent, warning me against desiring something beyond my lot in life. I should be grateful for all that we do have.

Much like I didn't know loss until Mama died, I was blessedly oblivious to the burden of financial hardship until the money ran out. I didn't understand what it meant to be discriminated against until I found myself faced with the reality of others' disdain as I tried to feed our family with our limited resources. I've been publicly embarrassed by my father's drinking and our failure to afford rent and groceries.

Moving to the city opened my eyes to harsh realities. On the Murray Estate, we were sheltered from the noise and the unfairness. I learned quickly to duck my head and do as was expected of me. Even here, at the hotel, it is easy for me to disappear into the woodwork.

I switch the vacuum off, my mood deflating with the machine's bag. As I wrap the cord around the handle, a new thought occurs to me. The vacuum needs power to be useful. A position on the eighth floor has its own power. Besides a better uniform and a raise in pay, the role distinguishes maids for their superior quality. I just need to find the courage to turn on the switch.

I work through the rest of the day, turning over the comparison in my mind. By the time I have changed out of my uniform and am leaving the hotel, I have changed my perspective on the eighth-floor position. If I were to get the promotion, my station in life would actually remain the same. I would, after all, still be a working-class maid. But my station within the hotel would be elevated. Maybe what first appeared to be a giant step is really only a small step in the right direction.

I peek at the time on my wristwatch and pick up my pace, eager to share with Louisa how I have reconciled her advice with my own view of who I am. I am relieved to understand that I do not have to be as brave as I thought. Louisa was right. I don't require a bucketful of courage to seek something better for myself.

I walk toward our meeting place, head held high and shoulders back. I am so much happier when I can be someone worth looking up to. I can hardly wait to tell Lou. As I turn the corner toward the clock, I spot my sister and wave to her, my excitement bubbling over. But she appears not to notice me. Louisa is talking with someone else. A few more steps garner me a better vantage point of the clock and my sister standing before it, an angry expression contorting her face. The clock chimes five in slow motion as the scene unfolds. I find myself frozen, unable to move.

CHAPTER 29

Friday, October 21, 1927
Louisa

I arrive at the clock two minutes before five. Derailed by my thoughts about Thomas and the play, I scan the sidewalk somewhat absentmindedly for Masao. Hopefully, the boy's mother will expect him home soon so I can simply give him the book and be on my way when Clara arrives. The sidewalk is busy, with the workweek coming to an end. Horns honk as cars and jitneys dodge one another. I tug my coat a little tighter around my body and insert myself close to the base of the clock, its large round face towering above me.

I think I hear someone call my name, but with the din of street noise, I can't be certain. Then I hear it again. The voice is closer now, and familiar, but spewing words with an angry force that makes me cower slightly as I turn to see who is hollering.

"Who do you think you are?" Gerald spits out as he reaches me in two long strides.

"What—what are you doing here?" I stammer, placing a

steadying hand on the clock's slender midsection. I take a step back, ensuring there is adequate distance between Gerald and myself.

"You have no idea what you've cost me." Gerald's finger is an inch away from my face, forcing me to back up.

The fury that has been below the surface of my skin for the past several weeks builds as I regain my footing. Does this man even know how impossible he is to work with? Putting aside his ability to pour cold water on an entire cast's performance, his judgemental disposition drove me out of the theatre this afternoon. He told me I was an imposter, unable to act and unworthy of his time. The nerve of him to show up in public, after overhearing my intended destination, makes me want to scream.

"What I've cost you?" I almost laugh at him. "Honestly, Gerald, I have no idea what you are talking about." I meet his eyes with a steely glower all my own. "Tell me, then, how in the world did I accomplish this great feat?"

"I've been cut from the production because of you." Gerald drops his voice to a whisper, shifting his body weight a few inches closer. I can feel the heat of his skin in the air between us, making me more than a little uncomfortable.

"In case you've forgotten, I left the theatre this afternoon. I am the one Thomas needs to replace, not you. As you have informed me several times, I am completely replaceable. You, on the other hand, apparently are not." I roll my eyes, mocking him before delivering my insult. "You don't strike me as a daft fellow. Were you truly not able to follow along?"

My ridicule only exasperates him further, resulting in a menacing tone. "You left, and he fired me. That is exactly what happened."

"Thomas would never do that." I wave my hand, and the book, emphasizing my point. "Thomas has put up with you for this long. He knows he is contractually obligated to keep you in the role. Opening night is weeks away. He'd be crazy to let both of his lead actors go this late in the process. Without you, there is no play."

"Would you please lower your voice?" Gerald seethes as he shakes his head. "That is where you are wrong, Miss Know-It-All. There is going to be a play. Just not one with me in it." Gerald bats his eyes mockingly. "Whatever you've been serving him, sweetheart, has certainly paid off. Clearly, his affections for you run deeper than any contract he signed with me."

I cringe at the insinuation that something inappropriate has been going on between Thomas and myself. The gall of this man to spread such a vicious rumour. I glance about the street, hoping we've not been overheard. "There is nothing between me and Thomas, and you know it."

"I don't know anything. Sweetheart."

I notice a few people slowing to assess us as they pass and consider, for a fleeting moment, what Clara will think if she stumbles upon this scene. This is my chance to set the record straight with Gerald. Through my own actions this afternoon, I've already vacated the role of Mrs. Craig, and with this man ready to tell bold-faced lies about me, I've got nothing more to lose.

I take a step toward him, squaring my stance for steadiness and pointing *my* finger into *his* face. "Did you ever consider that you might have been the cause of your own demise? You have been a disruptive, complaining, self-absorbed, mean-spirited man. Nobody is going to want to work with you once word of your reputation gets around town. You'll be known as the difficult actor. The one who derails an entire production with his holier-than-thou opinion of himself. The one who criticizes everyone at every turn and continually steps on the director's toes. No, there is nobody who will want to work with you."

I let out a shaky breath and realize I want him to know the truth. My truth. My voice softens. "Your actions have cost others their dreams. A play is about so much more than one person or one role. You have been cruel and unkind. You have been prejudiced against others for reasons I have yet to understand. You have ridiculed and lamented, and never once have you taken responsibility for your place in this situation. How can you be so selfish?"

"You have no idea what you are talking about." Gerald raises his voice so he is sure to be heard. He turns away from me, tossing the crowd an *is this girl serious* look. I realize he is using the crowd like he would an audience, taking from them the energy he requires to play his role. Is this the purpose of the loud, obnoxious, public confrontation? I don't see what he would have to gain from airing his dirty laundry.

I pause for a moment, watching his every move. How he positions his shoulders, his hands. Even his facial expressions seem rehearsed. This is an act. My mind races, examining our interactions over the past several weeks, trying to locate the missing piece.

He continues to posture, waving his arms as though someone has lit him on fire. I watch intently as he spews his monologue of lies. If I weren't the target of his rant, I would commend him for an excellent performance.

Gerald glances back to me over his shoulder, and recognition dawns on his face. He knows that I know. I shake my head slowly, squeezing my eyes shut against the truth. "How could you?" My voice is barely a whisper. "This isn't about you and your role. Why are you so intent to ruin the play?"

Gerald scoffs at my question. "You wouldn't understand.

You are well versed in getting exactly what you want with your pretty smile and your amenable little attitude. You can't possibly understand."

If his remarks weren't so condescending, I might ask if he truly thinks my smile is pretty or my attitude amenable. Instead, his sentiment makes my blood boil. I lift my arm, ready to clobber him with the book I am holding, when I remember the reason I have the book in the first place. I glance around the crowd, searching for Masao, hoping he is smart enough to remain out of the way. "What are you playing at? There must be a reason for all these shenanigans."

"You wouldn't believe me if I told you." Gerald's voice drops low, making the conversation private again.

"Try me." I cross my arms defensively over my chest, daring him to continue.

CHAPTER 30

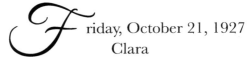riday, October 21, 1927
Clara

Louisa raises her arm, looking as though she is ready to throw something at the man. I rush forward, my immediate fear and inaction replaced by the overwhelming desire to remove my sister from the situation.

I move closer, but Louisa doesn't notice me. Her entire focus is on the man. A rather handsome man, I think to myself, save for the scowl lining his face.

Having been on the receiving end of more than one of her arguments, I can tell by her posture that Louisa is knee-deep in a battle she isn't likely to walk away from willingly.

"Try me." She taunts the man, and I instinctively step beside her, bumping her elbow with my arm.

I place a hand on her coat sleeve and tug. "Lou, what are you doing? People are staring." I glance about the sidewalk, noting the growing number of onlookers.

Louisa shrugs me off, her eyes remaining steady on the man before her.

The man takes a step forward, and I grip Louisa's coat sleeve tighter. He leans in and whispers, "I was paid by another theatre group to ensure Thomas' play did not make it to opening night."

"Are you kidding me? Why? What kind of actor wants a play he's starring in shut down?" The strain in Louisa's question lifts her voice, eliciting a glowering expression from the man. "What you are saying doesn't make any sense, Gerald."

Recognition dawns on me, and my head swivels for a better look at the man. So, this is Gerald, the man set to play Mr. Craig opposite Louisa's Harriet Craig.

"Will you lower your voice," Gerald hisses. "These aren't the sort of people you want to disappoint. Just pipe down and let me think this through."

Gerald takes a few steps back and paces in front of us. Back and forth. Back and forth. With his hand resting against his forehead, I can see he is thinking, but about what, I have no idea. Louisa's toe begins to tap, and I sense her mind whirring behind her cool gaze, fixed on Gerald.

I lean closer, speaking into Louisa's ear. "What is going on?"

Louisa, as though noticing me for the first time, looks my way with a startled expression. "I'm still trying to sort that out."

Gerald stops abruptly and turns to face us both. Leaning in, he places his mouth close to Louisa's ear, and I wonder if he is being clever or foolish, given Lou's inability to stand being placated. From my vantage point, all I hear is "if we pretend, maybe they will believe I still have power over the failure of the play," followed by the hiss of rapidly whispered words. Louisa's mouth drops open, and her hand covers the reaction.

As Gerald's words continue to fly, I can tell Louisa is considering what he is saying. A few moments later, she nods her head, almost imperceptibly, and I imagine the people gathering on the sidewalk leaning in to hear what's being said.

Gerald stands upright, meeting Louisa's eyes with a questioning gaze.

"Fine." Louisa drops her arms to her side and sets her attention on me. In a low voice, she says, "Clara, I need you to play along." She tucks a strand of hair behind my ear and touches her forehead to mine. "I will explain everything later. Right now, I need you to step aside and watch."

I open my mouth to disagree, but Lou puts a finger to my lips. "I need you to trust me, Clara." Louisa hands me a red book to hold before nudging me a little further away from where she stands. "Go wait over there. We are going to do a scene from the play. I promise, I'll explain it all later."

I shuffle a few feet away, turning my back to those watching from the sidelines. I catch Louisa's wink in my direction a split second before her face transforms.

"Ladies and gentlemen, thank you for joining us for this afternoon's taste of our theatre production of *Craig's Wife*, opening soon." Louisa's smile dazzles as she manages to draw the crowd closer, ensuring a circle forms around her and Gerald.

Gerald takes his mark and continues. "This"—he holds out his hand for my sister to take—"is Harriet Craig. She is the domineering wife of Mr. Craig. She is played by the very talented Miss Louisa Wilson."

Hands clasped, they bow together before jumping into a scene from the play. I watch, engrossed, as the two transform into a doting husband and an uncaring, money-hungry wife. The role reversal strikes me as uncanny to say the least, given what I know of the situation between Lou and Gerald.

Watching the crowd, I can tell they are enjoying the entertainment.

The short skit is wrapping up when I spot Masao at the edge of the crowd. His face is set with determination and a hint of worry as well. He steps forward, his fists opening and closing. I am trying to puzzle out the reason for his upset when his eyes lock on Gerald.

Masao pushes past those watching and marches into the centre of the circle. Gerald's eyes grow wide, signalling to Louisa with a wave of his hand and murmured words. "The boy."

Louisa is glancing over her shoulder when Masao hurls himself in front of her, his arms splayed out as if to defend her.

The crowd erupts with applause, many of them presuming the performance has come to an end. Louisa bends down, talking to Masao with a kind and gentle demeanour.

Straightening herself, Lou grabs Masao's hand on her left and Gerald's on her right, tugging them both forward into a theatrical bow. "Opening night is Friday, November eighteenth. We hope you will join us then," Louisa shouts to the crowd as they disperse, each onlooker continuing with their day.

I let out a long, slow breath, hoping the tension of the situation has resolved itself. I take a step toward them, wanting to ensure Masao is all right, but Gerald begins hissing at Louisa. I step back once more but remain within earshot, observing every move.

"I don't know who is watching." Gerald juts his chin in Masao's direction. "He could have ruined the ruse." Gerald's eyes shift from one side of the street to the other. "As long as they think I am still working to sabotage the play, I am safe."

Louisa pivots to meet Gerald's accusation with a sensible

response. "For heaven's sake Gerald, this is a public street. Masao didn't know. After he saw the way you treated me at the theatre, I can hardly blame him for wanting to protect me from you." Louisa cocks an accusatory eyebrow at Gerald and ruffles Masao's hair, her voice softening. "It's sweet and precisely what a good friend would do."

"You really don't understand." Gerald tugs on his jacket sleeves, his eyes darting nervously about. "Without a role in the play, I can't do what I was hired to. They will be looking for me."

"Who will be looking for you? That man from the street the other day? The burly one? Did he give you that shiner you had a while back?" Louisa glances around before returning her attention to Gerald. "This does seem all a bit cloak and dagger, you know. Is there anybody you can go to for help?"

Gerald shakes his head emphatically, his eyes squeezed shut.

"What did you get yourself into, Gerald?" In typical Louisa fashion, she presses on. "There must be a way out of—"

"No." Gerald cuts off Louisa with a tone that sounds as though he would like to boom the sentiment for all the city to hear. His need to conceal his predicament seems to rein him in.

After watching and listening intently to Gerald's distress, Masao tugs on Louisa's jacket. She bends at the waist to hear what he has to say.

Returning her attention back to Gerald, Louisa relays Masao's suggestion. "Masao here says that in Japantown the entire community comes together when someone needs help. He is sweet to suggest that perhaps these people would not think to look for you there."

Without warning, Gerald turns on Masao, lurching toward

him with fiery eyes. "Do you honestly think I would be safe in your ghetto, boy?"

Louisa and my eyes lock, both of us knowing that Masao's innocence is at risk, and perhaps his well-being as well, given Gerald's increasing level of frustration. We move as one. With the threat of physical harm and Gerald's vile slander, neither of us hesitates, knowing all too well that doing what is right will not likely be expected of two young women.

Louisa and I collide and form a wall, shielding Masao from Gerald's verbal attack. I drop the book Louisa gave me to hold. Reaching behind my back, I grip Masao's arm, squeezing it reassuringly.

Gerald, shocked by our quick actions, retracts. He raises his palms, defeated by our solidarity and our good sense. "I—I don't know what has come over me. This—this has all been too much. I am a doomed man, but I shouldn't have brought you into it." He stumbles backward, his expression filled with regret. "Please. Forgive me, Louisa. I am sorry—"

Without another word, Gerald turns and darts across the street, disappearing between the buildings a half block away.

As soon as Gerald is out of sight, we turn in unison and kneel in front of Masao, ensuring he is unharmed. Louisa examines his face and hands for cuts and scrapes before pulling him to her in a fierce embrace. "What a brave boy you are. I am so proud of you, Masao. So proud." Tears pool in Louisa's eyes, and I finally understand what she meant when she told me of her hope that the pebble she tosses into the water of humanity will ripple out and touch others' hearts. I should have known Louisa's pebbles would be the size of boulders, capable of moving mountains.

The clock chimes half past the hour, startling us with its reverberating sound. Louisa wipes the tearstains from Masao's cheeks before tending to her own. Picking up the red book,

Louisa dusts it off and hands it to Masao. "I believe this is what you came for, sir." She winks at him, garnering a welcomed smile from the boy. "We better get you home. Your mother is going to worry after you."

"I will be happy to accompany the lad home." Cookie's voice breaks through our bubble of secluded conversation.

All three of our heads tilt upward. Ms. Thompson and Cookie stand over us, bundled in winter coats that aren't warm enough to vanish the fraught expressions from their faces.

"We were on our way home when we happened upon the likes of you." Cookie sighs, reaching out a hand to Masao. "I imagine a lengthy explanation of this afternoon's events will be required, so you best fill me in. Quick as you can."

We stand, brushing the debris from our knees. Louisa rushes through a brief but lively rendition of what transpired on the sidewalk. Though she provides a complete explanation of Masao's involvement, she neglects to add any details regarding Gerald's odd behaviour. I don't push in front of the others, but I intend to ask her about it as soon as we arrive home.

After another hug, Masao happily accompanies Cookie to Japantown. I stifle a giggle at the pair of them, Masao skipping along while Cookie takes short, quick steps to keep pace with the boy.

"Well, I am certain you have both had a very long day." Ms. Thompson glances between us. "We don't want your father to worry either. You best be on your way home."

"Yes, ma'am," we say together, pivoting to walk toward the comfort of our apartment.

"Oh, and Miss Wilson," Ms. Thompson calls out, halting our steps.

We both pause, turning to reply.

She realizes her gaffe and stifles a chuckle. "My apologies.

Miss Clara Wilson. Please come by my office in the morning. A young lady with such gumption certainly deserves to be promoted." Ms. Thompson nods resolutely. "Very pleased to see you have located your compass, Miss Wilson. Very pleased, indeed."

CHAPTER 31

$\mathcal{F}$riday, October 21, 1927
Louisa

Clara is bubbling with excitement at having earned the eighth-floor position. To her credit, though, she is doing her best to tamp down her joy as we make our way home.

"So, the play?" Clara asks, her pace slowing to match mine.

My lips twist. "Cancelled, I suppose."

"Oh Louisa, I am so sorry. What happened? I mean, I know I saw something there." Clara flings an arm behind her, in the direction of the clock. "But how did things unravel so quickly?"

We walk past The Hotel Georgia, its bright lights offering me little to smile about as the sky shifts toward darkness. I fill Clara in on the disaster of this afternoon's rehearsal. She angers with speed when I tell her about the comment that sent me running from the theatre.

"That no-good louse." Clara blurts out the harsh sentiment as only a sister could. I try not to, but I can't help but smile at her loyalty. "Please tell me you didn't believe him for a minute."

My shoulders lift in an admission of guilt. "I did. I figured someone had finally found me out." I glance sideways at Clara. "I fear it is easy to believe someone when they're only confirming your own self-doubt."

"But Lou, you are talented." Clara pleads with me. "Even today, when you were putting on that bit of the play in front of everyone on the sidewalk. You were a shining star."

I disagree with my sister and throw her a look that says so.

Clara is undeterred. "You come alive when you perform. Even I believed you were Mrs. Craig, and I have lived with you my entire life."

"You're just saying that to make me feel better." I link my arm through Clara's. "Too bad it's so chilly. We should have ice cream to celebrate your promotion."

"Stop trying to change the subject." Clara admonishes me with a stern tone. "I believe in you. Like you believe in me."

A tear I've been trying to hold at bay sneaks past my lower lid and slides down my face. Clara reaches her gloved thumb to my cheek, tenderly brushing the moisture away.

We walk in silence for a few blocks, each of us trying to reconcile the day's events. I look up and see the lights on the corner of our apartment building. "Home," I whisper to myself, thankful to have arrived at our safe place, where I can rest.

"Louisa!" I hear my name being called and turn to see Thomas jogging toward us, face pink and jacket open to the chilly air. "Thank goodness. Louisa, I am so glad I caught up with you."

"Thomas. What are you doing here?"

"Thomas?" Clara asks. "The director Thomas?"

I roll my eyes at her, knowing she is reading more into his

presence than she should. I wave a gloved hand between them. "Clara, this is Thomas. Thomas, this is my sister, Clara."

"Nice to meet you." Thomas extends a hand for Clara to shake. His natural ability to slow down and make note of the important moments never ceases to amaze me. I suspect that is how he sees an entire production, one important moment at a time.

Redirecting his attention to me, he smiles. "You were right, Lou."

"Right about what?"

"You said it was as if Gerald didn't want the show to succeed." Thomas, not knowing what transpired between Gerald and me this afternoon, is still in the dark about Gerald's true motives. I realize with a sinking heart that I have to be the one to tell him.

"I did, but Thomas, there is something I should tell you."

Thomas doesn't let me explain further. "I know what is going on." He looks as excited as a nine-year-old boy going to a ball game.

Thomas shifts his weight, ensuring he has both my and Clara's attention. "Gerald didn't want the show to succeed. In fact, I don't think he even wanted the role of Mr. Craig. I heard a rumour a few months back but ignored it, wanting to give him the benefit of the doubt." Thomas waves a hand in the air to dismiss either his misjudgement or his genuine nature.

"Anyway, it seems Gerald ran up quite a debt with some not-so-nice guys. He gambled away the earnings from his last show and then some. Lost his shirt, so to speak." Thomas runs a hand through his hair, and my stomach does a somersault. "So, these guys, these people Gerald owes money, one of them has a kid brother who is eager to get into the theatre business."

Clara and I nod, glued to Thomas' every word.

"Well, this kid brother has a play he wants to produce. Apparently, not many theatres in town were willing to invite his kind of business connections into their midst. He got in touch with the owner of our theatre and put some pressure on him about securing a run of dates for his play." Thomas pauses to take a few breaths. "Thing is, our theatre is booked solid from now right through to summer."

The puzzle pieces are clicking into place. Gerald's hastily whispered story about being in trouble over some money. His job to ensure the play didn't make it to opening night.

Thomas lets out a deep sigh before continuing. "They hired Gerald to sabotage our play so they could steal the show dates out from under us. And since Gerald owed the brother money for his gambling debts, the stage was set."

"I'm so sorry. All this time, he's been working against you." I offer Thomas a sympathetic smile.

"Against all of us," Thomas asserts. "I can understand Gerald's motivation. He likely didn't feel as though he had much of a choice, backed into a corner like he was, but man he sure made things unbearable."

"Well, you were right about one thing." My tone is teasing, and I sense Thomas taking the bait.

"Yeah, what was that?"

"Turns out Gerald is an exceptional actor."

The three of us erupt in laughter, and I feel the tension of the past several weeks ease from my shoulders.

Thomas accompanies us the final block to our apartment building, the two of us sharing our insights and knowledge about Gerald's plan as we walk.

We reach The Newbury, and Clara begins to climb the stairs to the front door. "You go on ahead. I'll be in soon." I incline my head toward the building, letting her know I'll be fine.

261

"Don't stay out too long. You'll turn into ice statues out here." Clara pulls on the door and waves goodbye. "Lovely to meet you, Thomas."

"You as well, Clara." Thomas tucks his chin in a gentlemanly nod.

As the door closes behind Clara, I turn to Thomas. "So, what happens next?"

Thomas places a hand over his heart, bowing at the waist as he addresses me formally. "Miss Louisa Wilson, my leading lady, I am at your service."

"You haven't got a Mr. Craig. And I was quite certain you wouldn't want me back, given my swift and childish departure from the theatre this afternoon." I am thankful for the cloak of darkness to hide the colour in my cheeks.

"Your departure, as you call it, was surely swift but not at all childish." Thomas lifts my chin with one finger, drawing my eyes up to meet his. "Every actor faces doubts and insecurities from time to time. All of us do at some point. Some people simply hide it better than others."

"I used to be one of those. The kind who hid it better." My eyes fall to the ground, embarrassment creeping in to take up the space between us.

Thomas lifts my chin a little higher, making certain I am hearing him. "You are not alone in this. In our world of theatre, those doubts allow us to portray a character's vulnerability. I like to think of that annoying little voice of doubt inside my head as inspiration in disguise."

"Inspiration?" I can't remove the skepticism from my voice.

Thomas chuckles lightly. "Yes, inspiration comes in all shapes and sizes, and sometimes it appears in the one form it knows we can't ignore. Our insecurities."

I fold my arms across my chest and tilt my head in question.

"Think about it. Why is it so easy to listen to and believe our self-doubt? How come it seems like the negative voices inside our heads shout louder than the positive ones?"

I roll my eyes. "I don't know. How come?"

"Because they are the initiators of change. Those obnoxious negative beliefs are meant to push us toward something greater. They test our resolve and force us to be stronger and more capable. They are the inspirational seeds of all that we might accomplish in our lives. Sometimes all we need is a little water and sunshine to encourage our inspiration to sprout. I'll be your sunshine, Lou, if you'll let me."

Now, it's Thomas' turn to blush. He watches me without turning away, without hiding who he truly is, causing my heart to race. Unsure of how to react, my first inclination is to flee. Instead, I pause a moment to consider the options. Trusting Thomas' intent, I decide to stay and am rewarded with several minutes of his eyes on me. I've never felt more understood in all my life, and in this moment, I know I could tell this man anything and he would still look at me the same way.

A coy smile lines my lips as I tug the bulky wool gloves from my hands, shoving them into my coat pockets as the heat between us warms me through. "You still haven't solved the problem of the missing Mr. Craig."

Thomas chuckles again, and I am delighted that I can make him laugh so easily. "As they say, Miss Wilson, the show must go on."

"How so, Mr. Cromwell?"

"If you will allow me, I will be the Mr. to your Mrs. Craig."

I throw my head back in laughter. "You? How do intend to direct the production while playing a leading role?"

Thomas's face turns serious. "It's not as though I haven't memorized the lines. I have every line for every character in the play up here." Thomas taps the side of his forehead. "I know most of the stage notes as well. This is what comes from obsessing about a production."

"What's that? A well-prepared actor who is sure to steal the show?"

"So, that's a yes? You'll play Mrs. Craig?" Thomas leans toward me.

"Yes. I'll be your Mrs. Craig." I toss a hand playfully in his direction, intending it to land just below his shoulder, but Thomas catches my wrist. The world tilts as he slowly lifts my hand to his mouth, kissing my palm with a gentle brush of his lips.

Thomas lowers my hand but doesn't let it go. "I'll see you at rehearsal?" His voice is soft, kind, and reassuring.

"I'll be there."

"You should get inside before you freeze." Thomas guides me toward the stairs.

We stand in silence, watching one another until voices from across the street break our intimate moment. "You should go," he says. "I will see you at the theatre."

I nod in agreement. "I'm going to need to take my hand with me."

Thomas blushes again. "Of course. I apologize." He lets go of my hand and takes a step back.

Not wanting him to leave misunderstanding me, I back up my vulnerability with a bit of fear-induced inspiration. "Don't be sorry. It's the most comfortable my hand has ever been." At the top of the stairs, I wave a quick goodbye over my shoulder and enter the lobby, my knees weak and my heart still fluttering.

CHAPTER 32

riday, November 18, 1927
Clara

The opening night of Louisa's play is finally upon us. This is the first time I've seen the theatre up close. As I step into the well-appointed lobby, all I can think is that Louisa's description didn't do the place justice. I have to remind myself to close my continuously dropping jaw. When I saw the line stretched all the way down the street, shivers ran down my spine. I worry how Louisa might feel knowing this many eyes will be on her for the next few hours.

I hand our tickets to the man in the booth and beg him to let me keep at least one intact as a souvenir for Louisa. He smiles warmly and punches only a small hole in the corner of all three tickets.

Papa is dressed in his best jacket and tie, and even I am in a new dress. I allowed myself to be cajoled by Louisa's pleas to take me shopping before the event. Masao, slightly nervous in the crowd, tucks himself between Papa and me as his eyes roam the expansive lobby. We follow the signs to our section and wait in line for the attendant to check our ticket and direct us to our seats.

I follow Masao's gaze toward the shimmering chandeliers and the rich fabric curtains positioned at every lobby door and window, ready to block out any light from outside. I stifle a laugh when I notice him licking his lips as his roaming gaze falls over the refreshment centre. I bump his shoulder gently with my elbow. "We'll have refreshments at the intermission." Masao hugs me around my waist, his appreciation at being included in tonight's festivities evident.

Papa leans toward him and lowers his voice. "Sure is something, hey Masao? I know I've never seen anything like it."

The boy reveals his two missing front teeth in a wide jack-o'-lantern smile.

The line shuffles forward, and a fresh wave of giddiness erupts within me. I clutch our three tickets to my chest, eager to present them to the attendant and then tuck them away for safekeeping. My hope is to present Louisa with the tickets, a playbill, and a photo of her in costume on her birthday this January.

Masao swivels in place and waves enthusiastically behind us. I turn to find Ms. Thompson, Cookie, Rebecca, Hazel, and Jane, all dressed in their finest, entering through the lobby doors. They are almost unrecognizable with their hair curled and their cheeks powdered. I return their waves, delighted they have come to support Louisa.

I peek around the couple ahead of us in line. My heart skips a beat as the auditorium comes into view. I take in the plush red velvet seating and the stage decorated with ornate gold flourishes. No wonder Louisa was keen to spend so much of her time within these walls. The couple moves into the theatre, allowing us to step past the threshold and a foot closer to the attendant. Despite the gathering crowd, a hush falls over the theatre, sending a shiver of excitement cascading through my body.

I lift my eyes to the rounded ceiling and follow its lines to the most expensive seats in the house. The side balconies offer Vancouver's elite a clear view of the stage, and I am pleased to see those seats already filled. I nudge Papa, inclining my head toward the balconies. "Surely a good sign for the play, don't you think?"

Papa nods in agreement as we move forward once more. Handing our tickets to the attendant, I can no longer contain my enthusiasm. "My sister is in the play," I announce to the attendant, clad in a dark red uniform, with gold tassels hanging from his shoulders.

"Is she now?" He smiles at me as he examines our tickets. "You won't miss a thing, seated in the second row, miss." He hands me a program and extends his gloved hand, directing us toward the centre aisle. "Go all the way to the front of the stage, and turn left at row two. Enjoy the show."

"Thank you." I follow those in front of us to the centre aisle. Papa and Masao are quick on my heels as we walk down the sloping aisle toward the stage.

I am so excited I could almost burst. I place a calming hand on my stomach as I near the second row and edge past the seats between ours and the aisle. As I do, my attention is captured by the expansive stage cloaked by a thick, red curtain that I imagine takes the effort of several men to open and close.

Masao and then Papa follow me. We flip our seats down and are settling ourselves, removing jackets and gloves, when a strained shout interrupts our happy banter. "Excuse me."

My head turns toward the voice. Through a cluster of theatregoers, I see a man dressed in a red uniform with gold accents weaving down the centre aisle. He arrives at our row slightly out of breath and leans toward Papa.

"Excuse me, sir." He inclines his head toward me in a polite greeting. "Miss." Returning his attention to Papa, he lowers his voice. "I am sorry, sir, but he cannot sit here." The usher's pillbox hat is askew on his bobbing head.

Papa, understanding the man's meaning, shifts his body to shield Masao from the conversation. Papa doesn't say a word, directing his full gaze upon the man in uniform.

The usher lowers his voice even further, though his hurried approach has already captured the gaze of everyone nearby. "Sir, I do apologize, but the theatre has reserved seating for, well, for others." The man's eyes brush over Masao uncomfortably.

Understanding dawns on me, and I place a protective arm around Masao's shoulders, feeling the boy's posture drop in disappointment. "But we have tickets." I pull the tickets from my purse and show them to the usher. "My sister is playing the role of Mrs. Craig. Surely you can understand that we wish to remain in the seats she purchased for us."

"I am sorry, miss. The theatre has rules, and I am obligated to abide by them." The usher shuffles his feet, clearly uncomfortable with his present duty. He gestures half-heartedly toward the rafters at the back of the theatre.

Papa stands to his full height but lowers his voice to a murmur. "The boy may be of Japanese descent, sir, but he was born in Canada. This city, as a matter of fact."

The usher shakes his head solemnly and mumbles, "I wish there was something I could do."

All eyes are on us as Papa turns to Masao with a cheery tone. "How about you and I get a bird's-eye view of the show. I bet we can see the whole stage from up there, maybe even some of the backstage area too." Papa points to the hard, stadium-style balcony seating located in the furthest reaches of the theatre. "What do you say?"

Masao offers a disappointed smile and takes Papa's offered hand. The two of them slide from their second-row seats. Papa turns to me before retreating up the aisle. "You stay here. Your sister will be looking for you at the front."

A gathering of theatregoers, waiting for the situation to clear so they can settle into their seats, move to the side to allow Papa and Masao to pass. They are like two fish swimming against the current.

I hesitate, wanting to do right by both Papa and Louisa. Watching him depart with Masao, something stirs deep within me. My eyes dart around the theatre, at the velvet seats, the stage, and the heavy red curtain waiting patiently for the show to begin. All of this is intended for the city to enjoy. Sadly, not all are welcomed here in equal measure, even with a ticket in hand.

A couple is standing at the end of the row, motioning that they would like to pass me to reach their seats. I stand abruptly, knowing precisely what I must do.

"Excuse me." I step forward, forcing the couple to retreat into the centre aisle as I vacate the second row.

Spinning around, I spot Masao's dark hair as he leaves the section of the theatre that should be his to enjoy.

My eyes land on the three second-row tickets clutched in my hand. With a defiant shake of my head, I open my hand and let the tickets flutter to the ground. I can almost feel the ripple of my dropped pebble. I jut my chin, firm in my conviction and knowing who I am going to be in this moment, and march up the aisle to catch up with Papa and Masao.

I finally understand that hard work may be a means for me to rise above my station, but no amount of work will allow Masao to rise above prejudice. I can at the very least be by his side, giving him a hand to hold and maybe even my shoulders to stand on.

~

Louisa

Standing in the wings off stage left, I peek around the curtain, hoping to get a glimpse of Papa, Clara, and Masao. I scan the second row, but they aren't in their seats. I begged Thomas for the three second-row seats before the tickets were released to the box office.

Even as the female lead, I paid a premium for the coveted opening-night tickets, bringing a packed dinner from home to help cover the cost. With my hotel work hours reduced so I could ensure the play was ready for tonight, I have been trying not to burden my family by incurring additional costs. The other cast members spent their breaks at the local diner, enjoying hot sandwiches and cola. But I stayed back, ran my lines, envisioned the scenes, and demanded more from myself, determined to make my debut something I can be proud of.

"Five minutes to curtain," a stagehand whispers to me.

"Thank you," I reply over my shoulder, giving the theatre another scan. Lifting my eyes to the balcony, I shield them from the bright lights with one hand.

I gasp, and my hand drops to cover my mouth. Squinting again, I recognize the silhouettes of Papa, Clara, and Masao sitting close to the theatre's roofline in the furthest reaches of the balcony.

Moisture pricks my eyes. My heart plummets at the realization that someone has not allowed Masao entrance, despite the tickets I purchased. Although I am thankful that both Papa and Clara stood in solidarity with our friend, it is easy to see the cost of their gesture. The performance is two hours long, and the balcony is far from hospitable, given its bench seating and placement near the rafters.

I am proud of my sister. She has decided to do what she believes is right, and though she may do so timidly and with hesitation, she does it with all of her heart. I dab my eyes gently, careful not to ruin my makeup. This is an important night, and I must gather myself for what is ahead. I will deal with the seating arrangements after this evening's performance. By then, I will have earned the right to speak my mind in this theatre.

"Hey." Thomas slides up behind me, his breath warm on my neck as he peeks over my shoulder and through the curtain. "Don't be nervous."

My lips quirk into a smile. His belief in me is something to hold onto. "My premium ticket purchase."

Thomas leans closer, scanning the crowd. I use my finger to tilt his chin upward, toward the balcony. "On the benches? But—why?" He takes a step back as understanding dawns on him, pulling me away from the curtain as he moves. Shaking his head, he eyes me warily. "I can feel a battle coming on." Thomas' face softens into an assured smile. He pulls me closer and whispers in my ear. "But then again, I've heard the story about what happened at the clock. I can't imagine you backing down from a worthy fight."

"Three minutes to curtain." The stagehand is back, this time embarrassed to have caught us in a close encounter.

"Go." I shoo Thomas away so he can get into position on the opposite side of the set.

I sneak another glance toward the balcony and can't help but smile. Shuffling down the crowded row is Cookie. Mopping her face with a handkerchief while pushing her way through the crowd, Cookie appears undeterred. I watch with delight as Papa stands to greet our friend before offering her a seat between Masao and himself.

"One minute to curtain, Miss Wilson." The stagehand's words are laced with urgency.

"I'm coming," I say quietly as I follow him to my place backstage. I think about my family, Masao, and Cookie as I steady my breathing, nodding my readiness to Thomas. I've always thought one needed to be persuasive and strong, standing up against societal inequality with a loud voice. Maybe, though, it is our small, daily actions that inspire positive change. One person can surely change the world if they put their mind and heart to it.

Though he doesn't realize he is doing so, Thomas reaffirms my thoughts as the curtain opens. "Chin up, Lou. You are ready for this."

AUTHOR NOTES

Despite The Hotel Hamilton being a fictional hotel, *Meet Me at the Clock* takes place on the traditional, ancestral, and unceded territories of the of the xʷməθkʷəy̓əm (Musqueam), Sḵwx̱wú7mesh (Squamish), and Səlilwətaʔɬ (Tsleil-Waututh) nations in Vancouver, British Columbia.

You may have noticed several Canadianisms among the pages. For example, Canada used the imperial system of measurement until 1975 when the country switched to the metric system. You likely also noticed the many extra "u's" inserted into words, as is common in Canadian English. The British use of Ms. instead of Miss or Mrs. for *Ms. Thompson*, though contrary to US sensibilities given that Ms. was not a well-used term in the USA until the mid 1980s, was inserted purposefully as a nod to my Canadian homeland. Ms. was actually proposed as a neutral alternative to Mrs. or Miss as early as 1901.

I borrowed and tweaked the saying, "meet you under the clock" which may have also been spoken as "meet you under the Birks clock". From as early as 1907, Vancouverites have been meeting one another at this iconic landmark. In fact, as I announced information about this book's release, my cousin contacted me and asked me if the clock was indeed the same clock her parents used to rendezvous at while working in Vancouver. It is indeed, and I am thrilled to have that bit of personal family insight into the beautiful four faced time piece of history.

Though The Hotel Hamilton was at the height of luxury in 1927, in-room dining did not officially exist until 1931 when the Waldorf Astoria in New York City re-opened its doors after relocating to their Park Avenue address. A story that took place at The Hotel Georgia in 1950 actually inspired this mention in the novel. Apparently, Katharine Hepburn arrived in Vancouver and upon checking in at the hotel, handed the manager a list of her requirements. Since the film legend preferred to dine in the quiet of her hotel room, in-room dining was born at The Hotel Georgia that same day.

In the novel, the sisters take a leisurely stroll through Stanley Park, stopping at the site of The Seven Sisters, Prospect Point, and the zoo. The zoo began as a pound in 1888 and remained fully operational as a zoo until 1993, when the decision was made to move the existing animals to other locations and start shutting the facility down. A polar bear named Tuk, was the last remaining resident and due to concerns about his health, he could not be relocated. The polar bear enclosure was the final exhibit to close when Tuk passed away in 1997. I visited the zoo several times as a child and remember Tuk as the lonely last resident. If you are ever in Vancouver and visit The Vancouver Aquarium, located within the park, you can still see remnants of the zoo and animal enclosures near the aquarium's building.

Prospect Point continues to be a popular location as a walking destination and look-out spot within the park. I was inspired to include a refreshment stand where one didn't exist in 1927 as when given a too short stipend for proper operations of the lighthouse, the clever lighthouse attendant, Keeper Grove, set up a lemonade stand in the summer of 1909 to help subsidize his operational fund. He apparently did a thriving business with the tourists until the Parks Board shut him down the same year. I dedicate this imaginary refreshment stand to Keeper Grove and his industriousness.

I would be remiss if I didn't mention the Thanksgiving Day kerfuffle. I was well into working on this story when I discovered what I originally thought was an inaccurate detail about Thanksgiving 1927. Having already set the story around the autumn celebration, I was surprised to learn that the holiday was moved to July 1 in 1927 to coincide with Canada's Diamond Jubilee. Digging deeper, I learned Canada held the first North American Thanksgiving in 1578, which completely shocked me. I also discovered that what we today know as a traditional Thanksgiving on the second Monday of October did not exist until they officially declared it on January 31, 1957. From the end of the First World War until 1930, Canadians celebrated Thanksgiving alongside Armistice Day on the Monday closest to November 11th. In 1931, Armistice Day was renamed Remembrance Day, and the celebration of Thanksgiving was moved to a Monday in October.

Here is a little nugget for you. The pastry chef who is leaving The Hotel Hamilton for Montreal and hence the reason for Cookie's promotion, is Mr. Fournier. His name literally means, occupational name for a baker. The things authors do to entertain ourselves.

To say I ventured down a rabbit hole with Masao's interest in planting an apple tree, is an understatement. There is indeed a trick to getting an apple seed to grow into a tree. The process involves laying the seeds in a damp towel until they sprout. Only once the seeds have sprouted can you cover them with soil and expect a plant to grow. Of course, I haven't even touched on the topic of grafting when it comes to fruit trees which would have been the most successful method, but one that was likely not available to a little boy. Oh, and there really is a red book titled, *Apple Growing in the Pacific Northwest*. This was a fantastic discovery as the photograph for the cover of *Meet Me at the Clock* had already been taken by the time I started searching for a specific book Masao could look for.

Though the word *racism* didn't exist until 1928, and began being used commonly by 1935, the sentiment and ill treatment of Chinese, Japanese, Indian, Negro, and other non-European individuals did very much exist. When I researched Vancouver history it was impossible to miss the reality of such an ugly existence. From stories of Hogan's Alley to the anti-Asian riots to legal and binding real estate clauses that prevented non-European residents to rent or own property. The evidence of mistreatment was everywhere.

Louisa and Clara's approach to this mistreatment differs throughout the story, as I imagined they would in the real world. An author friend, Sharon Peterson, recently posted a moving social media post where she inspired me with her words. She said, if you see someone in a difficult situation, ask them if you can be of service. It sounds simple enough, but in fact, this act of care takes an immense amount of courage and concern for another person. We must put ourselves out there in a vulnerable way, knowing our help may not be accepted. But if we don't ask, how we will know if we could have made an unpleasant situation better? Life can be messy, unfair, and challenging, but what the sisters learn is that helping another human is like tossing a stone into a pond. Who knows how many lives that ripple will touch? My wish is that we go forward rippling out kindness on our paths to being people we can be proud of.

To learn more about the research that goes into my novels, subscribe to my author newsletter by visiting my website at tanyaewilliams.com and you will receive an eBook copy of *At the Corner of Fiction and History*.

ACKNOWLEDGMENTS

We may sit at our desks and write alone but we never truly create our stories without the help, guidance, and cheering of others. I owed a debt of gratitude to many for their continual support and encouragement.

One of the biggest perks of my job is getting to hang out with other writers. I swear, it is like jumping into a conversation mid-sentence, in a foreign language, and being completely understood. Seriously, it doesn't get better than that.

With that in mind, thank you to all the authors in my life who inspire, delight, inform, cheer, and let me know when I am overthinking things. I am listing those with books available by name specifically, so you can go and check out their stories, because inspiring me to be a better writer is precisely what they do.

To the ladies of The Eleventh Chapter, I am honoured to be included with the likes of you. Each one of you is beyond talented. Jenn Bouchard, Kerry Chaput, Jen Craven, Sayword B. Eller, Maggie Giles, Gloria Mattioni, Caitlin Moss, Sharon M. Peterson, and Colleen Temple.

To my HNS After Party friends, we laugh, we learn, we question, and we come together in support of one another. Thank you Shakurra, Dot Caffrey, Carla, Michelle Cox, Erin, Lisa Lane, Louisa Paschella, Kate, Kathy Scott Mejia, Pam, Martha, and Kate Thompson.

A huge thank you goes out to my amazing beta readers, Sophia Alexander, Kelsey Gietl, Diana Lesire Brandmeyer, and Kate Thompson. I gave you a very messy draft this time around and you all took it in stride and helped make it better. Without you, the story wouldn't be what it is today, and it would definitely be missing some comas. Thank you!

Thank you to my accountability partner and dear friend, Carla. We met in the hotel hallway at a writer's conference and she promptly invited me in for wine. We've been writing pals ever since and knew in an instant we were meant to journey through our writing careers together. We push each other, ask the difficult questions, and hash out plot lines until the story shines. Thank you for challenging and understanding me.

Thank you to my new writerly friends of the Pencil Dancers, together we can do ALL the things!

Victoria Griffin, you gave your all to this story and I am immensely grateful. Thank you!

The Hotel Hamilton book covers are a result of a photo shoot with a wonderful crew (thank you Emily, Kari, and Dave) and the vision of the incredibly talented Ana Grigoriu-Voicu who made it sparkle in a way that only she can do.

I am supremely fortunate to have a team of advanced readers who after six novels, are still with me, finding the hidden typos and offering support. You are the best and I am immensely grateful for your insight and dedication. Big hugs to each of you! To my newsletter readers, thank you for your continued support and excitement for each new story I share.

On a personal note, thank you to Kari, Donna, Tammy, Irene, and Judy (my real life pen pal), who understand when I am immersed in the story and patiently wait for me to look up from my computer screen. Thank you for delaying plans, checking in, waiting for emails and texts, and just generally supporting me in your own wonderfully, loving way.

I would be nowhere if it were not for a love of history and storytelling that originated in my family home. Thank you, Mom, Dad and the rest of my very large extended family for your support, inspiration, interest, and appreciation of what I do. I love sharing the stories with you!

To Dave and Justin, thank you doesn't even come close to what it means to have your love and support. Thank you for talking me through the rough patches and for celebrating every little milestone along the way. From idea, to research, to finished novel, you are there and I wouldn't want it any other way.

And to you, dear reader, arigatou gozaimasu, which translates to "thank you" in Japanese. Thank you for picking up this book and taking time out of your day to read *Meet Me at the Clock*. I hope the story made you smile, laugh, cry, and feel while exploring your own thoughts on family, life's challenges, and more.

ABOUT THE AUTHOR

A writer from a young age, Tanya E Williams loves to help a reader get lost in another time, another place through the magic of books. History continues to inspire her stories and her insightful view into the human condition deepens her character's experiences and propels them on their journey. Ms. Williams' favourite tales, speak to the reader's heart, making them smile, laugh, cry, and think.

ALSO BY TANYA E WILLIAMS

Becoming Mrs. Smith

Stealing Mr. Smith

A Man Called Smith

All That Was

Welcome to the Hamilton